DEDICATION

One of my favorite authors, Michelle Leighton, wrote,
"Every broken person's worst fear—that no one will be able to love us in
spite of our scars."

This book is dedicated to anyone who has ever been broken.
You are loved—scars and all.

PROLOGUE

~Jess~

EIGHT MONTHS EARLIER

Being a wallflower is definitely not my style. I normally work the room: socializing, making the rounds—enjoying myself. I usually know everyone and am rarely the outsider. Yet, here I stand, pressed against the wall in the living room of a house that is too small for this many people. It's Family Weekend at the University of Arizona, and we've come to see Gabe and watch his football game. Gabe is a junior and a wide receiver for the U of A football team.

I'm here for the weekend with the Garcias, since my dad is working. I normally stay with the Garcias, our neighbors in Santa Ruiz, when my father can't be around because of his job. They have watched me for at least four days a week for the last thirteen years while my dad spent his time climbing the career ladder. Dad is the Fire Chief for the Santa Ruiz Fire Department—I'm very much an afterthought for him. The Garcias, Gabe's family, have really taken me in and accepted me as a member of their family.

As I try to look normal while holding a red Solo cup of Diet Coke, I sneak glances at Gabe while he moves around his house, entertaining the people who are here at his party. Ava, Gabe's little sister, and my best friend, is talking to Josh, one of Gabe's roommates that she met on a previous trip to Arizona. Pulling my cell phone from my back pocket, I tap out a text message to Max, one of my friends at home.

What am I missing in Santa Ruiz?

Adrian and Me ;) How's AZ?

Hot.

God, if he only knew what my interpretation of "hot" really meant.

I can't imagine I'm missing much back home. The life of an honor-roll student in Santa Ruiz is about as exciting as watching paint dry, but normally Ava and I would be spending the evening with Max and Adrian, our two best "guy friends," going to dinner or to the movies.

As I wait for Max to text me back, I find Gabe again in the sea of people. Some tramp is hanging on his arm and whispering in his ear. When I lean forward to get a better look, I feel the cold drink run down the front of me before an overly large man falls into me, pinning me against the wall.

"What the fuck!" I yell, trying to push him forward so I can breathe.

"Ah, sorry," he says, laughing as he backs away.

I'm definitely out of my element here. The girls are gorgeous and hardly wearing any clothes while the boys are not really boys anymore, but men. And here I stand, in a corner, covered in an entire cup of cheap keg beer.

"Fucking great," I mumble to myself, shoving my phone into my back pocket while tugging at my fitted white cap-sleeve t-shirt that now looks as if it has been painted on. My denim shorts are wet down the front too, so not only do I have a wet t-shirt, but it also looks like I've pissed myself.

"What happened?" Gabe is laughing when he takes in the sight of me drenched in beer.

"What does it look like?" I ask sarcastically, glaring at the beast of a man that dumped his drink down the front of me. Gabe grabs my hand and pulls me through the crowded living room and down a hallway. Pulling the keys from his front pocket, he unlocks his door.

"You have to lock your bedroom door?" I ask him.

"We all do. There are so many people in and out of here, I don't want them messing with my shit," he says, pulling me into his room and closing the door behind us.

The room is dark, the only light coming from the glow of a small desk lamp. Gabe hasn't changed since he's left home; his room is immaculate. There's nothing on the floor, and even his desk is neat and orderly. He opens the closet door, pulls a navy blue t-shirt off a hanger, and hands it to me.

"Here, change into this," he says, brushing past me. He sits down at his desk and begins checking his e-mail. I back away a bit more into the dark, turning around so my back is to him. I pull my wet t-shirt off of me, toss it to the floor, and pull the clean t-shirt over my head. It's so big that it hangs past my cut-off jean shorts, and now it looks like I'm not wearing any bottoms. I can smell the laundry detergent on the shirt, but I can also smell the slightest hint of Gabe. I pull the collar of the shirt up just under my nose and inhale deeply. As I turn

3

back around, I see that Gabe is sitting in his chair, watching me.

"You look good in my shirt," he says quietly.

"Thanks for letting me borrow it." I smile and chew on the inside of my bottom lip nervously. His hazel eyes shift to rake over me from head to toe. I fidget with the hem of his too long t-shirt and my pulse starts racing. He continues to stare at me, not saying anything.

"What?" I ask him, tilting my head.

He pushes himself up from his chair and walks toward me, stopping to pick up my wet t-shirt. He stands up and inches closer to me so that we're face to face. I can feel his warm breath sweep across my cheek. I smell his light cologne, or maybe it's his body wash; whatever it is, it's perfection.

"I missed you," he whispers, our eyes never breaking contact. "I'm glad you came this weekend."

"I missed you too," I whisper back, swallowing hard. "It's quiet without you at home."

"Tell me how much you have missed me, Jess," Gabe orders, causing a slight tremble to roll through my body. I can feel my pulse beating in the back of my throat, making it difficult to swallow. Before I have time to reply, Gabe's nose presses against the side of mine, his lips mere millimeters from my mouth. I want so badly to just lean forward, to press my lips to his, but I'm too nervous.

"I've missed you . . . a lot," I stutter quietly. With a slight lean, his soft lips press against mine, and my head falls back just slightly. Gabe pulls my bottom lip into his mouth and gently sucks. My legs tremble as he moves his soft lips across mine and my stomach flips as he deepens his kiss. Pausing, he pulls away and holds my face with both of his hands. He looks deeply into my eyes, searching for unspoken desires. My heart races as my lips answer and I press my mouth to his, capturing the only thing I've ever wanted—him.

KNOCK, KNOCK, KNOCK!

"Jess, are you in there?" Ava yells through the door. The knocking startles me and Gabe walks over to the door and unlocks it.

"There you are," she says, pushing past Gabe and entering the room. "I was looking everywhere for you." She walks across the room, throws herself onto Gabe's chair with a loud sigh, and scrunches her eyebrows together at the sight of me in Gabe's t-shirt.

"Some asshole dumped an entire glass of beer down the front of my shirt, so Gabe let me borrow this," I say, tugging at the oversized t-shirt.

"Well, it's a good thing Mom and Dad are here now to get us, because you aren't going to get laid looking like a bag lady." She snorts, and I realize how ridiculous I look.

"Ava, don't fucking joke around about that," Gabe says, glaring at her.

"Relax, Gabe. Jesus," she says, jumping out of the chair. "Miss Goody Two-Shoes wouldn't give it up at a keg party anyway." Ava rolls her eyes. "Give Jess her shirt. We need to go unless you want Dad in here, shutting down this shindig."

Gabe hands me my wet shirt as Ava tugs me through his room. As I glance back over my shoulder, I see that he is standing next to his bed with his hands on his hips and a small smile spread across his lips. Those lips will be my downfall.

CHAPTER ONE

~Jess~

"What'cha reading?" he asks, jogging over to get the basketball that has rolled to my feet.

"Some romance series that everyone is raving about." I use my hands to shield the front cover so he can't see the picture or title.

I'm distracted by the sweat that's rolling down his large, muscular frame, along his golden bare chest, and over every last curve of his perfect abdominal muscles to the fine dusting of dark hair just below his belly button. I swallow hard, then lose track of that little bead of sweat as it travels even lower. All of Gabe Garcia is perfection in my eyes—he is my Adonis.

"Any good?"

"Oh, ah…"

"The book, Jess. Is the book any good?" He's laughing at me now. *Shit*.

I nod nervously and pull myself out of my Gabe-induced coma.

"Yeah, actually, it's really good. Anything is better than text books."

His hazel eyes look greener today as the sun is shining directly on his bronzed face. His eyelashes are long and accentuate his beautiful almond-shaped eyes, and his dark brown hair is a tussled mess from playing basketball.

"You might actually enjoy it more if you turned it the right way." He laughs, picking up the basketball and dribbling it back to the five guys that are standing there waiting for him. I look at the book I'm holding in my lap. He's right; I've been holding it upside down, as I've spent the better half of the last twenty-five minutes "pretending" to read it. Embarrassed that I've been caught, I toss my book into my large bag and fold the blanket on which I've been sitting. I glance over my shoulder and see him shooting free throws as I leave the park and walk down the street to his house.

I've known the Garcias since I was four years old. My dad moved us here to Santa Ruiz, California right after my mom died. He took a job as a firefighter and has made it his number one priority to work his way up the career ladder, literally, to become Fire Chief, which he finally made about five years ago. So while dad was burying himself in his career, our neighbors, the Garcias, essentially raised me.

I've had a crush on Gabe since I was around fifteen. For the past few years, I've watched him date other girls, go away to college, come home, and leave again. But last fall, on a visit for Family Weekend, something changed with us. We've never talked about that night, but the small glances, the touches here and there, tell me there's something more.

As I walk up the driveway to the Garcias' house, I realize this will be the last weekend that I will stay with them. Since Ava and I technically finished school yesterday, Dad made me a deal that I could start staying at our house alone when he was at work. After all, I'm eighteen, and it's really about time that he can trust his straight A honor student to take care of herself. Shit, I've been practically doing it for my entire life anyway.

"How was the park?" Angelica, Gabe's mom asks as I enter the side door that opens into the kitchen.

"Hot," I mumble, reaching into the fridge to grab a bottle of water.

"Yeah. It's a warm one today. Don't run until later, Jess; it's just too hot right now."

"I won't. I'm going to take a quick nap and then run later." I kiss her on the cheek as I move toward the stairs to take me to the bedroom that I share with Ava.

"Hey," Ava says as I toss my bag onto our bedroom floor.

"Still working on your speech?" As valedictorian, Ava is speaking at Saturday's commencement and has been obsessed with perfecting her speech. Truth be told, she could stand up there with nothing prepared and sound amazing; it's just her nature. She's personable, outgoing, and feisty.

"Yeah. How was the park?"

"Good until Gabe and the guys showed up. They were so loud I couldn't concentrate on reading."

I notice Ava isn't even listening to me because she's so wrapped up in writing her speech. Pushing the headphones from my iPhone into my ears, I turn the music on low and lie down on my bed. Closing my eyes, I try to fall asleep, but I all I can see is Gabe at the park: his eyes, the sweat, his bare chest—*shit*.

I finally calm down, my mind still wandering to where that little bead of sweat traveled to, as sleep slowly takes over.

I feel rested when I wake up; full of energy and ready for a run. Running is therapy for me. When I run, I don't think or feel. Stress, worries, or anxieties temporarily disappear—it's just me and my music. Lately, I've been pushing myself harder; adding more distance or increasing my pace. I will admit there is something slightly disturbing about the excitement I feel when my lungs burn or my legs want to give out, yet I continue to push myself harder.

I change into a pair of black capri running pants and a hot pink tank top. Standing at the full-length mirror, I look myself over from head to toe. I can pick out every flaw on my body in this outfit, which only motivates me to run faster, harder. I'm momentarily pulled out of my negative thoughts when there is a light rap on the door.

"Come in." The door opens slowly and Gabe peeks his head in. "Hey," he says with his deep voice and a smile.

"Hey."

"Ava in here?"

"Nope. I just woke up and haven't seen her." I shrug and pull my long hair off of my neck and onto the top of my head as I tie a binder around the messy bun.

"Going for a run?"

"Yeah."

"Want some company?" I pause at his question. He's never run with me before. I try not to smile. *Of course I want him to run with me.*

"Sure."

"You don't sound so convincing." He laughs and steps closer. With two quick steps, he's directly in front of me, and I still. My throat tightens up with him this close to me. I can smell the light scent of his body wash. I take in the sight of him in a pair of faded blue jeans and a tight white t-shirt. Our eyes meet and I feel his hand brush my shoulder. His fingers slide under the strap of my tank top, untwisting it. I hadn't realized the straps were twisted with those of my sports bra.

"You were twisted," he says quietly, his hand still on my shoulder.

"Thanks," I whisper, swallowing hard as I notice the flecks of gold sparkling in his hazel eyes.

"I should get changed. I'll meet you downstairs," he says, his hand falling from my shoulder, lightly running down my arm as he backs away toward the door. I release the breath I was holding and feel the adrenaline that is coursing through my veins. I grab my tennis shoes, sit down on the edge of my bed, and put them on. My heart is still beating rapidly and it amazes me that his touch can cause such an intense reaction.

I nervously rub my arms as I wait for him downstairs. A minute later, he comes bounding down the stairs. He's changed into a pair of black athletic shorts and a tight gray compression shirt.

"Ready?" he asks, placing his hand on the small of my back while guiding me toward the front door. His touch immediately sends a shiver through me. *How does he do that?*

"Ready."

"So where do you normally run?" he asks as we walk down the driveway toward the street.

"Today, I am just going down Main Street to the entrance of Washington Park, then back. It's about three miles there and back."

"You always run three miles?" he asks, stretching his arms over his head.

"Usually around five miles; today is just a quick three miles, though." I see his eyes widen when I mention I normally run further. "I'll keep my pace steady; just try to keep up," I say, starting into a slow jog.

"Try to keep up," he says under his breath as he jogs alongside of me. I keep our pace slow and steady and less of a run; more of a jog. When we finally reach the entrance of Washington Park, I slow to a walk and let him catch his breath.

"So that was three miles?" he asks between breaths.

Chuckling, I keep moving to keep my heart rate up. "No, that was a mile and half. We still have to run home to get our three miles in." He stands there with his hands on his hips and his head tilted backwards, continuing to take long, deep breaths. I can tell he's not used to long-distance running.

"Let's walk for a bit," I offer, and bump him with my shoulder.

"It's still hot out here, and I'm thirsty. How do you run every day in this heat?"

"I don't run every day, but I like running. It helps clear my mind. I just listen to my music and let my feet carry me. Sometimes, I run and don't even know how I got as far as I did. I like running." I shrug. He leads us into the parking lot of a convenience store and I glance at him out of the corner of my eye.

"Water?" he asks, opening the door. The cool air-conditioning greets us as we walk in, causing my skin to break out in goose bumps. He grabs two waters from the cooler, pays for them, and we retreat back outside to drink them.

Dusk is setting in and the streetlights have just turned on as we continue our walk back home.

"So, are you excited to graduate?"

"Sure, I mean, I've never disliked high school. I guess I'm just glad to be moving on to college now, you know?"

"Any idea what you're going to major in?" he asks, taking a long drink from his water bottle.

"I'm thinking about broadcast journalism. It's always interested me."

"That's right up your alley. You're gorgeous, and your ability to find shit out is impeccable." He laughs at me.

"Are you making fun of me?" I joke as I bump him with my hip.

"Me, make fun of you? Never."

"I'm surprised you didn't stay in Tucson for the summer," I remark, wondering why he chose to come home this summer.

"Coach wanted me to, but it's too hot, and…" His voice trails off before he continues. "I don't know; I guess I just wanted to come home."

"I'm glad you're home," I admit nervously.

"Me too."

It's times like this when we're sharing little pieces of ourselves that I want to be back in his bedroom in Tucson with his lips pressed to mine. I want so badly to know if he thinks about those few minutes we shared, and if they consume him as they have consumed me. Neither of us has discussed the kiss, and I can't help but assume he thinks it was a mistake. Shaking those thoughts from my head, I ask, "So what are your plans for the summer?" I take another drink of water. Of course, me being clumsy, I spill it down the front of me. Stopping, I screw the lid back on the bottle.

"I don't know. I was thinking about maybe taking a class or two this summer." He reaches out and runs his thumb over my bottom lip, catching me off guard.

"Water," he whispers as he runs his thumb across my chin. His touch is soft and slow, and I want him to do it again.

Trying to appear unaffected, I respond quietly, "But classes you take here won't transfer back to Arizona, right? These aren't your general requirements anymore."

He smiles at me and starts walking. "You're right; they won't transfer. This is why you'd be a great reporter; you think quickly and dig for more information." He chuckles.

"Then why would you take them?"

"Just exploring some different options, I guess. I haven't decided anything yet." He smirks at me.

"When do you have to go back to Arizona? Football conditioning starts mid-summer right?" He doesn't answer immediately. I can tell he's hesitating.

"Yeah, mid-summer. I'm not sure of the exact date," he answers quietly, his voice trailing off again. Something is bothering him, but I don't want to pry. *Oh hell, yes I do, but I won't.* He stops momentarily and looks at me. My stomach flips every time our eyes meet. I wonder if he can see how affected I am by him. He reaches his hand out and tucks a piece of hair that has fallen out of my ponytail behind my ear. "Can we not talk about Arizona right now?" he asks quietly.

"Sure." I drop my eyes from his, hoping that all of my questions didn't upset him.

"Let's just walk home. I enjoy talking to you and I can't do that if we're running."

"Okay," I respond sheepishly. The twenty-five minutes it takes us to walk the remaining distance home pass too quickly.

I could walk and talk to him for forever. Arriving home, I glance across the street to my house.

"Hey, I'm going to shower at home. Tell Mom I'm sorry we missed dinner. I'll head over as soon as I'm done."

"Sounds good. Thanks for letting me run with you."

"You're welcome to run with me anytime," I reply nervously. He nods and waits until I'm safely in the house behind a locked door before he leaves.

I strip my clothes off in my bedroom and walk across the hall to the bathroom, closing the door behind me. Catching a side glimpse of myself in the full-length door mirror, I stare for a minute. Sighing, I run my hand over my soft stomach, wishing I were as toned as Ava, who has a perfectly flat, hard stomach. Looking up, I move my hands to the one area I have Ava beat—boobs. I am blessed with large breasts. While Ava is overall toned and fit, her chest is as flat as a board. I am soft and curvy and have breasts to die for, or so Ava says. I guess the saying is true, that "you always want what you don't have," and I would love to lose some of my curves.

I turn on the shower and let the water warm up as I brush my teeth. I step into the warm spray and take extra care to loofah my skin, shave my legs and bikini area smooth, and let the conditioner set in my long hair a little longer than I normally do. The scalding water pelts my skin and helps relax my tight muscles.

When I finish my shower, I step out onto the small bathroom rug and dry myself quickly, twisting the same towel around my wet hair, securing it on top of my head. Using my favorite coconut scented lotion, I take extra care to moisturize my entire body.

When I open the bathroom door, my heart jumps to my throat—then stops altogether. Gabe's hazel eyes shift to mine, but not before looking me up and down, slowly. "What the HELL are you doing here?" I panic, frantically moving my hands to cover my breasts and stomach simultaneously. I'm desperately trying to hide myself, when I finally grab the towel off my head and stretch it out over the front of me.

His mouth twists into a small smile and his eyes light up. "Mom sent me over to find you. She wanted me to make sure you hadn't fallen asleep over here. I knocked on the door, but you didn't answer, so I let myself in. I was just heading to your bedroom to check on you when you opened the bathroom door and flashed me." He chuckles as if this is funny.

"Gabriel, I did not flash you." I never call him Gabriel, but I'm pissed. Actually, I'm more embarrassed than pissed. He stands there, smiling at me with his hands on his hips and his eyes fixed on the short towel that is covering me. "Can you wait in the living room while I get dressed and grab my things for school tomorrow?" I ask with a harsh tone.

When he turns his back and begins walking down the hallway, I quickly step into my room, shutting the door behind me. My heart is racing as I try to calm myself down. I quickly throw on some clothes and toss extra clothes for school tomorrow in my bag. I slip into my flip-flops, take a deep breath, and slowly open my bedroom door.

Standing in the hallway with his arms crossed over his chest, he looks up and our eyes meet. I blush and nervously drop my eyes to the floor as I move to walk past him. His hand reaches out and catches my arm, abruptly stopping me.

"What, Gabe?" I whisper, my voice full of embarrassment as I raise my head and our eyes meet again. His brown eyes shift back and forth between mine, down to my lips, and back up again.

"I don't want you to feel awkward about what happened. I didn't know you were going to open the door and be naked." His eyes stay focused directly on mine, and I hear the sincerity in his voice. "You're beautiful, Jess. I'm not gonna lie; it's going to be hard for me to fall asleep tonight with the image of you standing in the doorway so fresh in my memory."

Gabe thinks I'm beautiful? I've always felt like he looked at me like he would a sister. Not attractive, not beautiful, just—there.

My mouth falls open as I try to gather my thoughts to speak.

"Gabe, I…"

"Shhh…Let's go." He presses his finger to my mouth, letting go of my arm. He pulls my bag off of my shoulder and carries it, motioning towards the door. "We better get home before Mom sends the police looking for both of us," he says, smirking.

We walk quietly across the street and in the front door of his house. Gabe hands me my bag, and his hand brushes against mine, sending a wave of chills over me. He walks over to Mom and bends down to give her a hug and kiss goodnight while mumbling something about *trying* to get some sleep tonight. Rolling my eyes, I wave and say goodnight to Gabe's parents. I fly up the stairs two at a time and run into my room. As I shut the door behind me, I throw my bag on the floor and fall onto the bed in dramatic fashion.

"What's wrong?" Ava mumbles from her bed, her face buried in a book.

"Everything!" I say, covering my face with a pillow to hide my smile. I hear her book smack the nightstand and suddenly feel my bed sink. Ava tugs at the pillow over my face, and I hold onto it tighter.

"Let it go!" she squeals.

"No."

"Dammit, Jess." She yanks it again, this time pulling it from my grasp. Tossing the pillow behind her, she rakes her eyes over me in concern.

"Doesn't look like you're upset," she observes.

"I'm not upset."

"Then why did you say 'everything' was wrong?"

"You're really nosy. You know that, right?" I laugh.

"You're really evasive. You know that, right?" She grabs the pillow from behind her and tosses it to the top of my bed. She lies down next to me and we lie in silence, staring at the ceiling for a minute like we used to do when we were little girls.

"Can you believe we graduate in two days?" she whispers.

"Yes and no."

"I'm really going to miss you when I leave for Stanford," she says quietly.

Ava has been my best friend, and the closest thing to a sister that I will ever know. The thought of not seeing her every day pulls at my heart. "I'm really going to miss you too," I say, keeping my emotions in check. "Now get off my bed and leave me alone," I demand as I toss a small throw pillow at her, trying to lighten the mood.

"Tell me why you can't stop smiling and I will."

"Goodnight, Ava," I say, rolling over.

"It's obviously been a good night for you," she says, climbing into her bed.

"Love you, Ava."

"Love you too. You know I'm going to find out why you're smiling, right?"

"Goodnight," I say again with a little giggle.

"Goodnight, Jess."

CHAPTER TWO

-Gabe-

"Fuck," I mutter, stretching before getting into the shower. When I decided to go for a run with Jess, I didn't expect to run a mile and a half. I may be a football player, a damn good one, but I am NOT a fucking cross-country runner. I haven't done much cardio conditioning since the season ended last November. I love spending time with Jess, though, and I'd gladly run again tomorrow as long as I get to spend time with her—alone.

Watching her run about kills me. She has these legs that go on forever, and I can't stop thinking about having those long legs wrapped around me and all the things I want to do to her. She is perfection in my eyes with her soft olive skin and huge green eyes. She's lean, yet curvy, with breasts that any man would die to get his hands on. It's hard not to think about raking my hands and tongue over every square inch of that body when I'm with her.

Never in a million years did I expect to see her naked tonight. As I let the warm water run over me, all I can think about is what I saw when she opened her bathroom door. The images of her body, the curve of her hips, and the way her breasts hung keep replaying through my mind like a slide show. I'm as hard as a fucking rock, and it's killing me to know that she's lying in the room across the hall, so close—yet out of reach.

I struggle a bit with the feelings I have for her. Part of me thinks I should stop thinking about her like this—she's practically my sister, for fuck's sake; but she's *not* my sister. She's fair game, and I want her to be mine. For months, I've pushed thoughts of her to the back of my mind and fought the temptation to act on what I've been feeling out of fear. Fear that she looks at me as nothing more than an older brother, an older brother that crossed a line last fall in Arizona when I took a small taste of her. But tonight, after I told her she was beautiful, I saw that fire in her eyes, and that's not something you have for your brother. I know she wants more.

Finishing up my shower, I wrap a towel around my waist. As I stop just outside the bathroom door, I see a small stream of light sneaking out from under the bedroom door where she is lying. She's still awake. Touching the door, I'm tempted to knock—just to see her, to hear her voice, but doubt seeps through and I think better of it.

Lying in bed, I try to count sheep, run algebra problems in my head; anything to try to sleep so that I stop thinking about her and all of the things I want to do to her. No matter what I do, she consumes my thoughts. I see her lips, the small mole on her cheek, her green eyes. *Dammit!*

Reaching over to my nightstand, I grab my phone and I start typing a new text message to her. Pounding out a few words, I lay the phone on the pillow next to me and roll over to try to go to sleep, but when I close my eyes, there she is again.

CHAPTER THREE

~Jess~

When I wake up, I feel refreshed— happy. I'm rarely happy in the morning; in fact, I try not to think most mornings. Reaching my arms above my head, I stretch. My muscles were hurting last night, but this morning, I feel great.

It's Friday, the day before Ava and I graduate. School is officially done, but Ava has volunteered both of us to set up the gym for tomorrow's graduation ceremony. Lying here, I think about the last fourteen years and how grateful I am to the Garcias. I only remember bits and pieces of my mom, but I look at all the pictures of her and me together and can't help but wonder what today would be like if she were here.

I love Angelica, but I can't help but miss my real mom and consider how differently things would be with my dad if my mom were still alive. Would he work as much as he does? Would he have made his life about his career? Would I have mattered more to him?

Shaking off the missing-my-mom-blues, I hop out of bed and make my way to the bathroom. I wash my face and run a comb through my tangled, messy hair. Finishing up, I gather a few things off the counter and open the bathroom door. Standing there, leaning against the wall, is a shirtless Gabe.

"Jesus, stalk much?" I mumble at him, but it's hard not to smile at him at the same time. My lips curl into a small smile as I stand there looking at him. My thoughts immediately go back to last night. The way he raked his eyes over me as I stood naked, the look in his eyes of solid want—need.

"I wasn't stalking you. Remember, I live here too," he whispers, leaning into me. Taking a step backward, I feel my back touch the wall in the hallway. Taking another step into me, he traps me between his firm body and the wall. My pulse is racing, and I turn to look at the stairs, wondering what would happen if anyone saw us this close.

"They're all downstairs," he whispers into my ear, placing both hands on the wall, one on each side of my head. His warm breath sends a shiver through me and causes a small gasp to escape my mouth. Gabe presses his nose to that soft spot behind my ear and presses his lips to my neck, planting a light kiss that causes my head to fall back slightly. His light, musky scent causes a heat to take over my body, pooling between my legs.

My body begins to shake from being this close to him. His scent, the feel of his lips on my neck, and his tight chest pressed up against mine cause a low moan to escape from me. My right hand finds his muscular shoulder and he presses himself into me further as my left hand rests on his hip.

"Gabe," I whisper as my head falls back further, giving him better access to my neck.

"Mmm hmm." He mumbles against my neck as he runs his tongue softly up and down my neck, followed by light kisses.

"I…"

"Shh…" he says, stopping me. "Don't say anything; just feel it."

He pulls his lips from my neck, pushes himself off the wall, and steps into the open bathroom door. Turning back, he shifts his eyes up and down my body much like he did last night. My stomach flips as he closes the bathroom door, and I slide down the wall and sit on the floor. As I drop my head forward, my hair falls into my face, and a light sweat breaks out all over my skin. My heart is beating wildly and my hands are shaking.

"What the hell are you doing on the floor?" Ava asks as she bounds up the stairs and stops at my feet.

"Just a little light-headed," I lie, pushing myself off the floor.

"Are you sick?"

"No, just needed to rest for a minute." I swipe at the small beads of sweat on my forehead.

"Good, because I need your help today."

"Can't wait," I lie again.

I follow Ava into our room, get dressed, and throw my hair up into a messy bun.

"Up for a party tonight?" Ava asks quietly, looking around me and out into the hallway. Glancing at her, I raise my eyebrow in a non-spoken gesture to hear more. "Max and Adrian invited us to go to Xavier's party," she whispers. Xavier is our friend Adrian's older brother who graduated from high school the same year as Gabe. Gabe has a real problem with Xavier, and he's warned Ava and me numerous times to stay away from him.

"Sure. Sounds like fun."

I stumble down the stairs and into the kitchen with Ava, pour some coffee into a travel mug, and stir in some vanilla creamer. Mom is sitting at the table with Dad, drinking coffee and reading the newspaper. I catch Gabe in my peripheral vision sliding into the chair next to Mom, grabbing a piece of banana bread from the platter in the middle of the table.

"Morning, girls," he says, breaking off a piece of the banana bread and tossing it into his mouth. He shifts his eyes back and forth between Ava and me, but I notice he holds his gaze a bit longer on me.

Finally, Ava responds. "Morning. How are you this morning?" she asks, her voice dripping with sarcasm. Gabe is smiling, picking at his bread, but keeps his gaze honed in on me.

"Fine. Glad that I get to spend the day relaxing while you little ones are setting up the gym." He laughs before asking, "Any big plans for the weekend?"

"Us 'little ones' are going to a party tonight—with older boys," Ava says, engaging him for a fight. Mom sets down the paper and focuses on the conversation that is about to ignite in front of all of us.

"Pssh, where at and with who?" he asks, his tone more serious. His brown eyes dance back and forth between Ava and me while he waits for an answer. I sip my coffee and raise my eyebrows to him, in a gesture of my loyalty to Ava. He's looking for me to be the voice of reason here, but I'm not interjecting myself into this fight. I'm always responsible. I make good decisions. I've got a good head on my shoulders and I can go to a party and not get myself into trouble. That's my logic.

"Xavier Garza's. Adrian and Max are going with us," she spouts off. I elbow her in the side, and she shoots her eyes to me and mouths *Ow* while rubbing her ribs. Gabe face turns sour and I can see the muscles in his jaw clenching. I'm positive that sound is him grinding his teeth.

"Not a good idea, girls. Xavier is a douche bag; you know this," he says, shaking his head at us.

"Just mind your own business. We're both adults and can make our own decisions. I don't need my 'big brother,'" she says, making air quotes as she continues, "telling us what we can and can't do. So don't be an asshole." I gasp quietly when I hear her curse. I mean, we all curse, but just not in front of Mom or Dad.

"What the hell has gotten into you two?" Dad's voice booms. "The language around here is unacceptable."

"Sorry, Dad, but he's a douche bag," Gabe mumbles, shoving the last piece of banana bread into his mouth.

"It's Adrian's brother." Ava's voice lightens and is almost laced with sympathy. "And we're going with Max and Adrian, so we have protection from all the old pervs," she says, laughing now and implying that the guys from Gabe's graduating class are old. "Plus, you're friends with Xavier; that's why you don't want us to go. You don't want us hanging out with your friends, right?"

"The last thing I am is a friend with that piece of…"

"Gabriel," Dad warns.

Gabe rolls his eyes at us as Ava grabs her bag. She reaches her hand out as I drop my car keys into her palm. Glancing back at Gabe, I shoot him a small apologetic smile. He just stares at me, never breaking eye contact with me while shaking his head "no" at me. I just shrug my shoulders and head to the front door.

"Whatever. We're out of here," I hear Ava announce behind me as I walk outside. As I settle into the front passenger seat of my car, my phone buzzes. When I pick it up, the alert tells me I have new text messages, both from Gabe.

The first text message was received last night at 10:30 p.m.

Thanks for taking me on your run this afternoon. Don't be embarrassed about tonight, you're gorgeous. I mean it.

My pulse quickens and a smile crosses my face. But when I see his second message, the smile wipes off my face.

You are not going to Xavier's tonight. That guy is bad news. Not up for discussion.

Huh. I don't liked being told what I can and cannot do, but there is something sweet in the protective nature of Gabe's response, so I calmly type my response.

You can run with me anytime, I had a great time. We're going to Xavier's party. Max and Adrian will be there, we'll be fine.

Before I even have a chance to put my phone down another message comes through.

Dammit Jess, you're not going.

We're going.

I will tie you to my fucking bed. You. Are. NOT. Going

Tie me to his bed? I actually laugh at the thought, and then blush.

"What the fuck is wrong with your brother?" I bark at Ava. She just glances over at me, then turns her eyes back to the road.

"Is that him texting you?" she asks. "Just ignore him; we're going," she says as she pulls into the student parking lot at the high school. I don't bother texting him back; I just shove the phone in my bag and grab my coffee as she parks.

As we walk toward the front doors of the school, Ava squeezes my arm. "Thanks for coming to help me. I know this is the last thing you really want to be doing today."

Yeah, she's right; I'd rather be doing Gabe. Did I really just think that?

"Of course. I'd help you with anything; you know that." I smile while taking a drink of my coffee.

"I'm excited you agreed to come to the party tonight. It's going to be so much fun. Kind of a pre-graduation party." She bounces and claps her hands together excitedly. All of the back and forth with Gabe regarding this party this morning has me a little unsettled.

"Hey, why does Gabe hate Xavier so much?"

"I'm not sure. I've heard some rumors about Xavier, but I don't know what to believe. Plus, I'm kind of hot for his little brother if you haven't noticed, so I'm not looking to dig up anything that I might not want to know." She laughs.

"Yeah, Gabe's going to have a fucking field day when he finds out you're screwing Adrian," I say, raising my eyebrows and taking another sip of coffee.

"We're not screwing." She smacks my arms, almost causing me to spill my coffee.

"Yet," I mumble and laugh.

The gym looks like a war zone. There are folding chairs strewn everywhere, a small stage with a podium, and papers everywhere. Ava gasps at the scene, and her obsessive-compulsive disorder and type-A personality kick-in.

"Who made this mess? Who did this?" she asks as two custodians continue to unload folding chairs from a rolling cart.

"Stop right there!" she shouts as she heads off in their direction. I laugh and continue to sip on my coffee, which will hopefully motivate me to help Ava get this place in order. Max sidles up next to me and bumps me with his shoulder.

"Morning." His voice is groggy.

"Hey, Max. She talked you into helping her with this shit too?" I ask.

"Yeah, she's hard to say 'no' to, ya know?"

"Tell me about it. So tell me about the party tonight."

"It's at Xavier's apartment. That's all I know," Max says quietly, rubbing his hands over his face.

"What time are you coming to get us?" I ask, keeping my eyes trained on Ava and the hell she's giving those two poor custodians.

"Six o'clock sound okay?"

"Sounds good. We'll be ready."

The rest of the day flies by, even though the gym is nowhere near being complete. Ava agrees to stay and finish up the decorations with two teachers and the two custodians, who, at this point, all but hate her.

"I'm outta here," I announce to Ava. It's after four o'clock, and I need to shower and get ready for the party. I decided I'm going with or without Ava. I've planned my outfit in my head—deciding to wear my black strapless shirt with faded-blue skinny jeans. Pair that with my turquoise jewelry and my cute black ballet flats since I'm so damn tall. The outfit is comfortable and cute. It's all set.

Ava walks over to me as I grab the car keys from her purse.

"I'm sorry I'm ditching the party. I just want this to be perfect." She sighs, looking around the gym at all the work we've done, and all the work she still has to do. Max left hours ago, leaving Ava and me to finish decorating with the school staff.

"Shit. Did you let Adrian know you're not going? They're coming by at six to get us."

"No. You're going to tell them I'm not going when they come to get *you*. They'll try to convince me that this is fine, and I want perfect, not fine," she says, swinging her arm through the air at the gym around us.

"I know, I get it." It's not her personality to settle for fine; she wants perfect and perfect is what she'll get.

"Have fun tonight," she says with a wink.

"I will. Don't stay here too late. It's going to be perfect, Ava."

"I know, I know. See you at home later, okay?" She wraps her arms around me for a quick hug.

"How are you getting home?" I ask, forgetting that I am taking the car that we arrived together in.

"Mom and Dad. Don't worry about me. Go. Have fun." She waves me off.

CHAPTER FOUR

-Gabe-

Spending time with my older brother Luke has always been one of my favorite things. Being so close in age, he really has been my best friend. We're shooting hoops at the park by his apartment and this is the first time I've seen him since I got home from college last week. Aiming for a three-point shot, I toss the ball. *Swoosh.*

"Nice shot!" Luke says as he grabs the basketball, dribbling it back to the free-throw line to take one last shot for himself.

"Thanks. Pretty sure I just kicked your ass with that last game." I laugh as we walk toward the park bench to grab our waters.

"It's good to have you home," Luke says, taking a long pull from his water bottle.

"It's good to be home," I say, pausing as I use my t-shirt to wipe the sweat off of my forehead. "Actually, that's what I wanted to talk to you about." I take a quick sip of water. "I'm not going back to Arizona in the fall."

"Oh yeah. Why not?" he asks rather abruptly, taking another drink of water.

"Honestly, football isn't going to be my career. I've given this a lot of thought—meaningful thought." I pause for a moment before I tell him, "I want to apply to the fire academy."

"Seriously?"

"Dead serious. I'm not going back to Arizona."

"Told Mom and Dad yet?" he asks with a chuckle and a raised eyebrow.

"Nah, soon. I wanted to talk to you and tell you first."

"So you're just going to walk away from the scholarship?"

"I am. I just know this is what I want to do," I respond. I know he thinks I'm stupid to walk away from the scholarship with only one year left, but I have my mind made up.

"You know I'll support whatever it is you want to do, and I'd love to work with you, little brother."

"Thanks, man. I appreciate that. I'm going to head home and take a shower. Catch up with ya this weekend?"

"Sounds good," he says as we grab our keys and head toward our trucks. I breathe a sigh of relief, knowing that I have Luke's support; now it's telling Mom and Dad.

"What are you doing here?" I ask Ava, noticing her bedroom floor covered with papers.

"Just finished setting up the gym for tomorrow's graduation. Took us twelve hours because those asshats didn't follow the directions I left them yesterday. What does it matter to you anyway?" she bites at me.

"It doesn't matter to me. I just didn't expect to see you here."

"Well, here I am."

God, she's so fucking pissy tonight. "Where's Jess?" I ask casually.

"She went to Xavier's party with Max and Adrian just like we talked about this morning. Did you lose your memory, old man?" she says without even raising her head to look at me. She's in a fucking mood, and I can't deal with her attitude when she's like this.

But now I'm pissed off, my blood boiling. I told Jess not to go to that fucking party, but she went anyway, alone, without Ava. I walk across the hall into my bedroom, grab a set of clean clothes, and quickly change. All I can think about is what that fucking asshole Xavier will try to do with her. I've heard the stories firsthand of how Xavier gets girls drunk and takes advantage of them. Over my dead body will he fucking touch her.

The last place I want to show up is Xavier Garza's apartment, but I'm going to go get Jess even if I have to drag her out of there kicking and screaming.

"Why didn't she listen to me?" I mutter to myself.

Grabbing my wallet and keys off of my dresser, I head out the door. As I pull into the apartment complex, I can hear the music coming from the patio on the ground floor. I let myself in through there instead of going inside and using the front door. I immediately see Jess inside through the patio door, talking to Max and Adrian. When I see her smile, a sense of relief washes over me, but fuck if my pulse won't settle down. She looks amazing. Her hair is down and wavy, flowing down past her shoulders to the middle of her back. She's wearing jeans and a tight black shirt. She's stunning. Xavier is mixing drinks at the counter, and I watch him walk over to Jess, handing her a red plastic cup before walking away. My pulse quickens when I see her bring the cup up to her lips. That's all I needed to see.

When I step through the glass sliding patio doors into the main living area of the apartment, I hear, "What's up, Garcia?" from Xavier. Everyone turns to watch me as I walk through the living room toward the small kitchen, including Jess, who looks surprised to see me.

Giving him a curt nod, I respond with my intentions of being here. "Not much, man. I just came to pick up Jess." She squeezes the red plastic cup in her hand as she glares at me.

"Dating your little sister now?" Xavier laughs, taking a drink of his beer. Most of the room starts laughing at his remark, and it's taking great restraint for me not to fucking snap his head off his body right here in his own apartment.

"She's not my sister, Garza, and who the fuck I date isn't any of your business, got it?" I say through clenched teeth. My tone is aggressive and I've positioned myself inches from his face.

"Settle down, Garcia. Just giving you a hard time, man," Xavier responds, still laughing. He backs off slightly because he knows I don't like him and that I'll knock him out right here. I've done it before, and he knows I won't hesitate to do it again. I'm still in his face when I feel a gentle hand on my bicep.

I don't take my eyes off of Xavier until I hear Jess whisper, "Calm down, let's just go." Her hand is warm as her fingers tighten around my arm. Turning, I reach for her hand and start walking, pulling her toward the patio door that I just came in through. I see her wave and offer a tight smile to Max, who just nods his head at me as we leave. The party is silent now; everyone is watching us leave.

"Adios, Garza," I shout over my shoulder.

"Asshole," I hear him respond quietly. I can't help but smirk. I am still holding Jess' hand and I don't let it go of her until we reach my truck.

"What the fuck was that?" Jess asks as she slides into the front seat and slams my truck door shut. "I am not a toddler. I can take care of myself, plus nothing was happening in there. You embarrassed me in front of my friends," she scowls. Her cheeks are flushed with anger, which upsets me.

"*They* are not your friends?" I question and point towards the apartment.

"Max and Adrian are."

"Yes, Max and Adrian are. The rest of those assholes aren't," I say with a raised voice.

I'm feeling a bit of remorse for the way I pulled her out of the party, but that remorse fades as I remember why I came to get her.

"Listen to me for a minute. Xavier is an asshole. He's hurt girls before—intentionally. He gets them drunk and takes advantage of them." I pause as heat roils through me. I think about what could have happened to her tonight. "It's happened more than once, and I know this because I know someone it's happened to. I know you're friends with Adrian, but his brother is a dick."

Her head drops slightly forward, her hair falling over her shoulder. She looks so innocent, so pure. Watching her fidget with her hands, I make a vow to myself that no one will hurt her. Ever.

"Why didn't you just tell me that this morning?" she asks quietly, turning to look at me. "I wouldn't have come if I knew that," she whispers.

"Look, what's important is that nothing happened, and I'm sorry if I embarrassed you."

"Thanks for coming to get me."

"You're welcome. So, can I buy you dinner? Peace offering?" She nods her head as she gives me a small smile.

CHAPTER FIVE

~Jess~

While I am still absorbing the information Gabe just dumped on me about Xavier, I can't help but smile a little when I think about how protective he was. My heart flitters a little in my chest when I sneak a peek at him as we're driving to dinner.

"Where are we going?" I ask casually, trying to lighten the somber mood in his truck.

"Surprise," he says, taking his eyes off the road to look at me.

"I don't like surprises."

"I know you don't." He chuckles.

"Then tell me where we're going."

"No."

"Why?" I ask and then stick my bottom lip out in a pouty motion.

"The lip isn't going to work, Jess. The only thing that lip is good for is me biting it." Well, that shut me up.

"You know…" I start, pausing for a second. "You shouldn't joke around about that stuff. I might actually think you're serious." I smirk and raise my eyebrow at him.

He pulls into the parking lot of Mancini's Italian Restaurant, parks, and shuts off the engine. As he reaches for the door handle, he catches my left arm.

"Who said I was joking?" he asks with intensity and fire in his eyes. He maintains eye contact with me while my blood pressure rises to unhealthy levels. I swallow, trying to wet my tongue, which has gone dry.

"Were you joking?" I ask him quietly, maintaining eye contact. Studying his face, I want to run my fingers over the ridge of his jaw line, the straight line of his perfect nose, and his soft lips. As I wait for him to answer, he sighs, then releases my arm.

My eyes fall to his hand, which has dropped to the center console between us. When I look back up at him, I'm caught off guard by the quick movement of his hand as I feel it rest upon my cheek. Using his thumb, he traces my bottom lip back and forth, causing my breath to hitch lightly at his gentle touch.

"Let's go," he whispers, his hand falling from my face, leaving my question still unanswered.

We're seated in the very back corner of the restaurant in a booth where no one else is near us. Since it is evening, the restaurant has turned down the lights, and most of the light is radiating from the small candles situated on each of the tables. The atmosphere is romantic, and I can't help but notice how handsome Gabe looks right now.

Our server greets us immediately, and instantly sets her sights on Gabe; most women do.

"What can I get you to drink?" she asks with a devious smile, never looking in my direction or acknowledging my presence.

"Diet Coke," I answer abruptly. She glances at me, blinking her eyes in annoyance that I answered her first. She turns her attention back to Gabe.

"Iced tea." He answers her without ever looking at her, or even noticing that she's ogling him. She leaves quickly, but not before casting one last snarky look at me over her shoulder.

"What are you going to order?" Gabe asks, still paging through the menu.

"Just spaghetti; I'm simple like that," I say, setting my menu at the end of the table. An abrupt laugh comes from Gabe, catching me off-guard.

"You're hardly simple," he says, looking over his menu at me with both of his eyebrows raised.

"What's that supposed to mean?"

"Just that; 'simple' isn't a word I would use to describe you," he says sincerely. I blush at his remark.

"How *would* you describe me?"

"There's no one word to describe you, Jess."

"Give it a shot."

"Give me some time to think of a word, ask me again later." He smiles at me. His full lips stretch with his large smile. His teeth are perfectly straight and bright white against the bronzed skin of his face. I nod at him; just sitting with him, looking at him, and speaking to him has left me speechless.

"What are you going to get?" I ask curiously, turning the conversation away from me.

"Not sure yet."

Our bitchy server is back with our drinks, a breadbasket, and her shitty attitude. We place our orders, Gabe finally deciding on chicken Marsala. Our server never stops smiling at

Gabe; giving him flirty eyes and leaning into him with her hip against our table. I kick him lightly under the table to get his attention and flash him a tight smile.

"That'll be all," he says, sending our waitress on her way. "What?" he asks, looking confused. It amazes me that he doesn't notice the way women outwardly flirt with him.

"You know, I'm sure she'll just give you her phone number if you just ask," I say sarcastically. "Hell, she'll probably drop to her knees right here if you just asked her." A deep laugh erupts from him and he tosses his head back with laughter.

"Do you think she's the type of girl I should date?" he asks me, leaning in across the table, his arms folded in front of him.

"I don't know what your type is, Gabe," I shoot back at him, narrowing my eyes.

"I think you do."

"Well, why don't you save us both some time and energy, and just tell me," I demand, leaning in toward him. I hate that this table is a barrier between us.

Turning his head to the side, I can see him contemplating his response. "You want to know what my type is? I'll tell you," he whispers. "My type is..." He pauses for a moment before continuing. "I'll tell you after dinner." He leans back, trying to contain his smile.

"Are you kidding me?" I roll my eyes at him. "That's two things you have to get back to me on."

He erupts in laughter again. "I love getting you all worked up," he says, reaching across the table and placing his hand on top of mine. My eyes drop to our hands, and I look back up at him. I feel a wave of warmth run through me at his touch. He runs his thumb over the top of my hand and looks from our hands, up to me. His smile fades and a more serious look sets across his face.

"I wanted to apologize again, Jess. I'm really sorry if I embarrassed you tonight at Xavier's."

I let out a deep breath. I want to be angry with him, but I can't. Before I have the opportunity to respond, he continues. "It's just that, I don't know what I would have done if something had happened to you."

"Thank you for apologizing, again, but nothing would have happened."

"You don't know that," he says sharply.

"No, I guess I don't. But thank you for coming to get me." I offer him a small smile.

The waitress appears with our food, and I can't help but flash her a dirty look when she notices Gabe's hand stretched across the table on top of mine. I'm not really hungry, but I take a few bites of the spaghetti I ordered, trying not to make a mess of myself. I notice Gabe's demeanor has become a little more serious, and he seems distracted as if something is on his mind.

"Everything okay?" I ask, taking a small bit of the spaghetti that I've twirled around my fork. Looking up at me, he studies my face, and I can tell he wants to say something.

"You know you can talk to me," I urge, setting down my fork.

He nods at me, then looks down at his plate of chicken Marsala. As he pushes the chicken and pasta around, he takes a deep breath. "I'm not going back to Arizona in the fall."

I nearly choke on a spaghetti noodle. "What! Why not? Mom and Dad are going to flip the fuck out. What about football? Your scholarship? When did you decide this?" I ask, my thoughts all over the place.

"You just threw about four hours worth of questions at me." He laughs at me, shaking his head back and forth. "I'm going to tell Mom and Dad this weekend. I just had to make sure that my plans were set before I made this decision and told everyone."

"What plans?"

"What I'm going to do with my life, Jess. Why I'm staying here in Santa Ruiz," he answers quietly.

"So you're just giving up football and your scholarship?" I ask, my voice laced with concern. "You're staying here?"

Nodding his head, he takes a long drink of his iced tea. "I decided at the end of last semester that I really want to be a firefighter, like Luke and Chief. I can finish my studies here and hopefully get on with the department in Santa Ruiz."

I'm silent, more out of shock than out of disagreement. My mind is all over the place. I'm elated that he's staying, yet I'm scared for how Mom and Dad are going to react. I can sense his discomfort with telling me, but I'm so glad he did.

"Wow," is all that I can seem to say.

"That's it? Just 'wow'?"

"I mean, I'm surprised, I guess." I smile. "You know girls totally dig firefighters, right?" I joke with him.

"Yeah, I've heard that." He laughs.

"I'm glad you're staying," I whisper, not sure if I want him to hear me or not.

"Me too," he whispers back.

I notice he gets lost in his thoughts again. Our server sets the bill on our table, and he grabs it.

"Thanks for dinner," I say, hoping to pull his attention from his serious thoughts. "And thanks again for coming to get me from the party—I mean it." This time, it's me reaching out to touch his arm. Lifting his head to look at me, he slides out of the booth.

"You're welcome," he says quietly as he waits for me to slide out of my side of the booth. Reaching out, he takes my hand, pulling me gently to a standing position. Without letting go of my hand, he laces his fingers through mine as he walks us through the restaurant and out the front door to his truck.

"Hey, remember…you still have to tell me what your type of girl is," I say, mocking him from earlier.

He stops near the back of his truck and turns to look back at me. "How about I show you?"

CHAPTER SIX

-Gabe-

I'm going to tell her tonight. My heart is racing, and my palms are sweating. For over a year, I've been dancing around the feelings I have for Jess. I've tried telling myself that I can't fall for her, or I shouldn't fall for her, but the problem with that is, it doesn't work that way. She is a magnetic force that draws me in. Yes, physically, she's beautiful, but it's more than that. She makes me feel things I've never felt before.

"Where are we going?" she asks as she looks up and down both sides of the street that we're driving down.

"You'll see when we get there."

She smiles at me and gives me an exaggerated eye roll. It's a gorgeous night—warm, and the sky is perfectly clear with a full moon. I'm taking her to Washington Park where it's pitch black and we'll be able to see the stars. It's off the beaten path, so I can't imagine that anyone else will be there—all part of my plan.

As I park under a light in the small gravel parking lot, Jess jumps out of the car before I can get around to open the door for her. When we meet each other in front of my truck, I grab her hand; again lacing our fingers together as if she's already mine. We walk in the direction of the hill at the far end of the park; I can barely make it out, it's so dark.

"It's so dark," she says, barely audible. I can't tell if she's afraid or just stating the obvious.

"You're fine. I'm not going to let anything happen to you." I give her hand a little reassuring squeeze. Finding our way to the bottom of the hill, we stop and look up at the top.

"That's where we're going?" she asks, looking up the hill.

"Yep."

Climbing the hill takes us a few minutes, but when we get to the top, it's perfect. The moon is so bright that it illuminates all of Jess' gorgeous features, yet it's still dark enough that you can see every star in the sky.

"It's beautiful," she gasps, her head falling backwards as she looks up at the sky.

"I know. I knew you'd like it here. Come, lie down on your back." Both of us lie down in the soft grass next to each other, our fingers still intertwined. We lie close to each other, shoulder-to-shoulder and hip-to-hip. Taking her hand, I lay it on my chest, pressing it against the rapid beating of my heart.

We lie like this for a few minutes as I muster up the courage to tell her what I've been wanting to say to her for at least a year.

"Jess. I need to tell you something. Just please listen without saying anything, okay?" I tell her. She turns her head towards me. The moonlight reflects off of her face, illuminating her full lips.

"You're making me nervous."

"I told you not to say anything." I tell her, putting my finger over her lips to keep her quiet. Her lips separate slightly and a quiet laugh escapes. I squeeze her hand, which is still resting on my chest.

"Sorry. Go ahead."

"For months, I've had feelings for someone. She's my type of girl, the one I wanted to tell you about at the restaurant. She's beautiful and funny, smart and witty." I pause to swallow and to catch my breath, which seems to have evaded me.

"I've tried denying those feelings for her, not because I didn't want to care about her and not because I didn't want to accept my feelings for her, but because I'm afraid that if I tell her my feelings, she will think differently of me, and it will ruin our friendship." Her eyes never leave mine, but her grip on my hand loosens. She doesn't know I'm talking about her. Tightening my fingers around hers so that she can't pull away, I finally spit it out.

"Jess, what I'm trying to say is that *you* are all I think about. I want to hug *you* and kiss *you*, and love *you*. You may not feel the same way about me, but I had to tell you." She's still. Staring at me with wide eyes and no emotion on her face. *Fuck my life. I shouldn't have ever told her.* A small sigh escapes from me. "Every kiss, every touch damn near killed me. When you came to visit me in Arizona, I got to have just a little taste of you, not knowing if I'd ever really have you, in the way I have always wanted, has been killing me." I can't even believe I just told her that, but it's the truth. The taste of her lips, the smell of her neck; every one of those things has nearly sent me over the edge.

She sits up suddenly, and I once again tighten my grip on her hand so she can't fucking run away from me. I know I've scared her.

"Talk to me," I whisper. She drops her head, and her long hair falls forward so her face is hidden from me. Sitting up, she scoots to face me while tugging at me gently, coaxing me to sit up as well. The silence is killing me after my declaration to her.

When I sit up, we're facing each other, touching knees-to-knees. She takes a deep breath and raises her head.

"I'm afraid too, because I've had feelings for you for as long as I can remember," she says as I release the breath that I didn't realize I was holding. A sense of relief washes over me, and before she can say anything else, I lean in and press my lips to hers, needing her to feel how much I want her. When she drops her hands, I bring mine up to cup both sides of her face.

Relief washes over me when she kisses me back. We're both taking what we've been denying each other. The taste of her lips is something I will never, in all of my life, forget. Her lips are full and soft—and mine. Gently pushing her onto her back, I lie at her side, deepening my kiss.

I nip lightly at her bottom lip, and run my tongue across it. I can feel her heart beating against my chest, and all I can think about is how I want to take her right here, but then I don't. I want perfect with her, and in the grass on top of a hill is not perfect enough for her. I continue to kiss her across her cheek and behind her ear, and the low moan that comes from the back of her throat when I kiss that spot behind her ear gets me instantly hard. I need to stop now, but I don't—or rather, I can't.

Working my way down her neck and back up again, I hover over her slightly swollen lips. Weaving my fingers through her hair, I pull her face to me, pressing my lips to hers one more time. I've never kissed a woman like this before or had a kiss mean what this means. I'm in love with this woman. Madly in love.

"Thank you," she whispers against my lips as I still kiss her. Her hands are firm, gripping my biceps.

"For what?" I mumble, still kissing her. Now that I have kissed her, tasted her, I don't ever want to stop.

"For everything," she whispers, gently pushing me off her. She rolls herself on top of me so that she is straddling me. Grabbing my hands, she laces her fingers through mine and places them next to my head, holding them on each side of me while she kisses me. God, she's so fucking sexy. She repeats every kiss, every movement that I did to her, including nipping me on the bottom lip and the kiss behind the ear. God, I want her.

Slowing down, she sits up, and when I join her, I pull her to my lap as she wraps her legs around my waist.

"Now what?" she laughs, dropping her head to my shoulder. I breathe her in and let the smell of coconut invade my nose.

"This is just the beginning," I say to her, planting a kiss on her lips in between each word.

"Beginning of what?"

"Us." A huge sense of relief washes over me. I wasn't sure what I was going to do if she didn't reciprocate my feelings. A quiet laugh escapes her lips as she lays her head on my chest. We lie like this; in the silence. Her warm body pressed against mine feels natural, like she was made for me.

I shift slightly to my side. "Jess?"

"Mmm hmm."

"Last year, when I kissed you in Arizona." I pause as she sits up and whispers, "Yeah."

"I wanted to tell you all of this back then. I'm sorry I waited so long." When I see a hint of a smile, I continue. "Every text, every phone call, every e-mail since that night,

I've always wanted to tell you this. But tonight, seeing your face, touching your lips, holding you—this is exactly what I wanted."

"Me too," she whispers.

CHAPTER SEVEN

~Jess~

I want the drive home to last forever, but of course, those four miles and two right turns pass in the blink of an eye. I could have laid on top of that hill all night with him. Every dream, every wish, every hope of mine came true tonight.

"What are you thinking about?" he asks me quietly as he cuts the engine and we sit in the dark cab of his pick-up truck.

"Just how happy I am right now. In this moment, how everything I ever wanted just happened," and I pause, "and that I'm so afraid all at the same time."

"Why are you afraid?"

"I'm afraid that when I wake up tomorrow, this won't be real. I feel like you're going to wake up and realize you told your 'kid sister' you had feelings for her, and that you're going to regret everything you said to me tonight." I take a deep breath and hit him with one last punch. "And I'm so afraid that I won't be enough for you—pretty enough, smart enough—just 'good enough' in general for you." I cast my eyes down at my fidgeting hands. It was so hard to say those words, admit those insecurities, but it's the truth.

He grabs my chin, turning my head so that our eyes meet. "This is real. Don't ever doubt my feelings for you. For years, I've watched you, wanted you—waited for you." He moves his hand from my chin and cups my cheek. "Please don't be afraid, Jess. I promise I won't ever hurt you." I nod my head, and let his words ease my fears. "And don't you ever think you're not good enough for me, do you understand?" His voice is quiet yet firm.

"Yes," I whisper.

The front porch light turns on and pulls us from this moment. "We should get inside." Leaning across the console, he presses his lips to mine. His kiss is intense, hungry. He mumbles the words "this is real" against my lips in between soft kisses.

"Understand?" he asks me.

"Yes," I whisper back, pressing one last kiss to his lips.

I open my bedroom door to find Ava still working on her speech. She looks up at me, raising her eyebrow.

"You're home early. How was the party?" she asks, looking back down at the index cards she has notes scribbled all over.

"It's after midnight, Ava. That's not early." I laugh. "The party was, ah…good," I mumble as I strip off my clothes, throwing on a tank top and boxer shorts.

"Must have been one hell of a party. You're dead sober—looks like I didn't miss much." She smirks; her words dripping with sarcasm. Not acknowledging her comment, I roll my eyes and head to the bathroom to brush my teeth and wash my face. My pulse quickens, thinking about Gabe being in the room next door lying in his bed, and how badly I want to crawl in next to him and snuggle up to his warm body.

I splash cold water on my face to try to stop thinking about him. If I don't, I know I won't be getting any sleep. As I tiptoe across the hallway back to my room, I stop to glance at his closed bedroom door. There's a hint of light coming from underneath, probably from his TV. Smiling to myself as I replay the last few hours, I walk over to his door, resting my hand on the handle. Glancing over my shoulder to ensure no one is coming, I hesitantly open the door and step in, closing the door quietly behind me. He is lying on the bed; when he sees me, he slowly sits up.

I stand there, nervously tugging at the hem of my top as he stands and walks toward me. Pressing his body flush against mine and grabbing my hips, he whispers, "Miss me already?" He's so close I have to tilt my head to look up at him. Timidly, I slide my hands up his bare chest and around the back of his neck. With piercing eyes, he stands, staring down at me intently. My breathing is shallow, and nerves swarm in my belly as I gently pull him down to me.

Looking up at him, I close my eyes as he presses his lips to mine. Slowly, he moves his lips back and forth across mine. His tongue finds the smallest opening and urges my lips apart, and his kiss becomes more intimate. I gasp as he alternates between light and gentle, and intense, deep kisses. My legs shake slightly as my body is overcome by the intensity of this moment. We are both breathing erratically when he drags his lips away from mine.

"I should go," I say in a hush.

Pressing one last kiss to my lips, he whispers, "I don't want you to."

I reach behind me, grasping the doorknob. "I know, but I need to." I slip out of Gabe's room and cross the hallway back to mine.

"What's that smirk for?" Ava says as she catches me smiling.

"Nothing. I'm just tired and ready to go to sleep," I lie. Jumping into bed, I pull my comforter over my head to hide the smile that is still spread across my face. I'm positive this was the best night of my life.

"You're a terrible liar," Ava mumbles.

"Shut up, Ava," I mumble from underneath my comforter.

Thump
Thump

"Are you kidding me right now, Ava?" I scream as best I can with a raspy voice. There is nothing worse than being woken up by pillows being thrown at your head.

"No, I'm not kidding. You need to get up, now. We need to talk. I just got off the phone with Adrian and he told me about Gabe's little 'knight in shining armor' rescue last night."

Fuck. Sitting up, I sweep my long, messy hair from my face.

"He picked me up; so what?"

"So what?" She stands next to my bed with her hands on her hips and a smirk on her face. "God, it's been obvious for weeks. The not very discreet looks between you guys. The strange tension when you're around each other. I was just waiting for you two to slip up."

"Slip up?" I question her. "Gabe didn't want us going to the party, Ava. When he found out you weren't with me, he came to get me. That's all there is to tell."

"You're lying."

"No, I'm not."

"Yes, you are. When you lie, you get a rash on your neck. Your neck is bright red and it's starting to crawl up your cheeks. So just spill it, would you?"

Shit. Sighing, I place my hand over my neck and feel my pulse beating rapidly. "We've really been *that* obvious?"

"Let's just say, you two suck at hiding things. You don't need to be fucking Sherlock Holmes to figure you two out." She laughs, and I'm annoyed. "What were you doing last night anyway? You didn't get home until after midnight," she asks, raising her eyebrows up.

I decide it's best just to be honest at this point. "He came to get me from Xavier's and we ended up grabbing dinner at Mancini's. We just talked until we came home. Honestly, Ava, that's all that happened."

"What did you talk about?"

"Really? Does it matter?"

"Yes, it does."

"We talked about school."

"That's it?" she asks.

"No, that's not it, but I can't remember everything we talked about. Lots of things, I guess."

"Did you kiss?"

"Ava!"

"What? It's a valid question."

"I'm not answering that." I can feel my face flush.

She gasps, "You did. You kissed my brother. Ewwww."

I bury my face in my hands. I was not expecting an interrogation first thing this morning. "Look, I'm happy for you guys," she says quietly. "Just don't be touching each other in front of me—that's gross and not something I need these precious little eyes of mine seeing." She giggles, sitting down on the bed next to me.

As I look up at her, I can feel my face flush again with embarrassment. "I should have told you I had feelings for him," I admit.

"Nah, I can imagine it would be weird for you to talk to me about my brother," she says sincerely.

I nod my head and smile. "You know this is the first time I've ever had to keep a secret from you." I giggle.

"Is that why you always keep Max at arm's length? Because you like Gabe?"

"Kind of, I mean, I just never had feelings for Max; he's just a good friend. That's all."

"He's going to be heartbroken, you know?" She laughs.

"He'll be fine."

My phone rings on my nightstand and I can't help but be thankful for the interruption. Glancing at the screen, I pull it from the power cord and answer it. I mouth to Ava, "It's my dad," and she leaves the room.

"Hey, Jessie," my dad says excitedly into the phone.

"Morning, Dad."

"You excited? Today's your big day."

"Yeah," I say quietly.

"I'm really proud of you."

"Thanks."

"Say, the reason I'm calling is, I wanted to see if you wanted to grab dinner after graduation. I'm going to have to work again tonight, but wanted to spend some time with you before I head back to work."

"Sure, that sounds good. Hey, Dad, so now that I'm graduating, do you think I can start staying at our house? You said I could, but I wanted to ask again." There is silence on the phone.

"Let's talk about it at dinner. Pick a place, anywhere you want to go."

"Can we do Thai?"

"Sounds perfect. I'll see you at the school at three o'clock." And the phone clicks. This is the extent of conversations with my dad.

After I shower quickly and get dressed, I decide to head home, across the street, to relax for a few hours before graduation. Closing the bedroom door behind me, I hear Gabe's raised voice coming from the kitchen. I freeze momentarily when I hear the exchange between him, Mom and Dad, and even Luke. I tiptoe down the stairs and out the front door as quietly as possible.

I'm not home ten minutes when my phone pings, alerting me to a new text message. Fishing my phone out of my purse, I slide open the screen to see a new message from Gabe.

"Where did you go?"

I don't know why this makes me happy, but it does and I smile as I tap out my reply.

"Home."

"I'll be right over."

Those four words cause my pulse to quicken and my palms to sweat. I rush into the bathroom to throw some mascara on my eyelashes and swipe some lip gloss across my lips. I run my fingers through my long, wavy hair, hoping to make it look more manageable. Just as I finish up, the doorbell rings and my stomach flips with anxiety.

I pause momentarily before opening the door, taking a deep breath. Twisting the door knob, I open the door and Gabe immediately steps over the threshold and pulls me to his lips. His kiss is warm and sweet.

"You taste like cherries," he mumbles against my lips.

"It's my lip gloss."

"I like it." He finally pulls his lips off mine, but continues to hold me close to him.

"I like *you*," I whisper and press my lips to his for one more kiss.

Pulling out of his embrace, I walk to the couch and sit down, and he follows me. Settling in next to me, he pulls my hand into his.

"So what are your plans tonight after graduation?" he asks.

"Dad is taking me to dinner before heading back to the station," I say with a shrug.

"Luke mentioned they're shorthanded; he's headed into work after graduation too. So you'll be at our house tonight, then?"

"Not sure; I'm trying to convince my dad to let me stay here now."

"Why?"

"Because I'm almost nineteen; I think I can stay at my own house." I laugh.

"But I like you across the hall from me."

"I like you across the hall from me too, but it's time for me to grow up and stay on my own once in a while." I run my thumb over the top of his hand.

"I suppose." He smiles. "Is your dad going to be at graduation? I need to talk to him."

"He'll be there, but why don't you come to dinner with us tonight."

"Are you sure?"

"Yes, I'm sure. In fact, you'd be doing me a favor. I don't know what we'd talk about if we were by ourselves anyway. You guys can talk 'fire talk.'" I laugh. "Speaking of 'fire talk,' I heard you talking to Mom and Dad when I snuck out. How did it go?"

"They're warming to it. At first, they were really upset, but they want me to be happy." He pauses, deep in thought for a few seconds. "This makes me happy. You make me happy." He flashes a genuine smile at me.

"You better not have based this decision on me. What happens when you decide next week that you don't like me anymore? Are you going to run back to Arizona?" I ask seriously.

His head tips back and he laughs at me. "Don't talk like that. I'll never not like you. Ever. What are you thinking?" he asks in a serious tone.

"I think you're crazy, is what I'm thinking. But I love you anyway," I say, laughing. I hope that it came out as more of a joke, but I'm serious; I'm madly in love with him.

Chapter Eight

-Gabe-

Graduation was…just like any other graduation, but Jess was beautiful in her cap and gown and Ava's speech was a hit. We spent an hour after the ceremony taking an endless amount of pictures and now I'm ready to have dinner with Chief and Jess. I ring the doorbell and wait.

"Gabe, come on in, son. Jess says you're joining us for dinner," he says, offering me his hand for a handshake.

"Yes, sir," I say. *Why the fuck am I so nervous?* Jess comes around the corner, and my pulse quickens. She's wearing a long strapless casual black dress and sandals. Her hair is flowing down over her shoulders. Her green eyes are striking against her tanned skin and the dark dress.

"Jess." I nod my head at her.

"Hi." She smiles.

"Well, if you two are done gawking at each other, let's go," Chief says. Jess' mouth falls open, and I feel myself blush.

"Gabe, you can ride with me. Dad has to drive separately since he's going to work after dinner," she says. Once we're safely out of Chief's line of vision, I shoot my eyes to her.

"Did you tell him already? Jesus, I wasn't expecting that." I'm whispering, afraid he might hear me.

"No! I didn't tell him. Are we that fucking obvious?" she asks.

"That's exactly what I was wondering."

"Ava says we are," I admit.

"She knows?"

"She does now. Adrian told her you showed up at the party and dragged me out of there like a caveman."

I laugh at the caveman reference. "Good, one less person we need to stress about telling."

Leaning forward, she rests her head on the steering wheel for a moment and, when she raises her head, she just starts laughing. "Let's go," she says.

Our hostess seats us in a booth. Jess slides in next to her dad, and I sit across from them. I try not to look at Jess too much, but apparently, we're transparent, according to everyone around us. Chief orders a bunch of different entrées that we all decide to share, which makes it easy since I can't decide what I want to eat because I'm so nervous.

"So, Chief," I finally say, clearing my throat. "I have something I want to talk to you about." I glance at Jess and back to Chief.

"Sure, what's up, son?" he asks, his voice deep. His eyes shift between Jess and me.

"I've decided not to go back to Arizona in the fall." I pause, waiting to see his reaction.

He focuses his eyes on me for a few seconds. "Okay." he nods his head for me to continue.

"I've decided that I'd like to train at the academy and hopefully come on your crew as a firefighter."

He takes a drink of his ice water, sets his glass down, and plays with the condensation that is dripping down the side of the glass. "That's a big decision to make, son. Have you talked to your parents?" he asks, knowing they'd be concerned about my decision to not return to school.

"Yes, they were concerned at first. They didn't want me to toss away my scholarship, but they're supportive and warming to my decision. They're proud of Luke and said they'd be just as proud of me if this is what I really wanted to do."

"And is it?" He raises an eyebrow at me.

"Yes, sir," I say without an ounce of hesitation. Chief nods his head, and I can tell he's thinking about saying something. The silence is not helping my nerves.

"So the only reason you're leaving Arizona and your scholarship is because you want to be a firefighter? No other reason?"

I look at Jess; her eyes are open wide and she gives a slight shake of her head, as if to tell me not to say anything to him about us.

"Yes, sir."

With a large smile on his face, Chief finally speaks. "Well, then, let's get you enrolled in the academy as a recruit and get your classes scheduled. I'd love to have you on my crew." He reaches across the table to shake my hand.

Breathing the biggest sigh of relief, I glance across the table at Jess to see a small smile cross her lips.

For the next hour, Chief entertains us. Okay, let's be honest: he entertains me with story after story. I can honestly say it fuels my excitement. I love talking to Chief about my new direction in life and having his support as well. I could have sat here all night and listened to his stories of fires, medical emergencies, and even the bizarre calls they get. Jess is still smiling; I can tell she's happy for me. As we're finishing dinner, Chief directs his attention to Jess.

"Jessie, about our conversation this morning, I think it's fine that you stay at home. Just please check in with me a few times throughout my shift."

"Sure, Dad." She smiles at him, glancing back at me. Chief settles the bill and slides out of the booth.

"Thanks for dinner, Chief." I offer him a handshake.

"You're welcome, son. I look forward to bringing you on. Give me a call next week to discuss the details and next steps." He leans down, places a quick kiss on the top of Jess' head, and quickly leaves.

"You hardly ate anything," I say, looking at Jess' plate.

"I wasn't hungry and I want to go for a quick run when I get home."

"A run? I just ate an entire plate of Pad Thai!"

She laughs at me and stands, offering me her hand as she pulls me from the booth. Settled in the car, she inserts the key into the ignition. Stopping her from starting the car, I reach over and pull her into a kiss. I never want to stop kissing her. Taking my time, I explore her mouth, her neck, and her mouth again.

"Gabe," she mumbles against my lips.

I stop her from speaking by deepening my kiss. "Let's stay in tonight," I mumble back against her lips.

She pulls away from me. "Who said I was doing anything with you tonight?" she says, laughing.

"You don't want to spend the evening with your boyfriend?" I throw out, knowing that will get her attention. She turns her head to me quickly, her eyes wide.

"Say it again," she says with the biggest smile I've ever seen. She's biting her bottom lip as she waits for me to repeat what I just said.

"Do you want to spend the evening with your *boyfriend*?" I make sure to say it slow, enunciating the word "boyfriend," hoping she's affected by it.

"Yes, boyfriend, I'd love to spend my evening with you, but after our food settles, can we go for a quick run?"

"Are you going to try and kill me again?" I laugh, knowing that a quick run to her is a half marathon for me.

"No, just a few short miles, I promise. I'll let you win if you want to race," she says with a little grin.

"I always win. Remember that," I say, giving her a little wink.

CHAPTER NINE

~Jess~

I open the front door. Gabe is standing on my porch in his running shorts and a compression shirt, carrying a small duffle bag. I glance down at the bag and flash him a funny look.

"Moving in?"

"Want me to?" he says, stepping inside and planting a soft kiss on my lips.

"I'd love for you to," I mumble against his lips. As I toss his bag on the floor next to the couch, I catch myself smiling as I imagine going to bed with him every night and waking up wrapped around him every morning.

"Ready to go?" he asks, pulling me out of my short daydream.

"Yeah. Ready for me to kick your ass?"

"You promised you'd let me win, remember?" He winks at me and smacks my butt hard.

"Ow. I remember."

While we're stretching, I plan out our short run. I decide to take us down our normal route to Washington Park where we always run, this time actually running into the park and on the paved trail that winds through the park. It's a relatively short run there and back.

"Ready?" I ask him, jogging toward the street.

"Ready."

"Let's see if you can keep up this time, big guy."

About a mile and a half into our run, we're just inside the park entrance when I hear his breathing become a bit heavier.

"Jesus Christ, Jess. You said you weren't going to kill me," he says as I watch a small bead of sweat roll from his hairline, down his temple.

"I wasn't. I was just pushing us since it's a short run," I say, slowing our pace so that we're now in a light jog.

"Remember that hill?" He points at the hill where he brought me last night.

"How could I forget?" I can't help but smile when I see that hill. Slowing us down to a walk, we spend a minute catching our breath, but I notice Gabe keeps looking at the hill.

"Want to go back to the top?" He smiles at me. "Never mind; I can't wait that long to kiss you," he says, wrapping his arms around me and pulling me down into the grass just off the paved path. I can't help but giggle at how playful he's being. Holding my arms over my head, he runs his finger down my cheek to my neck, continuing all the way down to my stomach. Still hovering over me, he leans in as if to kiss me, but instead, uses his finger to start tickling me.

"Ahhhh!" I scream, which turns into a fit of laughter. He continues his attack, moving his hand from one side of my stomach to the other and up to my underarms. With my hands still pinned above my head, I'm helpless. I wiggle beneath him, trying to escape his hold.

"Tease," I yell at him while a tear runs out of my eye from laughing so hard.

"Got you, didn't I?" He laughs, finally stopping his assault as he collapses onto me. Pressing a sweet kiss to my lips, he rolls off of me and positions himself on his back at my side.

"That was mean." I giggle and slap his stomach softly.

"That was funny."

"I wanted you to kiss me." I pout.

"I did, when I was done tickling you."

Rolling back over, he straddles me and moves my arms over my head just as he did before.

"No. Not again." I laugh and try to lower my arms.

"Shhh…" He leans down and kisses me. Pressing light kisses to my lips, then my cheeks, my forehead, and even my eyelids. He kisses every inch of skin on my face and neck with gentle kisses.

"Gabe," I whisper against his lips, which have settled back on mine. "We need to finish our run."

He sighs and drops his head to my chest. Pulling himself off of me, he reaches his hand out to me to pull me off the ground.

"Fine, but we need to stand here for a few minutes. I can't walk right this minute," he says, shaking his head and adjusting his crotch. I can't help but laugh at my effect on him. Reaching out for my hand, he laces his fingers through mine and we begin walking. Suddenly, he drops my hand and takes off running, leaving me behind him. *Shit.*

"Damn you!" I yell at him, taking off in a sprint after him. He's running as fast as he can, and I know he's trying to beat me home. No way am I letting him win. We're on the last quarter mile, and I pass him in a full sprint. Rounding the corner of our street, we are about six houses away and I'm still in front of him by a few strides. Finally making it home, I run up onto my porch, using the railing to lean against while bending over, trying to catch my breath. Gabe is doing the same.

"Competitive much?" he sputters. Both of us have sweat running down our faces and his shirt is drenched.

"Look who's talking," I manage to say between breaths. Standing on the porch, we take our time catching our breath.

"What are you thinking?" Gabe asks.

"See that house over there?" I point at an angle across the street to an old house.

"Yeah. Old Man Johnson lives there."

"Every time I run or walk by there, I think about how beautiful that house must have been once."

"Don't bust his balls, Jess. He's old and can't keep it up."

"I know that." I roll my eyes at him. "I just look at all the potential it has. That small porch doesn't do that house justice. Imagine a full covered porch that wraps around the front and down both sides of that house." I find myself staring at this house, trying to see the beauty that's there, hidden behind chipped paint and dry rot wood. "With a porch swing," I say quietly.

"I love that you see potential where others see garbage," he responds, wrapping his arms around me from behind. We stand looking at that house for another minute.

"I wish someone could help him," I mutter.

"Dad has offered numerous times. He just tells him he's too old to invest the time or money to fix the place up."

"It's kind of sad. He's lived there his entire life; he raised his kids in that house." I can't help but think about raising kids in a house and the memories it must hold.

"Maybe that's why he doesn't want to change it. It holds too many memories for him."

"I was just thinking the same thing," I whisper. Gabe presses another kiss to my temple and unwraps his arms from around me.

"Let's go inside." He guides me towards the door.

"I'm going to grab a quick shower," I say, walking down the hallway. "You're welcome to use the other shower, or you can wait to use mine, unless you want to shower at home," I mumble over my shoulder, closing the bathroom door behind me.

I grab my robe, then I strip down and throw my sweaty running clothes on the bathroom floor into a pile. When I step into shower, the warm water pelts my skin. I stand still under the water with my eyes closed, and I can feel the dirt and sweat being washed away as the water massages me. I reach for my body wash with my eyes closed, and suddenly feel a hand on my shoulder. Quickly turning, beautiful hazel eyes are staring back at me.

"No sense in wasting water," he says, wrapping his muscular arms around me and pressing his mouth against my neck. Naturally, my head falls back, giving him more access to my sensitive skin. My stomach flips a little when his hands settle on my hips, pressing me against his firm body. Nervously, I place my hands on his shoulders; I've never seen nor been this close to a man naked, and to be pressed up against him has my mind racing. I gasp quietly as he gently nips at my neck.

I nervously run my hands down his firm chest to the hard ridges of his abs, feeling every muscle, every ridge, and goose bumps prick my skin. He groans against my lips as my hands explore him. I tilt my neck, and he moves his mouth there and finds that spot just behind my ear, leaving me trembling. I gasp, and my head falls back even further. The hot water from the shower is doing little to erase the goose bumps he has ignited across my body. My stomach is a ball of twisting nerves as his hands begin slowly exploring my body.

He reaches for the bottle of body wash and flips the cap open, squirting a generous amount into his hand. He starts massaging my arms and chest. My legs begin shaking as his large hands move up and down my sides, backwashing and massaging me. Reaching one of his arms around me, he finds my right nipple and gently pinches it, causing a shiver to spread across my trembling body.

"Tell me to stop if this makes you uncomfortable," he whispers in my ear. Pressing myself back against his firm chest, I balance myself as his other hand reaches around me, finding my other nipple and giving it a gentle pinch. Immediately, I feel the heat spread between my legs, and my stomach clenches as a small groan escapes me.

"Are you okay?" he whispers as he alternates between massaging my breasts and pinching my nipples.

"Mmm hmm," I mutter, and his hands move from my breasts to my stomach. I flinch and am self-conscious when his hands find my soft stomach, but he continues making small circles across my flesh with his fingers. He continues downward with one hand, reaching the top of my pubic bone, gliding until his fingers reach the pulsing flesh just below.

I gasp as one of his fingers slides across my labia, and I press back against him further, giving him better access. I can feel his erection pressing into my back, but I'm focused on the heat that has taken over my body and the feeling of his finger sliding gently back and forth across me.

Leaning into my neck, he whispers into my ear, "We need to get out of this shower. Now."

"But, I …" I start to say, but am interrupted immediately. I don't want him to stop.

"Now, Jess." He pulls the shower curtain back and reaches around me to shut off the water. Grabbing two large bath towels off the counter, he wraps one around his waist and the other around me. Stepping out of the shower, I reach for another towel and use it to towel dry my hair. Seconds later, I'm being pulled out of the bathroom, across the hallway, and into my room.

Walking to the edge of my bed, Gabe sits down, the towel still firmly in place around his waist. Pulling me towards him, he wraps his arms around my waist, resting his head on my stomach. My arms instinctively wrap around his neck, holding him in place. "I didn't want you to stop," I admit.

"I don't want to pressure you to do anything you're not ready for," he says, looking up at me, his eyes meeting mine. "You're not some girl I picked up at a party to take home and fuck. For as long as I can remember, I've cared about you, but now it's different; now I'm in love with you," he whispers against my belly, kissing it through the bath towel.

"I love you too, but I've never done this before," I admit nervously, pushing his head back slightly so I can look him in the eyes. I see confusion spread across his face.

"You never had a boyfriend before?"

"Yes, I've had a boyfriend before, but I'm a virgin," I whisper. "I've never let anyone touch me like you just did." He inhales sharply with what I've just told him.

"But, I saw your birth control pills on the counter. I assumed that you've…"

I interrupt, "I take those for other reasons. I've never *been* with anyone before." My heart is racing, and my hands are shaking with the admission that I'm still a virgin.

"I want nothing more than to touch you, be with you, and love you, but I will understand if you're not ready. I'll wait until you are," he says, his arms still wrapped around me. I nod my head as I take in the last few minutes: the shower, and my body's reaction to his hands touching me.

"Gabe?" I say, my voice trembling from being nervous.

"Yeah?"

I pull away from him and sit down on the edge of the bed, in hopes of stopping my legs from shaking. I've always imagined what my first time would be like, and I can't imagine anyone I'd rather give this to than him.

"I want you to be my first—and my last," I manage to say, my lip quivering. My entire body is trembling from fear, nervousness, and anticipation of this moment I want to share with him. "I don't want to wait any longer. I've always wanted *you*. Please, make love to me."

A small sigh escapes his lips as he turns toward me, pulling me into an embrace. Clinging to him, I can feel the rapid beat of his heart against my chest.

Urging me down to my back, he holds my head in both of his hands. His eyes are intense, but full of concern. "Are you sure? You will never get this back," he whispers. It comforts me to know that he is concerned about me and my feelings.

My heart is racing, and I can feel my pulse in my ears. "I've never been more sure about anything. I love you," I say, closing my eyes, a small tear escaping. Hovering over me, he wipes that stray tear, then tugs at the small knot in the towel that was holding it closed. The towel falls open and lies on either side of me. With a sharp inhale, I watch him slowly taking in the sight of me fully naked. Instinctively, I lay my arm across my stomach, and as quickly as I move it there, he pushes it away.

"You're beautiful," he whispers, his fingers trailing over my soft stomach. As I close my eyes, I feel his lips meet mine and begin their slow assault on me, moving to my neck, and down to my chest, finding my nipples. Savoring the feel of his lips moving across my skin, that newfound warmth spreads over my entire body again.

His tongue slowly moves around my nipple, and he takes his time, slowly alternating between each one. That intense heat between my legs is back, causing me to squirm lightly beneath him.

"Are you okay?" he asks, looking up at me. Nodding to him, he continues working my left nipple with his tongue while pinching my other nipple. Using his knees, he gently coaxes my thighs apart, and I feel his right hand move to my hip before continuing inward to my inner thigh. He circles his fingers on my thigh, causing my body to shake slightly from his touch. Settling himself between my legs, he allows me to get comfortable with his exploration.

His fingers trail upward, moving slowly to my center until he finds me, separating the soft skin he had been caressing just minutes ago in the shower. At first a gasp, but then small moan escapes me as he rubs gently—slowly.

"You're so wet," he says as his fingers continue to rub me lightly back and forth. I fight with my legs to keep them open as they instinctively want to close. I have never let a man touch me like this before, and while it feels amazing, I'm nervous. I can feel a pressure building in my lower abdomen, a sensation that causes me to catch my breath as the intensity comes and goes with each stroke. Pushing my legs further apart, he positions himself lower, kissing my inner thigh, removing his fingers from me and replacing it with his tongue.

"You okay?" he asks me again. My breaths are shallow, my nipples are firm, and my legs are still shaking, but I'm able to muster out a simple, "Yes."

"Tell me if you want me to stop."

"No. Don't."

I think he chuckles, but suddenly, I feel his tongue on me with one long stroke. I gasp loudly this time at the feel of his tongue as he licks me up and down. It's soft, yet rough. Gentle yet firm. It is when he finds that small patch of nerves that he gently sucks on that almost sends me over, and my legs begin shaking even more.

"Gabe," I whisper as I raise my hips and arch my back at the feel of his tongue. "Oh, God," I breathe out, my hips continuing to roll with the movement of his tongue. My hands find his head, and I grab onto his short hair as his tongue continues to push me further to the edge. My inner thighs are shaking as he holds them open; I've never experienced pleasure like this.

My heart is racing, my body is covered in goose bumps, and I feel that tremble in my abdomen building.

"Are you still okay?" he asks, pausing.

"Yes," is all I can muster. I feel him slip one finger into me, and I gasp at the pressure, clenching around his finger.

"You're so tight. Try to relax," he says as I nod my head so he knows I've heard him. His thumb is rubbing and gently applying pressure directly on my clit when I feel him slide a second finger inside of me. That trembling feeling is becoming more and more intense as I rock my hips with the movement of his fingers.

"Oh, God," I moan.

His fingers are moving in unison with my hips and his thumb is applying just the right amount of pressure. My thighs continue to shake and I feel the soles of my feet start burning as my toes curl. I close my eyes as I feel the most amazing release I've ever felt. My back arches more, and I gasp for air as ripples of pleasure run through my body. When he pulls his fingers from me, I watch as he moves them to his lips, tasting me. I'm mortified and curious at the same time as I watch him. Finishing, he crawls up me and simultaneously pulls the towel from around his waist, tossing it to the floor.

"I love you," he whispers, pressing his lips to mine. I can taste myself on his lips.

Still breathing heavily, I mumble against his lips, "I love you too."

Positioning himself between my legs, he settles in as he continues to kiss me slowly as I come down from my first orgasm. Finding that spot behind my ear, he licks and kisses me softly. I can feel that heat building between my legs again, brought on by the movement of his erection between my legs. The pressure of his pelvic bone pressing against me is causing another build-up.

"I want to make love to you too," he whispers in my ear. "But if you're not ready for that, please tell me now," he says, pulling back to look me directly in my eyes.

Brushing the hair off of my face, he kisses my temple. His eyes are dark, hooded, yet his touch is light and gentle. Closing my eyes momentarily, I nod my head. I can't imagine my first time with anyone other than him. Bringing both of my hands to his face, I pull his head down to me, pressing a needy kiss against his lips.

"Make love to me," I whisper against his lips. His forehead drops to mine as he lifts his hips slightly, pressing himself against my center. "Please," I beg him, my breathing rapid. He laces both of his hands through mine and places them on each side of my head. I squeeze his hands, to let him know I'm ready.

"Relax," he says. My pulse quickens with anticipation. As he gently enters me, I gasp at the slight pain of him stretching me. Taking a deep breath, I focus on trying to relax, and not the pain I feel from him entering me.

"I'm going to go slow. Just breathe," he says quietly, letting me adjust to him as he holds himself still for a few seconds.

"Just breathe," I recite to myself inside of my head. Keeping my eyes focused on his, my hands rest on his biceps as he pushes himself into me a little further and then a little further. I gasp with each inch he presses into me. It's painful, not horrible, but not comfortable either.

Once he's filled me completely, I close my eyes as I mumble, "Oh my God," and squeeze both of his hands again.

"Baby, are you okay?" he asks, pressing a kiss to my lips.

"Yes. Just give me a second," I whisper. Leaning forward, I kiss his shoulder and pull my hands out of his and move them to his arms to his back. When I relax and there is no longer any pain, just pressure, I rock my hips slightly, inviting him to do the same.

"God, you feel good," he says.

"So do you."

"Wrap your legs around me," he whispers, and I lift my legs, hitching them around his hips.

Taking his time with me, he moves slowly, and I can't help but take pleasure in the fact that the man I love is inside of me, skin to skin—making love to me. Closing my eyes, I want to remember this moment, just feel him as he moves back and forth. He's slow and gentle, and careful. Resting his forehead against mine, he continues to move, pressing light kisses to my face. Opening my eyes, I feel him harden more inside of me. His eyes grow darker and his pace quickens.

"Am I hurting you?" he asks, his breath hitching.

"No. You feel so good," I whisper in between breaths.

His breathing becomes more intense, and I feel him harden even more. Our breathing is rapid, and with two last thrusts, he moans, and I feel his warm release inside of me. He lowers himself onto me, and I can feel his heart beating against my chest. With his head lying between my head and shoulder, his soft lips and hot breath on my neck cause another wave of goose bumps to prick my skin. Overwhelmed with emotions, I hold him firmly in place on top of me, not allowing him to break our connection.

Taking a minute to recover, he lies there, still inside of me, and I'm not ready for him to leave me yet. "I love you. I will never get tired of loving you," he whispers with his lips still pressed against my neck. His breathing becoming less labored, and he pulls himself from me and settles at my side. Pulling me to him, he wraps me in his arms, his grip firm. I hear him repeat those words again, the most beautiful words from my perfect man. I close my eyes, burning this memory into my mind for the rest of my life. I cannot imagine this moment being any more perfect, or with anyone else.

CHAPTER TEN

-Gabe-

I have never been happier in my life. In the last month, I got the girl and was accepted as a recruit into the Santa Ruiz Fire Department. I spend most of my days training and taking my EMT classes at the local community college. Taking summer classes wasn't originally my plan, but getting accepted into the academy forced me to get them out of the way sooner rather than later. If all goes as planned, I should be finished with classes by the end of fall and, hopefully, an employed firefighter by the new year.

Jess is sitting on my bed, reading a smut book on her iPad while I get some studying done. I hear her close the cover on her iPad, stand up, and walk over behind me. She wraps her arms around my neck from behind me, and rests her chin on my shoulder.

"What is this?" she asks, reaching over my shoulder to pick up a packet from the stack of my notebooks.

"A study guide for that test I have tomorrow."

"Eww..." she says, studying the information I have to memorize.

"I'm not worried. I know most of the information. I just need to brush up on a few things," I say confidently.

"So, do you have time to sneak away?"

"Depends what we're doing." I wag my eyebrows at her.

"Is that all you think about?"

"Well, not all that I think about, but…"

"Okay, that's enough." She laughs at me. "I just wanted to go for a quick run."

"Sure. Let me just get changed and we'll go."

"I'll meet you out front in a few minutes. I have to run home and get changed," she says, setting the study guide back on my desk.

Pressing a kiss to my cheek, she leaves in a hurry. Jess is already stretching when I meet her in front of her house. Coming up behind her, I snake my arm around her waist and pull her into me, kissing the side of her neck. Her head falls back, and I hear a slight hum coming from her throat. As I gently nip her neck, I feel her shiver.

"Let's go, handsome." She smiles at me and smacks me on the ass playfully. Reaching out to try and smack her ass back, she yelps and takes off running. We complete our first mile quickly and turn around to head home, Jess is pushing me hard today, and I love that she challenges me. Coming up on the last half mile, she's in almost a full sprint. God, I love watching her run. Her hair is pulled into a ponytail, and her long legs glide through the air. I love running just to watch her. I'd be fine in a smelly gym on a treadmill if it wasn't for her. Slowing down as we come up on our street, our jog turns into a walk.

"Sorry, not much of a cool down today. I have to shower and meet Ava at the nail salon in about an hour," she says, pulling the binder out of her ponytail. Her long, dark hair hangs down past her shoulders. Taking a few deep breaths, I walk over to her. She is standing with her hands on her hips and her head tipped back as she breathes deeply. I reach both arms through hers and around her waist, and she drops her head forward, resting her forehead on mine.

"Hey, lover," she whispers, pressing a kiss to my lips.

"Hey. Quickie before you take a shower?" I ask with a smirk, kissing her neck.

"Gross. I'm sweaty." She swats at me.

"Yeah, so? It's usually me that makes you sweaty." I continue kissing her neck.

"Tonight, I'm all yours." She starts leaning back away from me, but I hold my grip on her.

"Oh, I plan to take full advantage of that." I smirk and squeeze her ass as she pushes me away.

"Go home, shower, and study. I'll be ready by six for dinner," she says, turning and walking away with her hips swaying. She has no idea how badly she affects me.

"Of all the places you could pick for dinner, you chose this?" I ask, trying to look appalled.

"It's pizza, Gabe." She rolls her eyes at me.

"We just ordered our food at a counter, and they gave us a number so they'd remember where to bring the food," I respond. "I wanted to bring you somewhere nicer than a pub."

"This isn't a pub, and I want pizza. This place has the best pizza in town. Didn't you ever come here in high school?"

"Ah, no."

"That's right. You were too busy being Mr. Jock and chasing tail to hang out at such dingy establishments like *this*." She laughs at me as her eyes scan the interior of the small pizza joint.

God, I love watching her laugh, the way her eyes crinkle just a little bit, and the way she tips her head back turns me on. There is an unspoken comfort with Jess. I've never been so at ease with another person in my life. Something inside of me was missing until we got together, and I never intend to let her go.

"So what's the plan for after dinner?" she asks, taking a drink of her soda.

"Bonfire at the house?" I ask, not knowing how she'll feel about that. Dad built this amazing fire pit in the back yard, and we spend most of our weekends with friends gathered around it.

"I'd love that. I want to spend as much time with Ava before she leaves," she says, her voice becoming quiet.

Ava leaves for Stanford in just a couple of weeks, so we've been making it a point to spend as much time with her as possible.

"I'm going to miss her when she leaves," she says.

"Me too."

"But it's different for you, Gabe. You still have Luke."

"Well, you'll have me."

"That's different. Who can I talk to about you? Or who's going to go get pedicures with me?"

I laugh. I'm not doing pedicures. "You can call her, text her, and even e-mail her. I know it's not the same as having her right here, but it'll work out."

Our pizza arrives and it's huge. I will also say, it's probably the best pizza I've ever had.

"So how did you find this place again?" I ask, taking another slice.

"This really hot guy used to bring me here, and we'd make out in the back corner." She points to a dark corner where there is an old Pac-Man video game, which has an "Out of Order" sign on the screen.

She laughs at me when I glare at her.

"I'm kidding. Geez, relax. The girls and I would come here after tennis practice."

"Your attempts at humor aren't very funny when you joke about other men."

"Yes, they are." She rolls her eyes at me.

"No, they're not."

"I'm hilarious."

I can't help but laugh at her now; she is so damn cute when she argues with me.

"Okay, you're hilarious, Jess."

"I know. I'm really glad we settled this," she says with a smirk.

"Hey, I have an idea," I say, taking another bite of my pizza.

"I don't know if I should be intrigued or scared. See, that was funny," she says, wiping her mouth with a napkin. "What's this idea of yours?"

"Maybe we can go visit Ava. You know, once she's settled, we can take a road trip and surprise her for a weekend." Her eyes soften and mist over as she thinks about my proposal.

"I'd love that," she whispers.

"I'd do anything to make you happy, you know that, right?" She nods and tears threaten to spill out of her green eyes.

"I love you, Gabe."

"I love you too," I respond. "Now are you ready to get out of this dump?" I joke with her.

"Yeah, yeah. I will never bring you here again." She laughs.

"Actually, I was hoping we could come back next week. That pizza was damn good."

"Told you." She laughs.

As I pull into my parents' driveway, I see there are quite a few cars already here. I even see Luke's truck parked in front of the house. Instead of heading through the side gate, Jess goes into the house, and, like a lovesick puppy, I follow her.

"Hi, Mom and Dad!" she announces as she walks through the door. My mom is at the sink, washing dishes, and Dad is sitting at the kitchen table, drinking a beer and supervising her.

"Hey, Jess!" my dad hollers.

He jumps up out of his recliner and makes his way to her, pulling her into a tight embrace.

"We miss having you around, but I'm glad Gabe is keeping an eye on you." He winks at her. "There's quite a crowd out there tonight," he says, nodding toward the backyard. Jess releases her hug on Dad and opens the patio door.

"'Bout time, lovebirds," Luke catcalls.

Giving him the bird, I ignore his comments, noticing that there actually are quite a few people here, more than the usual eight to ten that normally gather. Jess makes her way over to Ava, and I grab a beer from the cooler, taking a seat next to Luke.

"So how are classes going?" Luke asks, taking a drink of his beer.

"Actually, really good. I'm lucky that every one of my undergrad classes transferred over. All I need are the sixteen credits for the Fire Sciences degree. Once those are done, all I need is to pass the P.A.T. Jess has been running my ass off lately, so I'm hoping the extra cardio will help me."

Luke laughs. "Good. Can't wait to have you on board, bro." He takes his beer bottle and taps mine.

"Me too, man," I say, watching Jess move from group to group. She is a social butterfly, able to talk to and relate to anyone. She finally settles, sitting on the stone bench by the fire, talking with Ava. I can't help but smile when I see that they're laughing so hard, Ava is doubled over. Jess glances at me, and her eyes sparkle in the light of the fire. I never knew I could be so in love with someone, but she has completely captured my heart.

"I love you," she mouths to me.

"Love you too." I mouth back. Luke laughs when he sees us.

"So, how are things with you two?" Luke asks.

"Good. Really good," I say, watching her. "I'm happy."

"You look happy," he says. "Can I ask you something, honestly?"

"Shoot."

"Is she the reason you didn't go back to Arizona?"

I hesitate to answer for a moment because I wonder where this questioning is coming from.

"Partly. I love her. I really do, but I also know that I wanted to be a firefighter." I think back to a few months ago, when I made this decision and all the emotions involved. "Either way, this was a chance worth taking for me," I say, looking at Luke, and then back at Jess. "She's worth it."

"She is," he agrees with me. "I'm glad you're both happy."

"So am I, man. So am I."

CHAPTER ELEVEN

~Jess~

"Stop eye fucking my brother. It's gross," Ava says as she catches me looking at Gabe. I pick up another plastic cup and toss it into the trash bag.

"I'm not eye fucking your brother."

Picking up the last of the paper plates and empty cups, Ava and I make one last sweep of the patio, looking for anything else we missed.

"You know I'm really going to miss you when you leave," I tell Ava.

"I'm going to miss you too. I honestly can't remember what it was like before you starting living with us."

"Really? I remember so much about that time, probably because I had just lost my mom. I guess the trauma of it really ingrained in me everything around those years."

"Do you miss her?"

As I pause to gather my thoughts, I notice Gabe talking to Luke up on the patio near the house. I sit down on the built-in stone benches that surround the fire pit. I take a few moments to stare at the flames and remember the bits and pieces of my mom.

"Yeah, I miss her. I don't remember much about *her* particularly, but I have vague recollections of baking cupcakes with her and going to the library. She loved to read."

Ava sits down next to me, weaving her arm through mine and resting her head on my shoulder.

"You love to read too," she whispers.

A small smile settles on my face. "I guess I get that from her."

"And you look like her too," Ava says. "Almost identical."

I keep a small-framed picture on my nightstand of my mom and me. I catch Ava looking at it occasionally.

"I think so too. Do you think that's why he hates me?" I ask. "Because I look so much like her?"

She squeezes my arm. Ava knows I'm referring to my dad.

"He doesn't hate you," I hear Gabe say from behind us. Ava and I simultaneously turn our heads to see him walking toward us.

"Well, maybe he doesn't *hate* me, but he doesn't care much about me."

"Look, I can only tell you what I see." He sits down on the other side of me. "He loves you, Jess. He just has a really shitty way of showing you. I think losing your mom destroyed him. He knew that having you stay with us was what you needed, the stability of a family and siblings. We were a surrogate family for you, and he drowned himself in work as a coping mechanism. I guarantee you that man would lay down his life for you; he just doesn't know how to show you that."

Giant tears are rolling down my face as I absorb his view of my relationship, or lack thereof with my dad. I see Ava wipe tears from her cheeks too.

"I didn't mean for this to get all emotional." I laugh and swipe at the tears, trying to lighten the mood.

Lifting her head, Ava wipes her cheeks again. "Just because I'm moving doesn't mean I'll forget about you. I will miss your sassy ass every single day." She smacks my thigh and stands up. "And you have Gabe here to keep you, uh…busy." She winks at me.

"Good night, you guys. I'll see you tomorrow," Ava says quietly, leaving me alone with Gabe.

"Night, Ava."

"Night, sissy," Gabe responds.

We sit in silence for a few minutes, just watching the fire. Gabe's fingers are laced through mine. He brings my hand to his lips a couple of times placing small kisses across the top of my hand, and on each knuckle.

"You okay?" he asks.

"Yeah, sorry. I didn't think I would cry, but talking about it is still hard."

"You have every right to be upset. I can't imagine what it would be like to lose my mom."

Leaning in, I press my lips to his and taste a slight hint of the beer he had been drinking minutes before.

"Thank you."

"For what?" he asks.

"For loving me."

"I'll never *not* love you." Those words melt me a little more every time he says them. I press another kiss to his mouth, this one a bit deeper and more aggressive.

"I'm ready to go," I whisper against his lips.

He pulls my hand and nearly drags me across the street to my house, clearly ready to cash in on the alone time I promised him earlier. Shuffling into the house, I lock the door behind him and he is already down the hall and headed to the bedroom. I take over the bathroom to start getting ready for bed, tossing my clothes into the laundry hamper.

Looking at myself in the mirror as I'm rinsing face wash off of me, I see Gabe squeeze in and plant himself directly behind me. Resting his chin on my shoulder, he watches me finish washing my face and removing my make-up.

"What?" I ask, noticing the serious look on his face.

"I'm the luckiest man in the world, you know that, right?"

"You are, babe. You have so much happening for you right now, and I'm so proud of you. A few more tests and you'll be finished with school and then you can finally apply for a full-time position at the station. My dad is dying to bring you on." I turn and kiss him.

"Yes, that makes me happy, but I'm the luckiest man in the world because I have you." He rubs the side of my cheek with his hand.

God, this man knows what to say. Pushing me back gently against the bathroom counter, he presses his lips to mine while his hands skillfully catch the hem of my pink tank top, lifting it up and over my head. Sliding his hands from my shoulders, he finds my breasts, pinching both nipples, causing a slight moan.

"Like that?" he asks.

"Mmm hmm." I lean into him.

His lips move from my cheek, down to my neck, where he spends time kissing and nipping me. I feel his hands slide down my sides and over my hips, and he hooks his fingers in the top of my pink panties and pulls them down just past my hips, where they fall to my feet. As he lifts me onto the bathroom counter, his lips never leave my neck.

He positions himself between my legs, and I instinctively wrap them around his waist. He rests his hands just inside both of my thighs. Lightly circling his fingers, his hands move closer to my naked core. His fingers brush the sensitive skin of my labia, wasting no time finding where they intend to be. Running his fingers through my already wet lips, his thumb finds that sweet spot. I gasp loudly as my head falls backwards and I feel the tingling sensation take over me.

"Oh God," I mumble as his fingers find my entrance. Gently, he presses two fingers into me.

"Jesus," he groans, pulling his fingers out of me and dropping his boxer briefs to the floor. Pulling me forward to the very edge of the bathroom counter, he positions himself at my center and presses into me. I moan at the intense pressure as he fills me. Slowly, he moves in and out, nearly pulling himself completely out with each thrust. Every time I'm just about to peak, he slows his pace, this time stopping entirely.

"Don't stop," I beg. "Please."

My legs still wrapped around his waist, he pulls me from the counter, walking us to my bedroom. Bending over, he lies us down on the bed, never once separating us. Grabbing both of my hands, he places them up above my head and holds them there with one hand. Slowly, he begins to move in and out of me in perfect rhythm. I can feel my walls clenching as he brings me close to climax, but I'm not ready to go there yet.

Without thinking, I whisper loudly, "Stop!"

He stills. "Babe, what's wrong?"

He sounds nervous, and his body tenses. My legs are hitched around his waist, holding him in place on top of me.

Giggling, I say, "Nothing, I'm just not ready come yet."

He drops his head with a sigh.

"You scared me. I thought I was hurting you."

"I want to go on top," I whisper against his lips, unhitching my legs from around him. They fall widely, and he sits back, still inside me. He pulls my legs up over his shoulders, and thrusts himself forward, filling me. Doing it again, the pressure is intense, and once again, brings me close to the edge when he suddenly stops completely.

"Gabe, please…I'm not…ready…"

"That's what you get for scaring me." He thrusts again, this time pulling out of me. He drops my legs from his shoulders and lies down on his back while I position myself on top of him.

Bending forward, I press a kiss to his lips as I settle on top of him and slowly slide down, filling myself with every inch of him. It feels so different from this angle.

"Mmmm," he groans.

I place my hands on his chest, slowly moving my hips up and down. My breath quickens at the feel of him inside of me from this position. He is so much deeper when I'm on top, and it's an entirely different sensation. My pulse races with the different sensations my body is experiencing, and I can tell I'm not going to last much longer. Leaning back, I can feel him pressing against the very spot that is going to send me into ecstasy.

"Gabe," I breathe heavily. His large hands grip my hips tightly, forcing me up and down faster and harder. "I'm going to…"

"Come with me," he interrupts.

Falling forward, I do. My release is intense as I rest my head on his shoulder, and I let my body recover while taking in the intoxicating scent of him. There is nothing more comforting than his masculine scent.

"Babe, you can do that to me every day," he says, pressing his lips to the side of my face. Still trying to catch my breath, I slide off of him, rolling to lie on my back beside him.

"Babe?" Gabe asks.

"Yeah," I say with my eyes closed, my breathing still sporadic.

"Look at me."

Rolling my head to the side, I open my eyes.

"I will love you every day for the rest of my life; never forget that."

"I love that you tell me this every day," I whisper.

"It's because I mean it."

My eyes suddenly fill with tears. I've never felt like I belonged anywhere before, but in this exact moment, I know I belong with Gabe Garcia forever.

Watching Ava pile her belongings into Mom and Dad's car is bittersweet. Ava is headed to Stanford. I never doubted she'd get accepted with her grades and ambition. As she throws her last bag in the back seat, Gabe and I stand on the driveway, his arms wrapped around me from behind. She walks over to us, and my eyes fill with tears, my heart hanging heavy.

"You take care of my girl." Ava smiles and winks at him. He nods his head, trying not to get emotional like me. Wiping the tears from my face with the back of my hand, I try to compose myself.

"And you take care of my big brother," she says, walking over and placing herself in front of me.

"I will," I whisper.

"I'm so glad you have each other," she says quietly, looking down at her feet. "And I'll see you in a couple of weeks, right?"

Nodding my head, the tears continue to fall. My chin begins to quiver as my throat tightens up. She pulls me out of Gabe's arms and into a hug; we just hold each other for a minute. Selfishly, I don't want to let my best friend go.

"I love you, Ava."

"Love you too," she whispers.

"Get your ass in your car. Mom and Dad are watching us like we're a bunch of lunatics," I choke out, wiping more tears. Ava turns and walks to her car and Gabe pulls me back to him, wrapping his arms around me as I bury my head in his chest.

"Bye, Ava," Gabe says in a quiet whisper.

Peeking at her, I see her throw her oversized sunglasses on, flashing us her biggest smile as she backs out of the driveway. Waving goodbye to each other, I blow Ava a kiss, while Gabe smiles at me and wipes my tears as I reach out to hug him again.

"What am I going to do with you?" he says, laughing at me.

"God, I'm going to miss her."

"Me, too." He tightens his hug. "How about we stay in, order Chinese take-out, and watch *The Goonies*."

I can't help but laugh. "*The Goonies*, huh?"

"It's my favorite."

"It's a date," I say before I kiss him.

Chapter Twelve

-Gabe-

"Slow down," I order her.

"We're only thirty miles out," she squeals, speeding up even more.

"You're not going to be happy when you have a two-hundred-dollar speeding ticket." Scoffing at me, she smiles and lets off the gas just slightly.

"I can't wait to see her. So, you're sure she thinks we're coming next weekend?" she asks, tapping her hands on the steering wheel to the beat of a Train song on the radio. We decided to surprise Ava by coming up a weekend early. I dial Ava's number from Jess' cell, putting it on speakerphone.

"I'm a terrible liar," she whispers as the phone is ringing.

"Hey, Jess!" Ava answers.

"Hey, you. How's it going?"

"Good. Just headed back to the dorms after my last class. Remind me never to take a three o'clock class on Friday afternoons ever again."

"Big plans for the weekend?" Jess inquires.

"No; just studying. Adrian was going to try to come up this weekend, but he had to cancel. Something about his aunt being sick."

"That sucks. We can't wait to see you next weekend." Jess smiles, looking over at me. We pass a sign that says *"Palo Alto ten miles."*

Jess talks to Ava for the next fifteen minutes as we weave ourselves through the sprawling campus toward Ava's dorm. Finding a visitor spot, Jess kills the engine, gasping as she points toward a bench that sits just outside the large double doors of Ava's dorm. Sitting on the bench, on her phone, is Ava. Hurrying out of the car, we head toward Ava, who is paying no attention to the hosts of people coming and going around her.

"Look up," I hear Jess tell Ava.

"Oh. My. God," Ava screams, jumping from the bench and wrapping herself around Jess. Both girls are jumping and screaming, and I'm slightly embarrassed at the outburst that's happening right in front of me. Bending down, I pick up Ava's phone that she's dropped.

"I can't believe you guys are here."

"We decided to surprise you. Did it work?"

"Is the Pope Catholic? Of course it worked."

As I watch these two talk, it feels like time has stood still. They fall back into old patterns of completing each other's sentences, gossiping, and joking around with each other, all within minutes of seeing each other.

"You look good," Jess says, reaching out to touch Ava's hair. "The light brown makes your eyes stand out."

"That's what my stylist said. It's different, but I like it." She shrugs and runs her fingers through her hair. "Want to see my room?" Jess looks over to me as if she is looking for my approval.

"Oh, hey, Gabe." Ava walks over and places a kiss on my cheek.

"That's all I get? Oh, hey," I joke with her.

"Shut up. You know I love you," she says, picking up her bag, which is overflowing with books. "Let's go."

She walks to the double doors, and Jess and I follow. For the next two hours, we see Ava's room, take a short tour of the campus, and end up having dinner at a small sushi joint just off campus.

"So what do you want to do while you're here?" Ava asks, dropping a spicy tuna roll on the table since she can't figure out how to use chopsticks. I'm actually hesitant to tell them, but there is something I'd really like to do.

"So, uh…tomorrow, I was wondering if maybe we could catch the football game?" I know that neither of the girls are big football fans, but this would mean a lot to me, so I ask anyway. Jess and Ava seem to communicate through their eyes. No one says anything, and Jess sets her chopsticks down.

"You miss it, don't you?" she asks.

Nodding my head, I inhale a deep breath. "I do. Since Arizona is playing here this weekend, it kind of makes me miss it more," I answer truthfully. "I've played in this stadium twice, so I would like to catch the game if you are both interested, but I completely understand if you aren't."

Jess reaches out her hand and grabs mine, giving it a squeeze, while Ava studies me.

"What?" I ask her.

"Do you regret not going back for your senior year?"

"No, I don't regret it. I just miss it sometimes." Ava and Jess continue their non-verbal communication with each other until Ava finally ends my misery.

"Let's plan on it." She smiles, picking up another tuna roll, this time with her fingers. "But you owe me." She raises her eyebrows and shoves the roll in her mouth.

"Thanks." A small wave of excitement washes over me. "By the way, you're so gross. Use a fork." I shake my head and laugh at my sister.

"Fuck off. They don't have forks, and these little pieces of wood don't work for shit." She tosses her chopsticks at me, causing Jess to laugh uncontrollably.

"Some things never change," I say, shaking my head.

It's nice to see Ava and Jess both happy and laughing, and I'm actually excited and a little anxious to see the football game tomorrow. Leaving UA was one of the toughest decisions I've ever made, but I know it was the right decision. Pulling out my cell phone, I send a quick text message to Coach, letting him know I'm in town and would like to say "hello."

I notice Jess yawning, and realize that it's after eleven. We've been sitting here for hours, talking and catching up. Leaning toward her, I wrap her hand in mine and whisper, "Ready to call it a night?"

She nods, and I notice how tired she looks. "So what time should we pick you up tomorrow?" I ask my sister, who's playing on her phone, probably texting Adrian. Without even looking up, she answers.

"Ten thirty. We have to get tickets and the game starts at noon. Don't be late or you won't be seeing shit tomorrow," she says so eloquently. God, I miss my snarky sister.

"You two ready?" I ask, knowing damn well Jess is going to fall asleep if we don't leave now.

Walking to the car, the girls are whispering to each other and giggling. I swear it's like they've reverted back to being twelve years old. I can't help but smile as I watch those two. The car ride to Ava's dorm is quiet as Ava is still playing on her phone and Jess is trying to stay awake. We pull up to the large brick dormitory and Ava hops out. "Thanks for dinner," she says, sticking her back in the car before shutting the door. "Remember, ten thirty. Don't be late."

I pull into a parking spot at the hotel and kill the engine. Jess fell asleep just minutes after we dropped Ava off. Her head hangs slightly to the side against the headrest. I love watching her sleep. Leaning in, I press a light kiss to her soft lips, which wakes her.

"We're here baby," I whisper against her lips.

"Mmm," she hums against my lips, kissing me back.

"Let's get you to bed. We have a big day tomorrow." I say, unbuckling her seat belt. She rubs her eyes and reaches for her purse before opening the door. I meet her in front of my truck and take her hand to lead her inside. She curls herself into my side as the late fall air is cool and damp and we walk briskly to the entrance of the hotel.

Settling into our room, Jess heads immediately for the bed. She kicks off her shoes before throwing herself on top of the comforter. I unpack our overnight bags and finally settle into the bed, wrapping myself around her. I feel her wiggle out of my arms as I notice the sun peeking through the curtains.

"What time is it?" I ask with a groggy voice.

"Eight thirty. I didn't mean to wake you. I'm going to take a quick shower, go back to sleep for a bit." She disappears into the bathroom, juggling her clothes and toiletries in her arms. A small wave of anxiety rolls through me when I think about watching my old teammates hit the football field today, and I can say I'm slightly jealous that I'm not on that field.

Reaching for my phone on the nightstand, I turn it on and numerous e-mails and text messages fill my screen. Clearing most of them, I hear Jess finishing up in the shower in which I was hoping to join her. I knock on the bathroom door and wait for her to answer.

"Come in."

"You're done already? I was hoping to join you," I say, opening the bathroom door and entering the small bathroom. She is wrapped in a towel that just barely covers her tall frame, with another towel wrapped around her wet hair.

"I would have liked that," she says with a smile, pulling the towel off her head and letting her long hair fall against her shoulders. She leans in, pressing a kiss to my lips. Her shoulders are still beaded with water, and I brush my hands over them to wipe away the small beads.

"So, Coach just texted me. He wants me to stop by the stadium early to see the guys. Are you cool with that?"

"Really? That's great. Of course I'm fine with that. I'll just hang with Ava until you're done."

I pull her into my arms and kiss her cheek and neck. A little mewl sounds from her throat and she places her hands on my chest, giving me a slight push, breaking my contact with her neck.

"Hey, what was that for? I didn't get you last night."

"And you're not getting me this morning either. We're going to be late if you don't hurry up and shower, and I do not want to piss off your sister by being late."

I don't disagree with her, but I want to take advantage of that short towel and her naked little body underneath it.

"Tonight. You're all mine," I whisper into her ear.

"Tonight, we're going to a party with your sister." She laughs and grabs her clothes off the bathroom counter and walks out into the hotel room to change, closing the bathroom door behind her.

"After the party, you're mine," I yell through the door.

The bathroom door inches open slightly, and she pokes her head through. "I'm always yours, I'm not going anywhere. Let's just enjoy this weekend with Ava. When we get home, you can have me anytime you want."

She's right. This weekend isn't about Jess and me; it's about visiting Ava and spending time with her.

"Fine, but when we get home…"

"I know, I know…" she interrupts me.

Standing outside the football stadium, my stomach flutters with excitement like it used to on game day. It's a cool, sunny, fall day; perfect football weather. There are crowds of people already tailgating, and I'm waiting for Jess and Ava by the main entrance.

Catching up with Coach and the guys for the last hour made my weekend. I definitely miss football, but I have no regrets about my decision to move home and pursue my career as a firefighter. I twist the red UA t-shirt that Coach gave me for Jess in my hands, when I happen to see her and Ava heading in my direction. They are walking arm in arm, each carrying a large Starbucks coffee.

"How was it?" she asks, pulling out of Ava's arm and planting a kiss on my cheek.

"It was great. So good to see the guys and just catch up in person for a little bit."

"I'm really glad you got to see them." She smiles at me and laces her fingers through mine.

"Should we go watch some football or do you two want to stand here chit-chatting all day?" Ava asks sarcastically.

The rest of Saturday was spent watching football, with Arizona taking home the win, and stopping by several parties with Ava. I will say that I do not miss the days of drunken house parties. Waking up Sunday morning, I reach for Jess and find that she's not in the bed. Sitting up, I see her sitting in the bedside chair, reading on her iPad.

"Morning beautiful." She smiles and sets the iPad down on her lap.

"Morning, sleepyhead. I wasn't sure you were ever going to wake up."

"What time is it?"

"Nine. We have to bring coffee to Ava; she's not feeling well after the party last night and she has a huge exam she has to study for."

"Okay. We should probably get on the road anyway. We have a long drive."

Standing up, she starts pulling clothes out of the dresser. "Go shower and I'll get us packed up," she says. True to her word, she has everything packed by the time I'm done showering. We haul our bags to the truck and stop at the Starbucks just off campus. Jess juggles the coffees as I pull the truck into the visitor parking in front of the dorm. Ava exits the main entrance just as we pull up, carrying a large book bag on her shoulder.

"There you are," she sighs, reaching for the large cup of coffee Jess is holding out to her. "I owe you," she says, sipping the hot coffee with caution.

"You always owe me," I joke with her. Ava continues sipping her coffee and we stand in silence for a few seconds before Jess finally speaks.

"I suppose we should get going," she says quietly.

"Yeah, you have a long drive. Please drive carefully." Ava's voice cracks. "You know I hate goodbyes, so I'm just going to go, okay?" She reaches out and pulls Jess into a tight hug. "I'll see you guys in just a few weeks for Christmas break." I see Jess wiping a few small tears from her eyes as she nods at Ava.

Ava walks backwards, away from us. I open the door to my truck for Jess and she climbs in.

"Drive carefully. Love you guys," Ava yells again and waves, this time turning around completely and walking down the sidewalk toward the library. I watch my little sister disappear into the sea of brick buildings. Jess leans her head back against the seat and closes her eyes, and I know that it's going to be a quiet ride home.

It's hard to believe that Christmas is already upon us. I finished my last class and now officially have my degree in Fire Sciences. The physical aptitude test was last week, and I passed with flying colors. I interviewed for a firefighter position and am now just waiting to hear from Chief to see if I'm hired.

Jess finished her first semester at Santa Ruiz State University, and in true Jess style, she completed eighteen credit

hours. Nothing like piling on the classes her first semester;
she's always been an overachiever. I spent the last week
looking for the perfect promise ring to give Jess for Christmas.
This was, singlehandedly, the most stressful thing I've ever
done. I chose a vintage-style ring, with a small princess-cut
center diamond and smaller diamonds circling around it in the
shape of a square. The band splits from all four corners and is
gorgeous. It's a smaller version of what I'd want to give Jess
when I actually propose to her.

Today is Christmas Eve, and as usual, it's always busy.
Mom made our traditional Mexican dinner: tamales, green chili
enchiladas, rice, and beans. Jess and Ava always help Mom
prepare the food. After dinner, all the women baked traditional
American desserts: cookies, brownies, and fudge, followed by
us all going to midnight mass. As we leave the church, I see
Jess leaning her head against the passenger window, and I can
hear her faint breaths. I run my knuckles down the side of her
cheek, which wakes her, and she offers me a small smile.

"Tired?" I ask.

"Yeah, it's been a long day." She rubs under her eyes with
her fingers.

We pull into her driveway, and she starts opening the car
door when I say, "I'm going to run home and grab a change of
clothes. I'll be back over in just a couple of minutes, okay?"
Chief is working again tonight, so I'm staying with Jess. I hate
leaving her alone.

"Okay," she offers quietly.

"Don't fall asleep."

Sighing, she looks at me and says, "Not tonight. I'm too
tired."

"That's fine; just don't fall asleep."

It's almost two in the morning, and the adrenaline coursing through my veins has me wide awake. I say a small prayer that she doesn't fall asleep before I get back. I shove everything in a backpack. Dad is arranging gifts that we'll open in the morning under the tree. It doesn't matter that we're all adults, Santa is alive and well and delivers gifts to the Garcia household every year.

"See you in the morning, Dad," I whisper as I open the front door to leave.

"Night, *Mijo*. Don't be late tomorrow."

"We won't."

I can see the light is on in Jess' room as I jog across the street and up her front lawn. Warm air hits me as I enter the living room and I can hear the bathroom sink running, and assume Jess is getting ready for bed. As I open the bedroom door, I see that it's dark, with the exception of a small bedside lamp that is on. I quickly take the ring out of my bag and hide it under the pillow. Climbing into Jess' bed, I wait for her to return.

"There you are," she says as she enters the room, closing the door behind her. She walks to the bed, crawls in beside me, and snuggles up with her head resting on my chest. She runs her hand up and down my chest, spreading a small chill across my flesh. Her eyes are closed, but her hand is still rubbing me slightly.

"Hey," I whisper, shifting slightly under her.

"Yeah," she says quietly without opening her eyes.

"Do you have any idea how much I love you?"

Smiling with her eyes still closed, she rolls her head slightly, pressing a kiss to my chest.

"Yeah, I think I know. Do you know how much I love you?" she asks me in return, opening her heavy eyelids.

"I'm hoping I'm about to find out," I say, pushing myself up. "I've known you for almost fifteen years. Every day that I've known you, I've cared about you and wanted to protect you." Sitting up, she looks slightly scared, and her tired eyes are now full and tense.

"I want to be the man that loves you, forever. I know we're young, and I know we have a lot to do before we commit to anything more permanent than what we have already, but..." I pull the small package out from under the pillow and hand it to her. "Open it."

Fumbling with the packaging, she unties the bow and rips at the corner of the package, tearing all the paper off in one swipe. She pulls the top of the black box off, looking up at me when she sees the small velvet box inside. Pulling it out, she flips open the top of the velvet box.

"Oh my God," she gasps.

"It's just a promise ring. There will be a better ring someday. But for today, I promise you that I love you with everything that I am, and I want you to know that it is only you; it has only ever been you that I love." Swallowing a lump in my throat, I stop. Tears spill out of her eyes, and I reach to wipe them off her cheeks.

"I want you to remember this moment—right now. How much I love you."

A sob falls from her throat, and she lunges her body at me, hugging me and crying into my chest. When her crying fades, she pulls back from me.

"It's so beautiful," she says, looking at the ring that is still sitting in the box. Pulling it loose from its perch, I kiss her finger before I slide the ring on for her.

"Don't ever doubt my love for you. Ever."

"Never," she says, pressing a kiss to my lips. This may be the best Christmas ever.

CHAPTER THIRTEEN

~Jess~

Walking down the quiet hallway of Jefferson Hall, my shoes squeak against the freshly buffed marble floors. Sunlight peeks out from under my academic advisor's door. I stand there for a second before I knock.

"Come in," I hear Janet's cheerful voice say. Turning the knob, I push open the door to find Janet sitting at her desk, strumming away at her keyboard. Her chair swivels around, and she stands to shake my hand.

"Hi, Jessica! Nice to see you." Her handshake is firm and fast. This woman is seriously amped on coffee or energy drinks, or really just likes to work during the holidays. "Take a seat," she says, pointing to the chair that is perched next to her desk. Setting my purse on the floor next to the chair, I lower myself down, crossing my legs. Janet sits confidently in her chair, clicking away with her computer mouse.

"Thanks for stopping by to meet with me over the holiday break. I was reviewing this semester's classes and your previously earned credits. Because of your dual-credit classes that you took in high school, you're nearly done with your sophomore year of college," she announces.

"Huh?"

"You did take dual-credit classes in high school, correct?" She lowers her glasses at me, waiting for me to validate her statement.

"Yes."

"Well, when you started here this fall, you were only a few credits shy of an associate's degree. With the amount of hours you completed this first semester, you're well on your way to completing your sophomore year of college by the end of next semester."

"Are you kidding me?"

"Nope, kiddo. You are ahead of the game; well ahead of the game. At the rate you're going, you'll be graduating almost a year and half ahead of schedule."

"Really?" is all I can muster. One might be excited about this, but I'm scared shitless.

"Well, this is why it was so urgent that I see you right away," she says, looking back to her computer screen again, still clicking away with that damn mouse. "I see you have declared yourself a Broadcast Communication major."

"Um, yes," I validate, fidgeting with my fingers, still in complete shock at the news that's just been dumped on me.

"Well, darling, you need to start considering an internship. You need to build your resume. There are classes on campus for which you should register to take for the fall semester, but let's get you a head start on an internship. It is a required part of the degree. They are difficult to come by. The sooner you start looking, the sooner you'll land something. I'm worried if you wait until next summer, and don't find anything, you'll push back that graduation date over a silly internship." She's clicking away on her computer and talking at the same time. "Now, I've got a few contacts I'm going to e-mail you. Some are out of state."

My heart stops. "Out of state?" I whisper.

Janet stops typing and looks up at me. "You don't *have* to go out of state. I'm simply telling you that I have some contacts out of state. If you can line up something at a local television or radio station here locally, then, by all means, do so. What I am telling you to do, is get *something* lined up for the summer, and soon."

My mind is in a million different places right now, and I'm beginning to panic. *Shit.* I have to get an internship lined up quick, and I'm not leaving Santa Ruiz. I'm staying here with Gabe.

"Okay, I've just sent you an e-mail with a couple of different internships that are available to students of SRSU. I'd love to sit down with you after the holiday break to discuss your plans for the summer and see if I can be of any assistance to you. Sound good?"

"Yes, thank you. This was really unexpected news." I pull a tight smile onto my face. There goes a relaxing Christmas break; I'll now be too fucking stressed out about applying for summer internships. Grabbing my purse from the floor, I leave Janet's office as fast as I can.

Walking to my car, I feel my phone vibrating in the pocket of my jacket. A million thoughts are running through my mind. Sliding into the driver's seat, I pull the phone from my jacket and click the e-mail icon. There sits the e-mail from Janet.

Jessica,

It was nice to see you today. Per our conversation, I have enclosed a list of internships that I know are accepting applicants. Please read each description carefully for requirements needed to apply.

I skim the rest of the letter until I get to the bottom where I see an attachment to the e-mail. I click the attachment, which opens another letter. My eyes run the length of the page, and all I see are:

Phoenix, AZ…
Albuquerque, NM…
Dallas, TX…
Wilmington, NC…
Hattiesburg, MS…

I'm not leaving Gabe, even for a summer, which means I need to find something local, and fast. I call Gabe and wait for him to answer.

"Hey, baby. How'd the meeting go with your advisor?"

"Hey."

"Everything okay? You sound upset."

"I'm okay; just stressed out."

"What happened?"

"To make a really long story short, she wants me to find an internship for this summer. I've got so many credits that I'm almost done with an associate's degree."

"That doesn't sound like a problem to me. Why are you stressed?"

"Because it's all happening so fast. She sent me a list of internships, and all of them are out of state."

"Aren't there any around here?"

"Maybe, but I'll have to find it myself."

"So do it."

"You're not helping me calm down."

Gabe starts laughing into the phone. "Just try to relax, babe. We'll talk about this when you get home. Worrying right now isn't going to help you."

"I know, it's just…the thought of leaving you scares me." I wait for him to respond, but when the silence continues, I wonder if the call was dropped.

"So then don't take an out of state internship. We'll find you one here."

I can almost hear him smiling through the phone. Breathing a sigh of relief, I find my nerves settling just a bit. I love that we're a team, and in this together.

"I'll be home soon."

"See you when you get here. And, Jess."

"Yeah."

"Don't stress. It'll all work out. It always does."

"I hope so," I mumble.

Chapter Fourteen

-Gabe-

As I wait for Jess to get home, I sit on the tan plush couch in her living room, anxious to share my news with her. I'm worried that she'll still be stressed when she walks through the front door and I want her happy.

"What are you doing here?" she asks, stepping through the front door. She sets her purse on the sofa table and kicks off her shoes.

"Nice to see you too," I mumble, seeing her mood hasn't changed since we spoke.

Frowning, she turns and walks over to me, leaning down to give me a kiss. "I'm sorry, I didn't mean for it to sound like that. I'm glad you're here. I'm just surprised to see you, that's all."

"I let myself in. I wanted to be here when you got home. Have you calmed down at all?" I ask, not sure I want to know the truth. After pulling her arms out of her jacket, she hangs it on the back of one of the kitchen chairs. Walking over, she throws herself down on the couch next to me.

"Actually, yeah. I can deal with finishing school early. I just didn't want to have to leave you for a summer for a stupid internship. As long as I can find something here, I'll be fine." She reaches out to touch my hand.

"Don't stress over it. It'll work out; it always does," I remind her again.

"I know. How was your day?" she says with a sigh.

"Good."

"Oh, yeah. What did you do?"

"Watched some TV, went to the gym, and got a phone call," I say nonchalantly.

"From?" Her voice is full of curiosity.

"The Human Resources Department from the City of Santa Ruiz."

"And?"

"I got the job."

"I'm so proud of you, baby!" she squeals. "I knew you'd get it. When do you start?" She leans in, planting kisses all over my face. Her mood shifts considerably.

"Beginning of January. Chief is giving me the rest of December off."

"Good. We'll have the next few days to celebrate."

"I know a few ways we can celebrate. You know what they say relieves stress, right?" I say, and then kiss her.

"I've heard about that, but I'm not sure it's true."

"Maybe we should test the theory," I say, picking her up and carrying her down the hall to her bedroom. Laying her down on her bed, I settle in on top of her. My erection is pressing through my jeans, and I know she can feel it as she repositions herself underneath me, rubbing up against it.

"I need you," I say between kisses.

"Not yet," she whispers, pushing me gently against my chest.

Sitting up, she pulls her gray sweater over her head, and tosses it onto the floor next to my sweatshirt. She's wearing a black lace bra; my favorite color on her. Leaning forward, she kisses me while her fingers reach for the waistband of my jeans. Running her fingers just under the waistband, she moves them back and forth, teasing my skin as she makes her way to the button.

She works the button as I shift to my knees. Sliding my jeans and boxer briefs down my thighs, she stops them at my knees.

"Lie back," she tells me, pushing me backwards. Making quick work of her jeans, she kicks them off her feet, leaving on just her bra and panties.

"You don't have to do this," I say, but praying to God she wants to.

"I want to. I like doing this to you." She smiles.

Moving to the side of the bed, she lowers herself to the mattress and crawls over to me. Straddling me like she has so many times before, my erection is pressing against her through her panties. She wants to be in control this time, so I let her. I smile to myself. I love it when my girl gets naughty. Lowering her face to mine, we're forehead-to-forehead, nose-to-nose, and mouth-to-mouth. Her breath has a hint of mint, and her lips are full and soft as I lean forward to claim her mouth.

Jess pulls back from the kiss, confusing me, but she immediately lowers her mouth to my cheek, kissing me down to my ear. She nibbles on my earlobe, and I feel her warm breath against my ear, giving me goose bumps. Slowly, her kisses make a trail down my body, across my chest, where she lightly suckles my nipples, gently nipping at them with her teeth. I'm so fucking hard right now, and all I want to do is flip her over, rip her panties off, and take her.

Dragging her tongue down my stomach, she presses light kisses as she continues her way south. I'm full of anticipation and need, and I'm not sure how much longer I'm going to be able to lie here and take her sweet lips on my body. Closing my eyes, I will my body to calm itself. I feel her warm tongue brush against the tip of my cock, and my entire body shudders at the feel of her soft tongue licking my engorged head.

"Fuck," I moan as I reach out and wrap my fingers in her long hair. Pulling her mouth off of me, she looks up at me; a huge smile crosses her face.

"Put your hands underneath your head," she instructs. "No touching me."

"You don't play fair."

"Neither do you." She giggles. Shifting my legs further apart, she settles herself in between them. I do as I am told as I watch her take me into her mouth again, lightly swirling her tongue around my sensitive head. *Holy Fuck.* She's fucking perfect with her tongue.

"Jesus Christ," I inhale sharply, not from pain, but from her taking me all the way. I can feel myself against the back of her throat. She slowly raises and lowers her head, and my breathing quickens as I move my hips to match the movement of her lips.

Removing my hands from behind my head, I place them on the bed next to my hips, gripping the sheets as she sucks me harder. I'm so close to losing it, I'm not going to last much longer. She moves her eyes to mine, watching me enjoy her mouth.

"I'm going to come," I say through clenched teeth, trying hard to prolong this. Her eyes light up at my words as she gives me one last stroke down the underside of my shaft, sending me off. I groan with each pump of my release, and she takes it all, swallowing. She's so fucking sexy. Finishing me off, she crawls up my body and lies down next to me.

"That was amazing," I say through deep breaths. She lies on her side, curling up next to me, resting her head on my chest. My heart is still racing as she places her hand over it.

"Did you like that?"

"I always do," I say as I run my fingers through her hair.

"We need to do something about these panties and this bra," I say with a smirk. Looping my finger on the top of her panties, I drag them down.

"Oh, do we now?"

I pull her panties down and lift her foot to remove one side and then the other side. Running my hands up her legs, I bring myself back up her long body, touching every inch of her.

"Sit up," I quietly tell her.

I help her up, and unhook her bra from her back; pulling the straps down her arms. Her breasts are heavy and fall perfectly when she lies back onto the bed.

"I'm going to celebrate my new job by fucking you senseless," I grit out, leaning forward to suck her nipples into hard little buds.

Her eyes flash to mine, and I can see she's wondering where that came from. I've never *fucked* her; we've always been sweet with each other. She has never seen this side of me, but if my girl wants to play naughty, so will I. Pushing her legs apart and up, I hold her legs tightly in place and hover over her entrance, teasing her with just the wet tip of my dick. I insert just the head, removing it immediately after I enter her. I do this a few more times and watch as she squirms beneath me.

"I need you," she pants, biting her lip.

She is so wet. Every time I enter her, she seems like she's one thrust closer to losing control. Teasing her more, I use my tip to circle her entrance from the outside while running a finger over her hard nub.

"Please," she begs. I love when she begs.

Inhaling sharply, I can see her chest rising and falling with her hurried breaths. Her eyes roll back before she closes them altogether.

"Open your eyes and look at me," I order.

Snapping her eyes open, she finds mine and holds my stare. Working her over, I can feel her clit throbbing, and she's soaking wet. She wiggles beneath me, trying to press herself into me.

"I need to feel you in me," she begs.

It's almost painful to watch her as I press and pinch her hard little clit, rubbing her wetness all around her opening. Finally positioning myself against her, without any warning, I push into her fast and hard. The gasp I hear almost frightens me, until I see her lips turn into a small smile.

"Like this?" I say, thrusting forcefully.

"Mmm hmm." Her back arches as she moans.

With every thrust, her thighs tighten around me, and I can feel her nails digging into my back, which turns me on even more. Her walls tighten as she clenches around me, bringing me close to my second release. Knowing her body, I can see she is also close to climax.

"Not yet," I whisper.

"Gabe, I can't, I'm..."

"Not until I say." I pull back one last time. "Open your eyes and look at me. I want to see your eyes when you come all over me." Her eyes flicker open lightly. "Ready?" I ask. She nods.

With one last hard thrust into her, I pump my release. I lay myself down on top of her; we're both struggling to catch our breath. I'm still inside her, throbbing, and can feel her ride out her orgasm. Her walls are still clenching around me, drawing every last drop out of me.

"I'm pretty sure that was the best sex I've ever had," I sputter. She nods her head, breathing deeply and closes her eyes.

"Gabriel," she whispers. She rarely calls me "Gabriel," but there is something about her saying my full name that turns me on.

"Yes, baby?"

"I'm madly in love with you," she whispers as she turns into me and curls up again.

"You're mine forever," I whisper back to her, and I mean it.

CHAPTER FIFTEEN

~Jess~

With the holidays behind us, Gabe is pouring himself into his new job, and I have a full class schedule for spring semester. I was able to secure a part-time internship at a local TV station for the summer here in Orange County. I shared my good news with Janet, but she was less than enthused when she read the job description, none too pleased that I wouldn't be getting much hands-on experience. I'm pretty sure I'll be getting coffee and running errands for the length of my internship, but I just can't imagine leaving Gabe for the summer to take an internship in another state, so a glorified barista I will be.

Gabe's shifts are forty-eight hours, where he has to stay at the firehouse, and then he has four days off. However, he's been picking up at least an extra day, sometimes two days a week of overtime on his normally scheduled days off. He loves his job, but I don't want to lose him to his career like I lost my father. I appreciate that he works hard and loves what he does, so I've been tolerant thus far.

Gabe promises me that he's taking these extra hours to acquaint himself with his new job and gain more experience.

This leaves me alone—a lot. I miss him, my dad, and Ava. I miss my best friend, and am looking forward to spending time with her when she's home for spring break in a few short days.

The weather has been unseasonably warm for early March, so I've been sneaking in a run here and there. Between my studies, missing Gabe, and worrying about this summer internship, it's nice to clear my head, and running does that for me.

Gabe's shift ends in a few hours, and we're planning to drive to Santa Barbara this afternoon to get away for the night. He's been picking up so many extra shifts, that even when he's home, he's exhausted, so we stay in most nights. When he suggested a getaway, I jumped at the opportunity.

He wouldn't tell me where we were staying, or what we were doing, but knowing Gabe, he'll have me in bed the entire trip, ravaging every inch of me. Tossing a few things in an overnight bag, I zip it up and set it on the floor next to my bed.

My phone pings with a new text message.

Leaving now. See you in ten. Love u.

Just finished packing. XOXO

I quickly make my way to the shower. I want to get in and out before he gets here, or he'll join me, and we'll never leave on time. Rushing to finish getting ready, I throw on a pair of dark wash blue jeans, rolled up to my calf, and a fitted black tank top. I transfer my wallet, keys, and make-up from my current purse to a large black leather hobo-style purse, and slip on a pair of black Toms.

Lightly drying my hair, I pull it up into a messy bun, and throw on some light eye shadow, finishing off with some mascara and nude lip-gloss. When I hear my front door open, I know its Gabe.

"Babe, I'm in the bathroom. Just finishing up," I holler.

I can hear his heavy footsteps coming down the hallway. Gathering my hairdryer and brush, I open the bathroom door. He is standing with his back against the wall, in his tight blue Santa Ruiz Fire Department t-shirt and pair of athletic shorts. My heart races, as it always does when I see him. Flashing me a warm smile, he pulls me into a hug and holds me. As he presses his nose into my hair, I can hear him take in the scent of me.

"Coconut. I love when you smell like coconut," he growls. Pressing his lips to my head, he begins trailing kisses down my face, until he gets to my lips, gently tugging on my bottom lip.

"You need to shower and pack," I mumble against his mouth.

"I don't need to do anything except love you," he mumbles back. God, he turns me on.

"Let's continue this in Santa Barbara." I pull away from his kiss, turning from him as I head to my room.

"I'm already packed. I just need to shower and change."

"Well, hurry up. I'm ready to go," I say impatiently as I shove my hairdryer and brush into my bag. Turning around, I find him undressing in the middle of my room. He's standing there, buck naked, when he catches me looking at him.

"Something catch your eye?" he snickers.

"Get that hot ass of yours in the shower, now!" I point towards the bathroom. He's trying to weaken me, and it's working, but I can't let him know that. I hear him turn the shower on and find myself laughing at his antics. Thirty minutes later, we're on the road, headed to Santa Barbara.

"Where are we staying?"

"It's a surprise," he says with a grin.

"I don't like surprises."

"Well, get used to it. I'm going to surprise you for the rest of your life," he says, taking his eyes off the road to hold my stare. I have a type A personality. I like to have it all planned out and organized. I'm a control freak. Surprises give me anxiety.

Changing the subject because I'm annoyed, I say, "I can't wait to see Ava next week." I turn my head to look out the window, admiring the view on our drive.

"It'll be good to see her. Just don't get upset if she spends most of her time with Adrian. You know she's in love with him."

I chuckle, thinking of my best friend falling for the guy that we were both just friends with in high school.

"I know. I can't imagine being away from you. I don't know how they do it; long distance wouldn't work for me. It couldn't work. I need you." Gabe reaches over and takes my hand in his, giving it a squeeze.

"I need you too." I love the confidence in his words. He pulls my hand to his mouth and kisses the promise ring he gave me for Christmas. We spend the next few hours getting settled into the most luxurious hotel room I've ever seen. It looks out onto the Pacific Ocean. Standing on the balcony, I let the wind blow through my hair while Gabe finishes hanging his clothes. I can smell him before I feel his big arms wrap around my waist, pulling me back into him. I love his light musky scent; I could curl my face into his neck and just drink him in.

Standing behind me, he holds me tightly while we watch the water, not saying anything to each other; just being together. It's the most peaceful silence: comfortable and caring. Bending down slightly, he plants a kiss on the space between my neck and shoulder.

"I've got dinner reservations for us, but for the next couple of hours, we're going to christen every surface of this room. I'm taking you on the bed, the bathroom counter, up against the wall, and on the desk."

My head snaps around to meet his eyes. He's serious. *Holy shit.* Just hearing him say that has me worked up, and the heat within me is rising. Pulling me inside from the balcony, he lifts my tank top, pulling it off over my head. Kicking my shoes off, I reach for the button on his jeans. It's a flurry of clothes flying all over the room until we're standing naked in front of each other.

"God, you're beautiful." He brushes his hand over my shoulder and down to my breast.

"Mmm," I moan as his hands explore me.

Living up to his promise, he takes me on the bathroom counter, up against the wall, on the desk, and then he makes the sweetest, softest love to me on the bed. Lying here with my sweet man napping, I reflect on the past year. I truly feel like my life has settled, and it's all because of Gabe. While he sleeps, I gently kiss his cheek, whispering to him as I do every night when he's home with me, "I'll never love anyone as much as I love you."

I'm glad I packed a change of clothes as we walk into an exclusive restaurant on the property. Even in a dress and heels, I feel underdressed. Everything here is exquisite from the paintings on the walls to the linens on the table.

Our server brings the glass of sparkling water I ordered and Gabe's vodka tonic. We order the same meal: pecan-crusted sea bass.

"This place is beautiful," I say, taking a sip of my water.

"You're beautiful."

I can feel my cheeks flush at his compliments.

"Thanks."

"It's amazing how much has changed in the last year," he says, sipping his drink. "I've got a new job, you're in college and almost done." He winks at me, knowing how much this topic of my accelerated college career bothers me.

"I was thinking the same thing this afternoon. It doesn't seem that long ago when we were just kids playing at the park and going to Disneyland." I smile at the memories.

"Speaking of Disneyland," he says, his voice more animated. "Remember when you got lost and we spent an hour looking for you?"

"I was not lost for an hour," I correct him.

"You were too. I think you were maybe five years old."

"I remember. You found me in the line to meet Cinderella." Both of us start laughing.

"I was thinking about that the other day." He pauses, running his finger around the rim of his glass. "I think that is when I first fell in love with you."

"What? Really? You were nine years old."

"I know. But the feeling of losing you, not knowing where you were, if you were okay, or hurt, scared me. I'll never forget that feeling." Holding his gaze, I can't help but feel a sense of comfort in his words.

"You know, I've never been back to Disneyland since that trip. I never did get my picture taken with Cinderella. Maybe we should do that with Ava next week," I say excitedly.

"She can bring Adrian, so all four of us can go, a double date."
He laughs lightly as he runs his finger around the rim of his
glass.

"That would be fun." He smiles at me.

"I'm getting my picture taken with Cinderella this time!"
We raise our glasses and tap them together as he shakes his
head and laughs at me.

"Now if our food would hurry up, I have other plans for
you tonight," he mumbles and looks for our server.

Back in the room, I see Gabe rummaging through his bag,
pulling out a full plastic grocery bag. I kick my heels off and
remove my dress, hanging it up in the closet.

"What's in the bag?" I ask.

"Grab your jeans and a sweatshirt."

"Why? I thought we we're going to bed." I smirk at him.
"I'm ready for round four," I tease.

"We'll get to round four, five, and six in a little bit. I have
something else I want to do first."

"This better be good," I mumble, pulling my jeans and
my sweatshirt out of my overnight bag. Once we're finished
dressing, he grabs the bag and the keycard for our hotel room.

"Ready?" he asks, taking my hand and pulling me out of
the room and into the hallway. Waiting for the elevator, I ask
him again, "So are you going to tell me what's in the bag?"

"Maybe." He smiles and leans in to kiss me.

Crossing though the lobby, we take the back doors out to
the beautiful outside patio that leads to the resort pool and
beach. Walking down the stone steps, we finally hit the sand.

He leads me across the private beach until we come to a bonfire pit.

Setting the bag down on the sand, all the supplies are waiting and ready to start a bonfire. The wood is already in the pit, and there is a starter log waiting along with a multi-purpose lighter.

"Need some help?" I joke with him.

"I can do it."

"You may be a firefighter, but you're not very good at starting them."

He laughs at my joke as he looks up at me, still fighting to keep the lighter lit against the wind. Finally getting the starter log going, the rest of the wood quickly ignites. Sitting down in the sand, he grabs the bag and some long sticks and plants himself next to me.

"Dessert," he says proudly, pulling out a bag of marshmallows, chocolate bars, and graham crackers.

"I love s'mores." I beam, opening the package of marshmallows. Gabe slides them onto the sticks while I get the chocolates and graham crackers ready.

"Did you think of this all by yourself?"

"Are you doubting my romantic skills?" he says through his laughs.

"No, I just would never have thought of this."

I slide the soft, golden brown marshmallow off the stick and onto the graham cracker, assembling the first s'more.

"I saw it in the brochure." He laughs, and I smack his arm.

"Well, regardless, I love it. This is better than any dessert in that stuffy restaurant."

"This is dessert, part one. Part two is going to happen upstairs in just a little bit." He wags his eyebrows at me.

Reaching out, I offer him a bite of my s'more. Noticing some marshmallow on his bottom lip, I reach out and wipe it off. Catching my hand, he pulls my finger into his mouth, sucking the sweet marshmallow off of my finger. The movement of his tongue around my finger sets my body on fire.

"Let's go," I whisper.

"Mmm hmm," he responds.

CHAPTER SIXTEEN

-Gabe-

Throwing the last bag in the car, she looks up at me with her arms crossed and her bottom lip pushed out.

"I'm not ready to leave yet." Grabbing her face, I kiss her and gently suck her bottom lip in between mine.

"I know baby, but you have school tomorrow, and we have to call Ava to tell her about our plans for next weekend."

"We can do that from here," she pouts.

Pressing a kiss to the top of her head, I wrap my arms around her. "I'll bring you back here again. I promise."

Settling into the truck, the drive home is quiet. Jess has dozed off, and we're only a few miles from home. This weekend was confirmation of everything I knew I was feeling. I can't live without her. I've been busting my ass working overtime and picking up shifts at the fire station to save all the money I can for an engagement ring and a house.

I know that I'm bringing her back to Santa Barbara; this is where I will propose to her. I will do whatever it takes to make her mine forever. I want to build my life with her: marriage, house, kids.

"Shit. Oh my God!" she screams. I swerve my truck, reacting to her sudden outburst.

"What? Jesus Christ, you scared the shit out of me," I yell. A look of panic crosses her face, and she's dumping her purse all over the car seat. Shit is flying everywhere.

"Settle down. Whatever it is, you'll find it. Just please, calm down."

"Calm down? I haven't taken my birth control pills in three days." My heart stops.

"What did you just say?"

"You heard me." Her eyes are filling with tears, and she's still flinging shit all over the seat. Turning down our street, I pull up in front of Jess' house.

"Babe, this is going to be fine. It was just a couple of days. You'll find them at home. Just take them immediately, okay?" She nods her head at me, but I can see she's scared. Shit, so am I.

"I'll get your bags. Go find your pills, then you can cook me dinner, woman." I wink at her, trying to lighten the mood. I toss her bags in her room, then I sit on the edge of the bed. She went straight to the bathroom, and the sounds of her rummaging through drawers frantically fill the silent house. Kicking off my shoes, I lie down, curling up with her pillow. I love how everything smells like her.

"I can't find them anywhere," she shouts, walking into her room. I can tell she's reached a panicked state.

"Babe, calm down."

"You calm the fuck down, Gabe!" Jesus Christ, she's pissed!

"Sorry. I didn't mean to upset you. Just call your doctor tomorrow morning and see if they'll call you in a new prescription."

rebecca shea

She's biting her lip, and I can see her brain working. I know how she operates; she's retracing every day and trying to remember when the last time she took her pill was and where she was.

"I think it might have been more than three days ago," she whispers. Okay, that got my attention.

"How many days?" I hiss.

"Four or five. I'm not sure, to tell you the truth. What if…" I cut her off.

"No matter what happens, nothing will change my feelings for you. Please try to not stress about this until you call your doctor, okay?" Nodding her head, she comes to sit down on the bed with me.

"I'm scared," she whispers.

"I know."

Pulling her down, I wrap her in my arms and snuggle with her. I can feel her heart beating rapidly, and her body is tense. I know she's worried as hell. The rest of the evening is full of strained silence. We're both thinking about the "what ifs."

"Thanks for making dinner, babe," I whisper to her and gently kiss her ear.

"You're welcome," she whispers back with a fake smile.

I just want to ease her fears, but I know nothing I say will make her feel better.

"Let's go to bed," I say, gently tugging at her arm. Taking a deep breath, she pushes herself off the couch and into my arms, squeezing me tightly.

"Gabe." I can hear her voice break. I pull her back from me so I can look at her, and she stumbles slightly. "Please tell me, that if I am pregnant, you won't leave me? I don't think I could do this on my own."

Tears leak from her eyes and run down her cheeks. Cupping her round cheeks with both of my hands, I wipe her tears with my thumbs. When I pull her back into me, her body is trembling with sobs. All I can do is hold her while she cries and reassure her that it's not even an option.

"Listen to me." I tip her chin up, drawing her eyes to mine. "I will never leave you, ever. Do you understand me?" My tone is firm and aggressive. I'm not mad at her, but it hurts a bit that she'd question my commitment to her. "There is nothing, and I mean nothing, that will come between us. You are mine forever. When the time comes that we have babies, whether that's now or in the future, don't you ever question my love for you or them. Do you understand? There is no leaving. Ever."

With a big inhale, Jess squeezes me tighter and nods her head.

"I love you," I whisper into her hair.

"I love you too," she says, pressing her lips to my chest and kissing me through my t-shirt.

"Now stop stressing about this, please," I beg her. "Let's go to bed."

When I wake in the morning, I notice she is already gone. She has an early class on Mondays, but I usually see her out the door. We both went to sleep with a lot on our minds, and I know I was tired, but I'm just surprised I didn't hear her at all this morning. Grabbing my phone from the nightstand, I see that I have a message from Jess.

Coffee is in the kitchen. I'll be home around 2:00. I love you.

I miss you when I don't wake up next to you :(Love you more.

Waiting for her to get back from class, I go home to unpack from our trip. I plan to hit the gym, in hopes that I will relieve any lingering stress from the missing birth control saga. We normally run on Mondays after Jess' class, so I'll get my cardio in with her. That's the *only* cardio I'll be doing with her until we figure out our little problem. Where the hell did the pills just disappear to anyway?

Making quick work of the gym, and laundry, I'm waiting at home for her to arrive. I love being here when she gets home. As I'm thinking about her, I hear her car pull into the driveway. The front door opens, and my beautiful girl bounces through, looking happy and confident, and not at all scared like she was yesterday.

"Want to go for a run in a bit?" she asks, walking by me and tossing her bag onto the floor.

"Sure. You look happy."

"I am happy." Her eyes twinkle. "Let me get changed and we'll go."

She hurries off down the hallway. Grabbing my tennis shoes, I lace them up while waiting for her. My phone rings, and I check the screen. "Shit," I mumble to myself.

"What's up, Chief?" I answer, already knowing why he's calling. He wants me to pick up a shift. Hanging up, I know she isn't going to be happy.

"Babe," I call out.

"Almost ready," I hear her respond.

Walking down the hallway, I open her door.

"Chief called." It's not hard to ignore the giant eye roll she does.

"Let me guess," she says sarcastically. "You're picking up a shift?" And that happy girl that bounded through the door just vanished.

I pull her into me. "It's just half a shift, twelve hours," I grumble. But I know the extra money will help me get a ring on her finger faster, so I agreed to pick up the shift, knowing that it might upset her.

"I know you love your job, but when will you ever say no? I don't want to live like I did growing up, never having my dad around. I want a man that's going to be around for my family and me. I feel like you're turning into my dad," Jess spits out, pushing away from me and reaching down to grab her tennis shoes.

"I'll never be your dad," I snap at her, pissed at the insinuation.

"Kind of looks like you already are," she fires back at me, tying up her tennis shoes and not making eye contact with me. A rush of guilt rolls over me. She thinks I'm choosing work over her.

"I will call you later," I mutter. She still won't even look up at me. "I love you." Getting no response, I step it up. "I'll make it up to you, I promise."

"Sure you will."

"Jess, please stop acting like this."

"Just go," she says quietly. "We'll talk tomorrow."

CHAPTER SEVENTEEN

~Jess~

As I jog down our street, I see Gabe getting in his truck to leave. My breathing is fast and ragged because I'm pissed off that he keeps putting his job before me. I understand that he's still new and he's learning, but he picks up every extra shift that he can. This is exactly what my dad did while I was growing up, although he did it as a way of burying his feelings and keeping himself busy after my mom died. My insecurities are telling me Gabe would rather be at work than spend time with me.

Running down Main Street past the little Italian restaurant we went to, I plan to run another mile down to Washington Park. This park holds many fond memories for me, and it's absolutely beautiful this time of year. There is a small creek that winds through the park with a paved running path that follows the banks of the creek. I turn up the volume on my iPhone music just slightly as I let the burn of my lungs wash away the anger that I had when Gabe left me at the house.

Running faster than I normally do, I push myself harder so that I can get a good workout, but also, to get home quickly. My legs are stiffening a bit from starting out so hard. I make it down Main Street and into the park entrance in a little less than twelve minutes; that's fast for me. I'm pleasantly surprised and happy with my time.

The park is absolutely stunning. There are spring flowers and cattails growing around the banks of the creek. With the light breeze, you can smell the fragrance from the flowers. It's almost a citrusy smell, very calming. The grass is bright green and has been recently cut, and the trees are mature with full, large leaves. I notice several other runners coming out of the park in the direction that I'm heading; we wave as we pass each other.

The path curves around the creek and is lined by large oak trees with branches that reach out over the path. The setting sun behind the trees makes the path a bit darker than it actually is this time of day. It's a gorgeous late spring evening. My earphones are plugged into my iPhone, and when Pink comes on, I turn it up just a bit more. Taking my eyes off the path to look at my phone, I feel myself falling to the ground.

My face hits the grass hard, and I can see my phone slide across the ground and into the tall grass that lines the edge of the creek. *Shit*. Rolling over to see what has knocked me over, or what I tripped over, I see a fist coming straight at my face. Trying to block the fist, I'm too late, feeling the excruciating blow to the side of my head. Hearing myself gasp, I see white stars before everything goes black.

Beep... Beep... Beep...

Hearing the beeping of machines, I can feel the heaviness of my eyes. Struggling to open them, I can see the darkness through the blinds covering the only window in the small room. Slowly lifting my head, I am overcome with nausea, and I can tell that I have been medicated.

I have the worst headache I've ever had, and with each beat of my heart, I can feel my head pound. Raising my arm to feel my face, I can feel the slight pull of the IV that is placed in my hand. I can hear hushed voices, one of them Gabe's, coming from just outside my room. I need to find the call button, knowing there is one here somewhere. I've never been hospitalized before, but I spent a good portion of my toddler years lying in a hospital bed with my mom and remember her pushing that button when she needed a nurse.

Trying to sit up, every muscle in my body aches. What the hell happened to me? I feel like I've been hit by a car. Lying back down, I close my eyes, trying to remember anything. I remember running, and falling, and that's where my memory stops.

Hearing the quiet squeak of my door, I slowly open my eyes and turn my head towards the door. Gabe walks in, making eye contact with me. Rushing to the bed, he presses a kiss to my forehead before he sits on the edge of the bed and holds my hand.

"When did you wake up?" he whispers, pulling my hand to his lips and kissing my knuckles gently. My mouth is so dry when I try to speak that nothing comes out. Closing my mouth, I swallow a couple of times, and I'm able to squeak out a few words with my voice breaking.

"Just a minute ago. Why am I here? What happened?" He squeezes my hand, but hesitates to say anything.

"You're okay, Jess. You're going to be okay," he says, his eyes bloodshot and full of unshed tears, sounding more like he's convincing himself. I haven't seen him cry since he was eight years old and broke his arm after he fell off his bike. He is the strongest person physically and emotionally that I know.

"Why are you crying?" I ask him. Without answering, he stands up and leans over me, pressing a gentle kiss to lips. Dropping my hand, he reaches his arms underneath my shoulders, pulling me into a hug, his shoulders shaking gently as he squeezes me a bit harder. Reaching my arms up and around his broad shoulders, I squeeze him back as best I can. I'm weak, and I don't have the strength to squeeze him harder.

"What happened?" I ask him again.

Pulling back from me, he kisses my forehead again and then my cheek. Running his thumb over my left cheekbone, I feel pain and the pressure, even though his touch is gentle and caring.

"I have to go tell the doctor that you're awake. I'll be right back, okay?"

I nod at him in acknowledgement. Turning to walk away, I notice now that he's wearing his work t-shirt that has "G. Garcia" written across his right chest and on the back it reads "Santa Ruiz Fire Department." He must have come straight from work. As I still try to piece together what happened and what day it is and what time it is, I hear my door open again. In walk a doctor and a nurse with Gabe and my dad standing behind them.

"Ms. Harper," the doctor says. "I'm Doctor Lefson. I'm glad to see you're awake. How are you feeling?"

Shrugging, I look back and forth between him, the nurse, and Gabe.

"This is Jennifer, your nurse. Mr. Garcia, Mr. Harper, we'll need you to step outside while we talk to Ms. Harper," he instructs, nodding at the door.

"No, he can stay." I reach my hand to Gabe. He looks to the doctor for approval before moving over to the side of the bed and pulling my right hand in between both of his. My dad turns and quietly leaves the room. "We're going to check your vitals and get some blood work first, but we need to talk to you about what you remember."

"I don't know why I'm here or what happened," I say. "I don't remember anything." He lowers his eyes, looking to Gabe. Dr. Lefson moves towards me and pulls his stethoscope off of his neck, setting it at the foot of my bed.

The silence in the room is deafening, and Gabe nervously rubs my hand between both of his. "Will someone please tell me why the fuck I'm here?" Hot tears sting my eyes and Dr. Lefson casually sits his right leg on the free space at the end of the bed, looking at me cautiously.

"Jessica, this evening you went running and you were attacked. Upon arrival, you were unconscious, so we performed a CT scan, which showed no internal bleeding or broken bones."

I breathe a sigh of relief. The way everyone has been avoiding my question, I thought maybe I was dying. "Well, that's good, right?"

"You have swelling and bruising to your face and eyes, but it appears most of your physical injuries are minor. However, we need your consent to perform an additional examination." Dr. Lefson's voice is soft and quiet. Gabe holds my hand tightly offering little reassuring squeezes. "When you were brought in, you were unclothed from the waist down. We have reason to believe you may have been sexually assaulted."

A heat washes over me like I've never felt. My ears burn and my throat constricts.

"We'd like to further examine you and check for additional injuries or evidence." I can't think. I can't feel. I just nod my head in approval.

"Okay, Jenny and my colleague, Dr. Jordan, will perform the examination. We will need you to sign some paperwork allowing us to collect evidence and take pictures if needed. It will be important and needed for prosecution." He's so fucking robotic with his words. Like this is shit he says every day. "The exam is very thorough, and can take a couple of hours. Is there someone else," he looks at Gabe and then back to me, "that you'd like to have here with you?"

Shaking my head no to him, I squeeze Gabe's hand.

"I need to do this alone," I whisper, and look up at Gabe. His eyes are still full of unshed tears, and he doesn't immediately move. Squeezing my hand one last time, he releases my hand and walks to the door, pausing before he opens it and then exits.

"Dr. Jordan will be in shortly. Jenny has all the paperwork and will walk through everything with you." He nods, grabbing his stethoscope and leaves through the same door Gabe just did. For the next two hours, I was swabbed in multiple places, had my fingernails scraped and cut, and had my blood drawn. I waited for them to finish the exam and confirm what my body already knew.

I was given multiple antibiotics and an emergency contraceptive pill since I had missed my birth control pills. The last few hours were like an out of body experience for me. Inside, I wanted to cry, to hurt, but nothing came. After taking their pictures and bags of evidence, I'm finally alone.

Curling into a ball, I lie in this cool hospital room and try to feel something: hate, anger, sadness, but all I am is numb. I hear the door to my room open and the quiet footsteps stop near the edge of my bed. I know it's him. I don't need to see him, or hear him. I have always been able to feel his presence.

"Jess?" he asks quietly.

"Go away." My voice is flat, emotionless.

"No. I need to be here with you."

"Please, leave."

"Don't push me away, please. I love you," he pleads with me.

"I know you do. I just need some time." My voice breaks, and finally the tears come. I can't fight them, and they roll down my cheeks as sobs escape me. The bed shifts, and I feel him slide in behind me, his large arms pulling me gently against the front of him. He's curled around me, spooning me and holding me so tightly, my ribs hurt with the pressure from his arms, but having him next to me is the most comforting feeling in the world.

"I'm not going anywhere," he whispers into my ear. His voice is quiet but shaky. I can tell he's crying by the sniffles I hear between the words he's whispering. "We will get through this, together. You and I. Nothing will break us, ever. Not this. Do you hear me, Jess? Nothing. We're unbreakable."

God, I hope he is right.

CHAPTER EIGHTEEN

-Gabe-

Holding her in my arms while she cries herself to sleep breaks my heart. I can feel her body trembling, and I'm helpless to all of it. All I can do is hold her and reassure her that she'll be—that we'll be—fine. I want to believe that. I watch her as she sleeps in my arms, finally resting my head next to hers, and I breathe her in.

Lying here, I listen to her soft breaths, holding her, feeling her body continue to shake in her sleep. I am certain that even though she is sleeping, she is not at peace. Who the fuck could hurt her like this? I will do everything in my power to find this sick fuck and make him pay. Sliding my arm out from underneath her, I try to move as quietly as possible so that she will not wake, knowing she needs the rest for her body to heal.

Sliding out of the bed, I can't help but stare at her, curled into a protective ball on this stiff hospital bed. Her beautiful olive skin has lost all semblance of its color and is pale. Her face is marked purple and pink with large bruises, and is slightly swollen under her eyes. My beautiful girl looks like a small child, scared and helpless. I quietly leave her room to go home, shower, and change quickly.

Chief is still sitting in the waiting room, sitting in the same chair he's been in for the last six hours. He still hasn't spoken to her, but has sat vigil outside her door. We came here together when we got the call. It was the paramedics from our station that responded, and one of the most difficult calls I've ever received. While little was communicated, other than her initial injuries, we all knew what had likely happened.

While I was the one who flipped my shit, punching water coolers and kicking trashcans across the emergency room and eventually the waiting room, Chief sat stoic and quiet. At times, I'd find his face buried in his hands, whispering quiet prayers.

Chief listened quietly and let me ask questions when the doctors would update us on her condition, only nodding his head when the facts were spoken. Closing the door to her room behind me, I try not to startle him.

"Chief, I need to run home quickly. I'll be back in about an hour. She's asleep, but I don't want her to wake up alone. Will you go sit with her?"

With a single nod, he pushes himself up from the stiff chair. While he's only in his late forties, he looks as if he's aged since last night. His face is somber and ashen and his hair a mess. Quietly moving past me, he stops, meeting my eyes for the first time since we arrived.

"How is she?"

"Hurting." It's the only word that comes to mind. Physical, emotional, and mental pain is all I see when I look at her.

Chief nods his head and enters her room. I watch him as he slowly makes his way to the foot of her bed, standing over her. For the first time ever, I see emotion from Chief. A single tear rolls down his cheek as he watches her sleep. Moving to the side of her bed, I see him plant a soft kiss to the top of her head before sitting down to take watch over her.

I notice that Ava's car is parked in the driveway when I get home. She must have left school early when I texted her to tell her Jess was attacked on her run. Entering through the side door of our house that opens into the kitchen, everyone is sitting around the dining room table in silence, cups of coffee littering the table. Mom, Dad, Luke, Ava, and Adrian all sit quietly, looking at me for any updates.

I glance around the table, not knowing what to tell them or what Jess would want me to tell them. I politely nod at all of them, but feel the lump forming in my throat, so I retreat and move through the living room and up the stairs to my bedroom. I can't talk about this right now as I'm still trying to process everything myself.

Taking the steps two at the time, I slam the bedroom door behind me. Kicking off my shoes, I throw myself onto my bed and bury my face in my pillow. Willing myself to breathe deeply, I try to calm myself down when all I feel is anger and rage roiling through me. I hear a light knock on my door, and I know its Ava.

"Go away," I mutter into my pillow.

Tap Tap Tap

Finally, the door squeaks open and I feel the side of my bed sink.

"Please tell me what happened." Ava's voice is soft and quiet as she sets her hand on my back. "Please," she begs.

With my face still buried in my pillow, I just shake my head back and forth. I can't talk yet.

"Gabe, I'm going to go see her. Tell me what I can expect, please."

"No. Don't go there," I say, pushing myself up from my pillow. Rolling onto my back, I place my hands underneath my head, staring at my ceiling. "It's bad." Those are the only words I am able to speak

"How bad?" Ava's voice breaks. Lying there, I ignore the question because I don't know if I should tell her. Her voice is firmer with me when she asks again. "How bad is it? Answer me, god dammit."

Finally making eye contact with her, my eyes are stinging with tears. Blinking to keep them from spilling out, I feel them finally break free of their confines, spilling down and into my hair. I shift to look at Ava, who is sniffling, wiping tears from her own face. Looking at her hurting causes me to lose the little bit of control I was holding onto. Jumping from the bed, I am no longer able to control the bile rising from my stomach. Running into the bathroom, I slam the door behind me as I make it just in time to lose everything that was in my stomach.

Showering and changing, I make my way back to the hospital, winding through the hallways to Jess' room. Chief stops me outside the door, pressing a hand to my chest.

"Can't go in; she's being interviewed," he says so calmly and matter of fact. Peering through the window on the door, I see two detectives, a man and a woman, talking to her. Her eyes are downcast as she stares at her fidgeting hands.

"When did she wake up?"

"About ten minutes after you left."

"How was she?"

"Quiet."

Taking a seat next to Chief in one of the chairs outside her room, I study the exhausted face of the almost unrecognizable man sitting next to me.

"You should go get some rest." He shuffles his feet, crossing them underneath his chair and releases a quiet sigh.

"I know I haven't been the best father to her. I know I haven't always been there for her like your family has. I just didn't know what to do with a little girl by myself..." His voice trails off. "...and I know Jess loves me, but she's going to need *you* now more than ever. She doesn't trust or need me like she trusts and needs you."

I nod in acknowledgement of his words. Swallowing the newly formed lump in my throat, I say, "I know." My stomach turns and clenches into a knot. I'm so fucking angry that I couldn't keep her safe. I couldn't protect her like I'd promised her I always would.

The door to her room opens and the two detectives make their way out. Both nod their heads at us as they pass. I stand to go see Jess, while Chief follows the detectives and stops them down the hall as I enter her room. She's lying there, all curled up in a ball again, not crying or sleeping, just lying there. Her eyes are devoid of any emotion at all.

"Hey, baby," I whisper, leaning down to kiss her cheek. She pulls away from my touch, not wanting me to kiss her.

"Baby, look at me," I tell her gently. "Jess, please," I beg. Her eyes finally shift to me. "Ava wants to come see you. Would you be okay with that?"

"No," she replies. Her throat is tight, and her words are barely audible. Her eyes instantly flood with tears, spilling down onto her pillow. Her lips and chin tremble as she closes her eyes, causing more tears to fall. Reaching out to touch her arm, she flinches at my contact.

"Everyone is really concerned about you and wants to see you. Mom hasn't slept and has prayed the rosary about a hundred times."

Jess knows my mom worries, and when she worries, she prays the rosary in Spanish. The nurse enters the room quietly, making brief eye contact with me before dropping her eyes to Jess' balled up form on the bed.

"Sweetie, you get to go home in just a bit. We're just waiting on your discharge papers," she says quietly. "Do you want me to help you get changed?" she asks.

"I can help her," I mutter angrily. I'm her fucking boyfriend. I will help her get dressed. Jennifer nods at me, pulling the curtain beside the bed on her way out.

"Let's sit you up," I say, pushing the incline button on the remote that's attached to the bed.

Once sitting, I grab the bag I brought back with me that has clean clothes in it for Jess. Slowly dropping her long legs off the side of the bed, her feet almost touch the floor. She drops her head as her legs hang there with her oversized hospital gown hanging down past her knees.

"Stand up," I whisper as she pushes herself off the bed, balancing herself on wobbly feet.

"Turn around." I place my hands on her arms and guide her to turn around. I reach for the ties on her pale blue hospital gown, gripping the top tie. I gently pull it and watch the top of the gown fall off her shoulders. Pulling the second tie, the gown falls open further. As I grasp the third and final tie, she presses her hands to the front of the gown, over her chest, holding it in place so that it won't fall to the ground.

Urging her to turn around again so that she's now facing me, her head is bowed, and her arms are tightly crossed across the front of her body, still holding her gown. Opening the bag on the bed, I pull out a pair of panties and a bra. Lowering myself down in front of her, I hold each side of the panties, and she slowly steps into them one leg at a time. Raising them slowly, my arms reaching under her gown, I pull them onto her hips.

Reaching for the bra, Jess stops me. She takes the bra from my hands and turns around so her back is facing me. The hospital gown drops to the floor as Jess reaches through each arm of her bra and fastens it behind her back. I hand her favorite pair of worn blue jeans to her and she takes them from me. Before I'm able to do anything else, she has grabbed her navy blue tank top, and is pulling it on over her head. I hand her a khaki lightweight jacket to put on over her tank top and drop a pair of black flip-flops on the floor for her. I even remembered to pack some make-up and accessories in case she wanted to wear them.

She looks in the bag and sees the gold bangle bracelets and gold earrings and shoots me a small, stiff smile. Grabbing her make-up bag, she moves towards the small bathroom. Shuffling her feet slowly, she winces slightly as she moves. She flips the light on in the small bathroom and sets her make-up bag in the sink. Her long brown, wavy hair hangs loose down the middle of her back. I stand, watching her move slowly, methodically, and with little emotion.

Raising her head for the first time, she looks into the mirror, and a loud gasp escapes her mouth. Her hands fly up to her face, and she starts touching her cheeks and her eyes. Quickly, I move in behind her, holding her shuddering shoulders.

"It's just bruises," I remind her. "They'll heal quickly."

She runs her fingers over her cheek, and then under her eyes. Turning her around, I try to pull her into a hug, but she wiggles out of it.

"Why won't you let me touch you? Please, let me hug you," I plead with her. Pushing around me, she walks back toward the bed when the nurse appears again.

"Ready to go?" she asks, waving Jess' discharge papers. Jess nods her head and grabs her bag. I reach to take the bag from her shoulder, and she quickly shifts her shoulder so that I can't take it, scooting past me again as she heads for the door.

"Is my dad out here?" she asks me without turning around.

"Yes, but I'm taking you home," I snap at her, not meaning to. Stopping dead in her tracks, her back still to me, I move up to her. I don't touch her as I stand just inches behind her.

"Why won't you talk to me? Why won't you let me help you or touch you?" I beg her for answers. Without turning around, I get my answer in the coldest tone I've ever heard.

"I need my dad to take me home." My heart breaks.

CHAPTER NINETEEN

~Jess~

Dad is rearranging clutter in his pick-up as I sit on the front bench seat, leaning my head against the window. I watch Gabe standing outside the entrance to the hospital, his hands stuffed into the front pockets of his jeans, his shoulders hung in defeat, as he just stares at us. I think he mouths the words "I love you" to me, but I lower my eyes and pretend to not see him. I don't know why I'm pushing him away. He is and has always been everything I have ever wanted or needed.

"Hungry, kiddo?" my dad asks. "You need to eat something," he says, seemingly concerned for the first time in his life. Funny that it's food and eating that he's concerned with. I shrug my shoulders, knowing that nothing will help the sick feeling in my stomach. Today is a gloomy, overcast day. The sky is full of dark, ominous clouds, much like my mood.

"Can we just go home? You can pick up food later, okay? I'm just really tired."

"Sure thing, sweetheart."

Walking into our house, I drop my bag by the front door and kick off my flip-flops. Walking down the hallway towards my room, I peel off my jacket and toss it onto my bedroom floor, kicking my door shut behind me. I toss myself onto my bed, and I gasp, realizing how badly my ribs hurt. I gently pull my chenille blanket over me, and for the first time, I feel like I might be able to sleep.

I jump when I hear the doorbell ring. Forcing myself to sit up, I notice I am drenched in sweat. Slowly shifting to get out of bed, I hear a light knock at my door.

"Can I come in?" Dad says.

"Yes."

"This was just returned to you," he says, handing me my phone. "They, ah, had to keep it last night to go through it, check it for evidence."

I take the phone from his hand and wipe some dirt off the front of it. I push the little round button at the bottom and unlock the screen, seeing that I have multiple notifications for e-mails and text messages. I toss the phone over to my bed, not ready for contact with the outside world just yet.

"I think I'm finally hungry; can you pick up some Chinese?" I ask.

"Of course. Anything in particular you want?"

"I would love some kung pao shrimp." A small smile crosses my dad's face.

"Anything you want. Do you want me to invite Gabe over?" I don't even hesitate when I answer him.

"How about just you and me tonight, Dad?" He nods, but looks at me questioningly.

"Sure thing, sweetheart."

I hear him grabbing his keys and locking the front door before I hear the rumble of his truck taking off down the street. I realize for the first time that I have not showered since yesterday morning and I know I have traces of that man on my body. Stripping myself of all my clothes, I move as quickly as I can into the bathroom, turning the water on as hot as it'll go.

I grab my toothbrush and brush my teeth. I then pull out some mouthwash out from underneath the sink. Swishing a huge mouthful around, I let it sting the insides of my mouth before spitting it into the sink. The bathroom is filling with steam as I step into the shower. Turning it down just a little, it's to the point where I can just barely tolerate the heat. Letting the water run down my head, my face, and my body, I grab my loofah and pour body wash all over it, frantically washing my body.

I want all traces of last night off of me. I scrub my face, my arms, my legs, and stomach. I drop the loofah to the floor of the shower and grab my body wash, squirting some in my hand. I lower my hand between my legs and gently rub the scented soap between my legs. I'm sore, and for the first time, I realize how violated my body is. No one other than Gabe has left his mark on me, and here I feel where another man has been, uninvited.

Finishing my shower, I wrap a large bath towel around myself. Walking to my bed, I reach for my dirt-covered cell phone. Opening the main screen, I open my text messages and text Gabe.

I need you. Please come over.

Drying myself, I wait impatiently to see if he'll respond. It must not have even been a minute that I sent that text message, but I hear Gabe unlock the front door, close it, and re-lock it. The sounds of his heavy footsteps are just outside my door and then there is a soft knock.

"Everything okay?" he asks, concerned. His hand is still on the doorknob as he stands in my doorway, looking at me standing in nothing more than a bath towel.

"Close the door," I say. Following my instructions, he slowly moves to close the door, yet keeps his distance from me.

"Make love to me," I tell him.

"Jess," he sighs, walking towards me with pained eyes.

"Make love to me." I raise my voice at him. He's standing in front of me, each of his hands holding both of my arms.

"You're not ready for that. Your body needs to heal," he says quietly.

"I need to feel you, please. All I feel is him, and I need to feel you," I cry.

"I want nothing more than to make love to you, but we have to let your body heal."

"Screw you!" I lash out, pulling myself out of his hold. "This disgusts you, doesn't it?" I say, dropping my towel to the floor and pointing to my bruised body. He stands there, moving his eyes up and down the front of me, taking in the sight of my bruised and battered flesh. He's shaking his head no, but I know what he's thinking.

"Say it!" I yell at him. "I disgust you, don't I?"

"Stop saying that. You'll never disgust me." He's angry and I can see him shaking slightly.

"Then make love to me. Please," I beg. My tone has gone from angry to sad. Tears are threatening to spill out of my eyes while he stands looking at me. He has never denied me sexually, until now.

He speaks quietly. "I can't. Please understand this is not good for you, for us."

"Get out of here!" I cry, tears finally spilling down my face. My body is shaking, and my chest is heaving. I feel like I could pass out. Bending down, I reach for the towel I dropped to the ground and wrap it around my body tightly. He doesn't move. His hands are balled into fists, but his sympathetic eyes remain on me.

"Get the fuck out of here!" I yell at him again as I turn quickly and walk away, making my escape into the bathroom across the hall.

Locking the door behind me, I sit down on the toilet seat and grab another bath towel to bury my face and the sounds of my sobs in. After minutes of crying, I finally hear Gabe's shoes carrying him down the hallway. Holding my breath, I hear him pause, opening the front door and then closing it with a light click of the lock. It's then that I drop the towel I was holding in my shaky hands to the ground. I slide off of the toilet and onto the cool tile floor and curl into a ball. I know I've lost him.

CHAPTER TWENTY

-Gabe-

As I walk in the front door of my house, Ava nearly jumps into my arms.

"That was quick. How is she?"

I honestly have no words for what just happened. I've been trying to wrap my brain around the last twenty-four hours and everything Jess is experiencing. I'm so confused; she's pushing me away one minute, then pulling me back in the next, then pushing me away again. I shrug at Ava as I watch the confusion settle in on her face.

"I don't know. I honest to God, just don't know," I mutter, feeling the back of my throat tighten.

My worst fears settle in. I'm afraid I've lost the girl that I've always known; the sweet, innocent girl I've fallen in love with. She's emotionally broken; a shell of the Jess I knew. Mom and Dad walk into the living room where I'm standing with Ava. Mom pulls me into a tight embrace, holding me just like she used to do when I was young. It's amazing that a mother's embrace can still have the same effect when you're an adult.

"*Mijo*, how is she?" Mom whispers to me as she continues to hug me.

She only calls me "*Mijo*" when she's concerned. As I shrug my shoulders, Dad moves in on our hug and wraps himself around both Mom and me. I allow myself to cry again, not for me, but for Jess. For that broken spirit I just left crying in her bathroom, for everything that has happened to her, and everything I couldn't do to protect her.

As I pull myself together and wipe the stray tears off of my face, Mom gently tugs my hand and leads me to the couch. I throw myself down, sinking into the soft leather couch and stretching my legs on the coffee table. Ava quietly sits down next to me and leans her head on my shoulder.

It's so quiet in here. None of us know what to say or what to do, so we sit silently, deep in thought. I realize that in some instances, there are no words to be spoken. The mere presence and support of your family is all the comfort and love that you need.

Finally breaking the silence, I explain every detail of what happened, as best we know it. Mom sits and cries, as does Ava, who is holding my hand. Everyone just sits and listens to me talk and cry.

"Jessica has been through a very traumatic physical and emotional experience," Dad says, shifting in his seat. He knows that anything he says to me will not truly bring me peace, but he tries.

"She needs time. She is going to be erratic with her emotions; you have to accept that and be patient."

Nodding my head in agreement, I know this, but I want her better. I want *my* Jess back. Standing up from the couch, I head to my room to try to sleep, when all I want to do is to lie in bed, curled up next to her, breathing in the smell of her coconut-scented skin. I think of her lying in her bed all alone, wondering if she's afraid, what she's thinking, and if she's missing me as much as I miss her.

Looking out my bedroom window, I can see the front of her house, including her bedroom window, which is dark. Chief's pick-up truck is in the driveway, and the porch light is on. I consider going back over there to try to talk to her and explain myself better, but I talk myself out of it. "She needs time," I hear my dad saying. Lying back down, I close my eyes and try to let sleep come to me. I'm beyond exhausted.

I wake up to the sun peeking through my blinds, and it startles me. I am almost always awake before the sun is out. Rolling over quickly, I look at my alarm clock and it reads ten-thirty. Jumping out of bed, I get myself together quickly and am easily ready in fifteen minutes. My stomach is in knots, and I just want to get to her house. Throwing on jeans and a t-shirt, I run down the stairs, leaving without speaking to anyone. I could hear Mom, Dad, and Ava in the kitchen, but I'm too nervous to talk to anyone. I need to see Jess.

The walk across the street is almost unbearable. Chief's truck is gone, and I hope that she is home. He most likely is back to work already.

"Bastard," I say under my breath as I knock on the door.

I can hear the lock click, and the door slowly opens, but only halfway. Jess is standing there in a black tank top and a pair of black underwear. Her swollen, bloodshot eyes bring out the bright green color of her irises. Even swollen, bruised, and crying, she is the most beautiful woman I've ever seen. Taking a deep breath, I collect my wits and gather my strength.

"Can I come in?" I ask quietly.

She opens the door all the way, and steps back, allowing me in. I walk into her living room and she closes the door.

Taking a seat on her couch, she drapes a large cream blanket over her long, bare legs.

"Can I sit down next to you?" I ask, careful to ask her for permission. Jess still hasn't said anything to me; she just watches me with those cautious, swollen eyes.

"Yes," she finally says.

I move next to her and sit down, reaching out to push her long hair back off of her shoulder. She flinches when my fingers brush the top of her shoulder, and I pull my hand back immediately. The thought of my touch hurting her, or upsetting her, sends bile to my mouth.

"Um, Jess…" I say, pausing when she pulls her eyes from mine and looks at her hands, which are folded in her lap. "There are a million things I want to say to you and to tell you…" She still won't look at me. *Fuck.* "I love you. I have always loved you…"

"Stop. I need you to listen to me for a minute before you say anything else," Jess says, interrupting me mid-sentence.

Giant tears roll down her face. I reach out slowly, pausing for her permission to wipe them off of her cheeks, and she pulls back from me again. *What the fuck?*

"I need you to let me go," she says.

My stomach clenches and my heart is racing. I feel like I might vomit.

"Two days ago changed who I am and who I will be forever."

I can't even listen to this.

"Are you breaking up with me?" I ask angrily. I'm not angry; I'm hurt. Before I even let her answer, I continue, "You are not leaving me, Jessica. You do not get to throw us away because of what happened to you."

She raises both of her hands to cover her face. The tears are leaking out from underneath her hands, running down her arms, and her entire body is shaking.

"I love you. But please stop pushing me away. We will work through this together."

She shakes her head no, never letting her hands leave her face. She gasps for breaths in between her sobs. My body is shaking from my emotions, which are fluctuating between sadness and anger. Why is she pushing me away?

"Is that what you really want? You want me to let you go? Say it again. Mean it." Her face is still buried in her hands, and her entire body is trembling.

"Tell me right now that you really want me gone, *for good*, and I'll leave you alone. Is that what you want?" Dropping her hands from her face, they fall into her lap almost lifeless.

"Look at me," I whisper. She raises her head slowly, looking directly at me. "Do you really want me to leave you?" I take one of my hands and slowly reach it out to touch hers. She doesn't pull back from my reach this time. I tighten my hand around hers, squeezing it lightly, and she squeezes mine back gently.

"I need you to leave," she chokes out, pushing my hand away. My heart stops in this moment. I swear to God, the world stopped moving. I gather what little strength I have and, on wobbly legs, stand up.

"If that's what you want, Jess. I'll go."

She drops her head forward and wraps her arms tightly around her waist. Her body is limp as she quietly nods her head yes at me. I don't know how my legs carry me to the front door, but they do. Reaching for the handle, I pause, turning back to look at her. Opening the door slowly, I step onto the front porch.

I offer up the few words I have left in me. "I will love you forever. *Forever*. Don't you ever forget that." I summon the energy to slowly shut the door on everything I have ever loved and walk away to the sounds of her loud sobs inside the house behind me.

Chapter Twenty-One

~Jess~

I rest my head on the edge of the toilet seat and try to catch my breath in between my bouts of vomiting and crying. Wiping my nose on the sleeve of my shirt, I muster the strength to push myself into a sitting position. My lungs are burning, and my stomach won't stop clenching, causing me to dry heave. I just pushed the most important person in my life, the only man I've ever loved, out of my life, and I'm not even sure why. Another wave of nausea hits, and I'm hunched back over the toilet again, spewing nothing but stomach acid, as I haven't eaten much in two days. Closing my eyes, I rest my head back on the toilet seat. I know it'll be just a matter of time before I throw up again.

I wake up, realizing I must have fallen asleep on the bathroom floor. My face is pressed to the cold tile. Pushing myself up to a sitting position, I am overcome with dizziness and my head is pounding. I feel hung over, but I know it's from the hours, make that days, that I've spent crying and throwing up. Taking a minute to get my bearings, I stand up and walk myself over to the sink. Grabbing my toothbrush, I spread a sizeable amount of toothpaste across the soft bristles and brush my teeth and mouth.

Standing upright, I catch my reflection in the mirror. I don't even recognize myself. I am a shell of what I used to look like. My skin is pale and light compared to my normal olive skin tone. I'm still covered in bruises; some have started to heal, casting a greenish-yellow hue to them. My brown hair is stringy and dry, unlike its normal full, bouncy waves. My lips are light pink, cracked, and dry, instead of plump and bright pink. I don't even know who the fuck I'm looking at in the mirror. A single tear falls from my eye, and I watch it trail down my cheek, falling as it lands on the bathroom counter.

For two weeks, I've stayed holed up in my house. I've successfully avoided any contact with Gabe, Ava, and any of the Garcias, for that matter. I've ignored phone calls from the detectives working my case, and calls for follow-up doctor appointments. I've successfully shut the rest of the world out. Dad has spent almost every day working—his coping mechanism—and I have spent two weeks on the couch, watching bad reality shows—*my* coping mechanism— remaining numb to life outside of my own. I waver back and forth between blaming Gabe for going to work that night, to understanding that this isn't his fault. I want so badly to find a reason to hate him, so that my actions in pushing him away are justified, but my heart could never hate him.

Last week was spring break, and so far for this week, I have skipped all my classes. One week of missed classes won't set me too far behind, but I'm just not ready to face the outside world yet. I've been dodging calls and voicemails from my academic advisor. I know she is calling to discuss my internship, and that is the furthest thing from my mind. Janet's ears must have been burning, as my phone rings again, and her familiar number flashes across the screen.

"Hello?" I answer quietly.

"Jessica? This is Janet, Janet Collins from SRSU. I've left you a couple of voice messages. We need to talk about your internship. We have a problem." As if I can deal with one more problem in my life right now. I sit, silently crying, listening to dead air, not even sure I care about what she has to tell me. Finally, I sniffle, breaking the silence.

"Jessica, are you all right?"

"Actually, no, I'm not," I speak, barely audible.

"It's just an internship; we'll get you another one," she says. I didn't realize that my other one had fallen through, but I guess that's why she's calling me.

"Your local internship was cancelled due to mandatory cuts at the station. They couldn't take on supervising interns while they are reducing staff. They just don't have the resources," she says, sounding regretful.

"I understand," I respond, still sniffling.

"But I have an opportunity I want to talk to you about. I know you don't want to leave California, but it's a really, really good opportunity. I'd like to discuss it with you. Will you please be open to speaking with me about it?" Silence fills the phone line between us.

"Sure," I whisper.

"Good. Be at my office at three o'clock. We have to jump on this fast." She doesn't even say goodbye before hanging up the phone. When I check the time on my cell phone, I see that it's already one o'clock, and I need to shower and see if I can somehow make myself look presentable. Dragging myself off the couch, I decide it's now or never to face the real world.

Hesitantly, I knock on Janet's office door.

"Come on in."

My hand shakes as I turn the doorknob and push the door open.

"Hi," I offer sheepishly. Typing, ever so fast on her keyboard, she swivels her chair around with a huge smile on her face, until she sees mine. A quiet, yet audible gasp escapes her as her smile fades and concern washes over her face.

"Hi. Take a seat." Her voice is quiet and her posture has become more rigid. "Before I get into all the details about this internship, I have to ask you if you're okay? Your face…"

I interrupt her. "Is bruised, I know. Am I okay? I don't know. I'm all over the place. This is the first time I've left my house in damn near three weeks," I mumble.

"I have to ask you this, so please don't be offended. Did your boyfriend…" I scoff at her insinuation that Gabe would ever hurt me. He would never.

"No. He didn't, and he's not my boyfriend anymore. If you must know, all you have to do is read the newspaper or watch the news," I interrupt her as my voice breaks.

Her eyes grow with my admission, and she inhales sharply. "Washington Park?"

I nod as tears blur my eyes. I hear her chair roll over to me, and a small, soft hand rests on top of mine.

"I'm so sorry," she whispers, causing me to flinch.

"Don't be sorry; it's not your fault," I whisper. "Just please tell me about this internship. Tell me something so that I stop thinking about all of this." I wave my hand up and down my body from my face to my feet. Nodding, she pulls her hand away and rolls her chair back to her desk. Wiping my tears with the back of my hand, I listen intently as she describes what very well may be an escape from my miserable reality.

When I leave Janet's office, my head is spinning with everything she just dumped on me: internship, North Carolina, guaranteed, leave in three weeks, school credit. I think I left her head spinning with everything I dumped on her as well. Before I left Janet's office, she sat and cried with me, and listened to me, and reassured me. It was the first time in two weeks that I felt like talking to someone. Maybe I would come out of this on the other side not completely shattered. I have to decide in the next week if I'm going to take this internship in North Carolina, as they want me there on the first of May. I would be missing the last three weeks of school, but the internship counts as credit, and Janet has arranged for me to test out of the remainder of my classes should I decide to go. She claims it's an opportunity too good to pass up.

North Carolina. I've never been there. Janet tells me it's on the water and that it's beautiful. I would be leaving everything I have ever known here in California, but then it's not like I have anything here anymore. I've pushed Gabe, Ava, and everyone else away, and Dad has buried himself in work again. It's actually an easy decision. I need to take this internship. I need to do this for me.

This is the first time I've been out of my house since Dad drove me home from the hospital almost three weeks ago. It's bright and sunny and warm. I drive home with my windows down and feel the fresh air whip my hair around, slapping me in the face. Turning the corner onto our street, I try not to look at the Garcias' house as I drive by. Remembering the excitement I used to feel coming home, turning the corner and onto our street, anxiously looking to see if Gabe was home, I find myself caught in the same habit. I look. His truck is in the driveway for the first time in two weeks. I assume he's been staying over at Luke's apartment, as far away as possible from his house and me.

My heart beats a little faster, knowing that he is just across the street. However, for the last two weeks, I've ignored his calls and texts until he finally stopped sending them. After I pull my car into the driveway, I raise the windows and step out. The smell of the blooming flowers on the citrus trees catches me, and I throw my head back as I close my eyes and just breathe. I breathe in deeply the scent of those citrus blossoms and feel the warm sun on my face. For the first time in two weeks, a sense of peace falls over me, if only for a few short seconds.

Raising my head, I open my eyes, and push the button on my key fob, locking my car doors. Looking back to my car to ensure I'd shut the windows, I glance up to see Gabe standing in his driveway, staring at me. He doesn't smile or wave at me, or show any emotion toward me at all. He just stares at me, and I stand frozen, staring back at him; the sweetest man, the only man I've ever loved, stands in defeat.

Lowering my eyes down to my feet, I raise them slowly, to find him still standing there, staring directly at me. His stance is firm, but his shoulders are slack. I raise my right hand slightly to indicate a half-hearted wave. He doesn't move; he just stands and stares at me. Turning myself around, I walk slowly up the front porch and into my house, glancing back at the man that I love, who looks so broken. By the time I lock the door, set my purse down, and peek out the window, he and his truck are gone. I promise myself that before I leave, I will talk to him.

CHAPTER TWENTY-TWO

-Gabe-

For the past four weeks, I've sent Jess countless e-mails and text messages, and I have gotten nothing in return. I never leave my phone; it's attached to my hand. Every time there is a ping, or a chime, or a ring, my heart stops, hoping she'll have finally decided to respond to me, to provide me answers, a glimmer of hope, a "fuck-off," something—anything. It's the silence that is killing me.

I walked away from her four weeks ago because that's what she wanted; that's what she asked me to do. A piece of me died that day. I was never a sap or believed in true love and fate and all that bullshit, until I lost her. I know I'm only half alive—half functioning. I'd do anything she asked of me, anything, including walking away, if that is what she wanted—and it was.

For most of the last month, I've stayed with Luke because I can't bear to be across the street from her, knowing I can't walk over to check on her, kiss her, hold her, love her, and protect her. I lie in bed every night, and I'm assaulted with the memories of us. Everything good in my life was Jessica. She made me want to be a better man, a better boyfriend, a better person. She made me think of marriage and family, and goals, where most of my friends were thinking about the next chick they were going to bang.

The last time I saw her was two weeks ago. I stopped by Mom and Dad's to pick up a few things to bring to Luke's apartment. When I tossed my bag in my truck, I didn't expect to see her car pulling into her driveway. It froze me. Literally. Everything in me stopped as I watched her step out of her car and lean her head back, tilting her face up to the sky. I could see her eyes were closed, and I wondered in that moment what she was thinking, what she was feeling. I stood there watching her, and for a moment, she looked peaceful, young, and innocent; not hurt, scared, and broken.

She was pale, much lighter than I've ever seen her and she looked like she had lost a lot of weight. Her normal beautiful, curvy frame was devoid of any shape; stiff, thin, and bony. Regardless, she was still the most beautiful woman I've ever laid eyes on. I didn't expect her to turn and look at me, to catch me staring at her. With a small flick of her wrist, she gave me a forced wave and a stiff, half-hearted smile. I swallowed the lump that was forming in my throat when I realized that we'd come to a place where she wouldn't talk to me, and smiles and waves were forced.

Clenching my fists, anger and hurt coursed through my veins, yet at the same time, I couldn't help but stand and watch her. Just to see her, to know that she was okay, was a relief. I watched her slowly move up the steps of her patio and into her house; watched her shut the front door. I left when I knew she was safely inside. Jumping into my truck, I drove to Luke's apartment, my sanctuary as of late.

I've spent the last few weeks working as much as I can. Picking up extra overtime shifts, and covering for guys who want an extra day off. Work has been my escape. Ironic, that is exactly what Chief is doing. I have to force myself to not ask him about Jess. I keep work strictly professional and only speak to him about work related matters. Chief spends as much time here as I do, and it pains me to know that she is alone at home dealing with her pain. I want nothing more than to call her, to hear her voice, but she has made it clear she doesn't want to hear from me. So two weeks ago, I stopped reaching out to her.

I'm off this weekend, and I plan to move the rest of my stuff from Mom and Dad's over to Luke's apartment. Luke convinced me that it might do me good to move in with him, to distance myself from Jess, and I reluctantly agreed. Pulling into the visitor space at Luke's apartment complex, I throw my truck in park and just sit, contemplating this next step in my life—moving in with my brother. I was saving to buy Jess a ring and a house, and here I sit in the parking lot of my brother's apartment. I feel my anger rise as I think about how in a matter of minutes, one run in the park, has changed the course of my plans—of *our* plans, forever.

Minutes have passed when I hear a tap on my window. It catches me off guard. I turn to see Luke. Wondering how long he's been there, I grab my bag off of the passenger seat and open my door, sliding down onto the pavement.

Luke must see the despair in my eyes. "You okay, man?" he asks quietly with a pat on my shoulder. I nod and offer the best lie that I can.

"Yep," Luke sighs. I know he wants to say something, but he refrains. I'm on edge, and he can tell.

"Hey, Ava invited a few people over to Mom and Dad's tonight, like old times," he says. Everyone is trying to move forward, as we've all been stuck in a holding pattern for the last month. "It would be good for you to…you know… take your mind off things for a while."

"Yeah, I'll stop by," I say, knowing damn well I'm not in the mood to socialize. Everyone has been worried about me. Ava sends me endless text messages, Mom calls me at least three times a day, and Luke is always just watching me. The guys from the station, and even the couple of girls that work there, have been more than tolerant of my mood swings. They've been great in giving me space to deal with everything that has happened.

"I invited Heather. She's off tonight," Luke says shyly. He's had a crush on Heather for months now.

"Good," I say, realizing I have a small smile on my face. I think this is the first time I've smiled in weeks. "Play it cool, my man…play it cool." I smirk. Where I was graced with social skills, Luke was inherently quieter. Luke laughs a big laugh.

"That's the plan, G. Hey, I'm heading to the gym. Be showered and ready to go, and I'll swing by to pick you up around seven."

"Sounds good. See you in a bit."

I shower and move things around my new room, making space for the last few belongings I plan to bring over this weekend. My phone pings, and as usual, I jump to grab it, hoping the message is from Jess, but it's a text from Ava.

Gabe, please promise me you'll come over tonight.

I'll be there, sis.

Good. I love you.

Love you too.

Luke picks me up promptly at seven o'clock as he said he would.

"Ready?" he asks.

"Yeah."

"You okay?"

Nodding my head, I say, "Yeah, it's just the first time since everything happened that we've had one of these, so I don't know what to expect, or think."

"It'll be fine. Just try to enjoy yourself," he reassures me.

Ava texted us and said there were a few more people coming than we're normally used to, which also has me a bit anxious. As we park in Mom and Dad's driveway, I catch a glimpse of light peeking out of Jess' bedroom window. The entire house is dark, except for her bedroom. I know Chief is at the station, and all I want to do is walk over there and force her to talk to me. Luke sits quietly with me while I stare at her window.

"Let's go have a beer, man," he says quietly.

Grabbing the cases of beer Luke brought, we walk through the side door that opens into the kitchen. Mom is at her usual perch, whipping up food while Dad is asleep in his recliner. Through the glass patio door, I can see that there are quite a few people in the backyard, and I'm wondering who Ava invited.

"Hi, Ma," I say, walking over and placing a kiss on her cheek. She's made her homemade guacamole and is arranging chips and salsa onto a large platter.

"Ah, *Mijo*, I'm so glad you came." She flashes me the warmest smile. I've been so caught up in my own misery that I've distanced myself from the people who care about me and love me, and a wave of guilt runs through me. Her eyes shine with concern as she leans into me and pulls me into a hug.

"Carry this platter out back for me, will you please?" she asks, breaking our hug.

"Ma, we don't come over here for you to cook for us, you know."

"I know, *Mijo*, I love doing it, though. I love when all my kids are here." Her voice cracks slightly, and I know she's missing Jess as much as Ava and I are.

Carrying the tray of chips, salsa, and guacamole outside, I set it on the large patio table where an assortment of other snacks has been placed. Standing back, I survey who is here, wishing that Jess were floating around the crowd, talking to everyone like she used to do. I loved watching her move from group to group, talking to everyone and making everyone feel welcome. Shaking that thought, I locate the cooler and grab myself a bottle of Dos Equis.

"What's up, man?" Adrian, Ava's boyfriend, fist bumps me.

"Not much. Finally off for the weekend," I say, grabbing the bottle opener. Popping the top, I tilt the bottle to my lips and let the cold, crisp beer slide down my throat. In two swallows, I finish half the bottle.

"Good to see you," he says, passing by me and heading into the house. Looking around at the people in my backyard, I see Ava talking with a small group of girls; they are all leaned into their small circling, whispering and giggling. I see Luke chatting with Heather, the EMT from work, and I smile. Grabbing another beer, I open it and make my way over to see how he is handling his crush on Heather before Max stops me.

"Hey, Gabe."

"What's up?" I'm really not in the mood to deal with these punks, but I know Max was close to Jess, and maybe he's heard from her.

"Not much. Just wanted to say 'hi,' and was wondering if you've heard from Jess. She won't return my calls or texts."

"Same here," I snap at him, taking a sip on the new beer in my hand.

"Yeah, okay. I'm sorry. I didn't mean to upset you. I'm just, um, worried."

"Look, if anyone hears anything, I'll have Ava call you, all right?"

I feel guilty for snapping at him. It's clear that everyone cares about her and she isn't talking to anyone. With a nod, he turns to walk away.

"Hey, Max," I call after him.

"Yeah." He stops and turns around, but makes no attempt to walk back toward me.

"If you happen to hear from her first, will you please let me know?"

With a tight smile, he nods again. "You know I will," he says before turning to walk back to the small group gathered by the fire pit.

CHAPTER TWENTY-THREE

~Jess~

It's hard to believe that two short weeks ago I agreed to move myself across the country for an internship, leaving behind the few things in my life that I have ever loved. It didn't take much thought for me, honestly. Gabe deserves better than me, at least better than the "damaged me." He deserves someone who isn't so damaged, someone that is whole and can love him without the insecurities I have, that I will probably always have.

I know that I will never love anyone the way I love him, ever. Maybe I'm making irrational and impulsive life decisions right now by pushing Gabe away, and moving from the only family I have ever known, but this is what I have to do, for him and for me.

I'm planning to leave early in the morning. Hopefully, I can slip out of town unnoticed. Not that anyone would notice I'm gone anyway, aside from the Garcias, who I haven't seen in over a month.

Stretching a piece of packing tape over the last box, I seal it up and push it away with my feet. I lean back against my bed, pulling my knees to my chest, and take in the sight of my bedroom. I've spent more time in this room the last three weeks than I have in all of the last fourteen years. The light pink walls are faded and in need of new paint. The hardwood floor could stand a good cleaning and polish. As of late, this room has been my haven, and a small part of me is sad to leave the comfort of its confines.

Grabbing the small blue and white plaid keepsake box, I pop the lid off. I know I'm torturing myself, but maybe it will be cathartic; a sort of symbolism to my fresh start. Rummaging through the contents, I can't help but smile and tear up at the memories one small box can hold. Ticket stubs to the Train concert Gabe and I went to a couple of months ago, pictures from Santa Barbara, notes he had hidden in my backpack, and the ring he had given me for Christmas; a promise to our future. I shoved the ring in the box the day I asked him to let me go.

Tears fall down my cheeks as I shuffle through all the pieces of my life that mean so much to me and shove them back into the box, except for the ring. Standing up, I unclasp the white gold delicate chain that hangs around my neck with a small diamond cross and slide the ring onto it. Reaching around my neck, I clasp the necklace and tuck the cross and ring under my t-shirt. I slide my hand to my chest, and feel the cross and ring beneath the palm of my hand. Pressing it against my heart, I know that is where Gabe will be forever.

I know I can't leave without saying goodbye to Angelica and John. It's been killing me all week, knowing I was going to have to talk to them. I haven't seen them since before I went for that run. Glancing at the alarm clock on my nightstand, I see that it's almost eight o'clock. Mustering up the courage, I grab my jacket and throw it on over my t-shirt and slide my feet into a pair of Toms. I look at myself in the full-length mirror that hangs on my bedroom wall and take note of what I look like—I'm a mess. I'm just going to go say goodbye, and I'm making it fast, so this will have to do.

Locking the door behind me, I step down the stairs from my porch, stopping suddenly when I see the street lined with cars. They haven't had a get-together in months. My chest tightens as my eyes scan the cars and I see Ava's, Adrian's, and Luke's, along with a few others I don't recognize. As much as I want to see Gabe, I don't think I have the strength, and my anxiety lessens slightly when I don't see his truck parked in the driveway, or on the street.

Shuffling across the street, I tuck my hands into the pockets of my jacket. I'm so nervous and scared, and for the first time since I decided to leave, a wave of nausea overcomes me. Standing at the front door, I raise my hand and knock lightly. I think to myself that if I knock lightly enough, maybe they won't hear me. I can then leave, knowing that I tried, but was unsuccessful in seeing them. I owe them more than a half-hearted attempt though, so I knock again, this time a bit harder. It seems so weird to knock on the door of a home that was basically mine for over fourteen years. Where I could walk in anytime unannounced. It was my home.

The door cracks open slightly and there stands John with a look of disbelief on his face. A small smile washes over his face as the door opens wider, and he pulls me into the house and into his arms, squeezing me tightly. Pulling my hands out from my pockets, I wrap my arms around him in return. This is the first real touch I've encountered in weeks. Tears fill my eyes and a lump forms in my throat.

"*Mija*, we've missed you," he says, tightening his squeeze. It's a comforting embrace, and hearing John call me "*Mija*" warms my heart. They have always considered me their daughter and have never treated me as anything less.

"I've missed you too," I choke out as a tear slips from the corner of my eye. Pulling out of John's strong arms, I wipe my cheeks with my fingers and take a deep breath to calm myself.

"Sit down, please." John motions to the couch.

"I can't," I say, dropping my eyes to the floor. "I just came to say goodbye." That lump is back, stuck in the back of my throat, stopping me from saying anything further.

"Goodbye?" he questions me.

I nod my head in short, fast movements. "I'm leaving tomorrow morning. I've taken an internship on the East Coast," I say, my hands fidgeting. I've always looked to him for guidance and support, and here I am, just telling him what I'm doing.

He stands, looking at me as he nods his heads slowly, running a hand over his face. Looking up, I notice Angelica standing in the entryway between the living room and kitchen. She's wiping her hands on a dishtowel.

"Why so far away?" she questions me as she walks towards me, closing the distance between us.

Shrugging my shoulders, I can feel my chin quiver as I force the words, "I just have to." Not able to say anything else, the tears overtake me again and Angelica is now pulling me into a hug.

"*Mija*, please," she begs, hugging me and rubbing my back. "We are here for you. *All* of us." I know that she is implying Gabe as well when she says "all of us."

"I know," I whisper back.

"Then stay. Let us help you," she pleads with a whisper in my ear.

"I can't. I have to do this," I say, trying to pull out of her arms. She won't let go, and her hands are now holding my upper arms. Running her eyes over me from head to toe, she studies every inch of me as if it's the last time she'll see me, and it very well may be.

"When is the last time you ate? You look too skinny," she says, releasing my arms. She offers me a kind smile and a gentle kiss to my cheek before she turns and heads into the kitchen.

"I really should go," I whisper to John. Standing there, with his arms at his side, he nods his head and looks back towards the kitchen.

"There are a few folks out back who would be really disappointed if they didn't get to say 'goodbye' to you." I swallow hard, knowing who he means. "They've been worried sick about you. You stopped taking their calls and returning their text messages. I hope you will at least go say 'goodbye' to them."

I know I owe them this. At the very minimum, I owe my best friend, my sister, a goodbye. I nod my head in agreement and move slowly towards the kitchen to the patio door. Just as I'm almost out of the living room, John's words stop me. "You know you can always come home to us. We will always be here for you."

Looking over my shoulder at the man who was more of a dad to me than my own, I offer him a small smile. "Thank you," I say as I walk into the kitchen. There stands Angelica at the kitchen sink, her hands resting on the counter as she stares through the window into the dark backyard. I'm met with the most mouthwatering aromas as I stand there and watch her. Everything I ate growing up with the Garcias was spread across the counters: enchiladas, tacos, rice, beans. My stomach immediately growls in hunger, but stops quickly when I see the patio door and realize I have to walk out back and say goodbye to Ava.

I reach for the patio door handle, but stop again to look at Angelica. I can't help but smile at the woman who raised me, taught me how to cook, comforted me while I was sick, went to my school conferences, and is the closest person I'll ever have to a mom. For almost fifteen years, she has cared for me like I was her own. Looking at her, I am comforted by her presence, and for the first time, I'm feeling sad to leave the Garcias behind.

Turning back to the door, I grasp the handle and slide it open. Stepping onto the stained concrete patio, I can hear the sounds of laughter and conversation from the small groups of friends gathered around the fire pit. I scan the backyard, looking for Ava, and find her snuggled under Adrian's arm.

As I take in the group of people gathered around the fire pit, my heart thuds rapidly with nervousness but nearly stops altogether when I see him. Gabe has his arms wrapped around a tall, blonde woman, embracing her in a hug. She looks to be around his age and is pencil thin. Her arm is thrown around his neck with her head tipped back, and she's clearly laughing at something he said to her.

My heart sinks as I watch him pull out of his embrace with the mystery woman, and I see the wide smile that covers his tan face. I can't do this. I can't see him with someone else. I'm not strong enough for this. *But this is what I want him to do. This is why I asked him to let me go, so he can be happy.* My hands are sweating and my eyes fill with tears. An angry heat takes over my body as I feel my chest tighten and struggle to breathe. Turning quickly, I make a run for the patio door just as a firm hand catches my elbow, stopping me before I can move any further. At the very same time that hand connects with my elbow, I hear my name.

"Jess?"

Snapping my head in the direction of the body holding me hostage, I see Luke gripping my elbow. He is clearly shocked to see me standing here in his backyard. I try to pull out of his grip, but he tightens his hand around my elbow to keep me from running away. When the sound of my name comes from Luke's deep yet surprised voice, the backyard goes silent.

Looking back over my shoulder, I can see everyone has fixed their attention on me. Ava, Adrian, Max, Gabe, and even his leggy girl, who I now recognize as Heather, the EMT from the fire station where Dad, Gabe, and Luke all work. *How fucking convenient.* As my eyes continue to shift from person to person, Luke breaks the silence.

"How are you?"

Glaring at Gabe, who is still standing ridiculously close to Heather, I flash him the meanest look I can. I want him to know I'm pissed, even though I don't have any right to be. I cut him loose. This is what I wanted.

"I'm...just leaving," I say, my voice cracking. "I just came to say goodbye." My eyes drop to the concrete patio as giant tears spill down my face.

"Goodbye? Where are you going?" Ava's voice is frantic as she moves quickly from Adrian's embrace over to my side. Luke still hasn't let go of my arm, holding me firmly in place. She is now standing directly in front of me, blocking my exit to the patio door.

"I leave tomorrow," I tell her, meeting her glossy eyes. "I'm moving out East for an internship." I barely manage to say the words through the lump in my throat.

"Where?" she asks quietly.

"Please." I beg her with my eyes to stop asking me questions I'm not ready to answer. "Just, out East."

"Why? Please, stay here. I'll transfer back. We can get through this—together." Her voice breaks, and I watch the giant tears spill from my best friend's eyes. Wiping them with her sleeve, she continues, "We'll get an apartment together. Just, please don't go."

"I can't," I whisper as I watch more tears fall from her eyes. "I have to go." I jerk my arm back, pulling away from his vise-like grip. I mouth the word "bye" to Ava, who is standing with her hands over her mouth, choking back sobs. Because I'm a glutton for punishment, or maybe because I never stopped loving him, I turn to take one last blurry look at Gabe. Even through my tears, I can see him clearly. His mouth has tightened into a straight line, and he's stepped forward away from Heather. One of his hands is flexed into a fist and the other is holding a beer bottle that looks as if he could crush it if he squeezed it any harder. I can see the veins in his arms as he's flexing his hand around the beer bottle.

As I turn back toward Luke and Ava, I see the side gate is open and know that this is my fastest escape out of this backyard. Taking a deep breath, I gather myself and walk quickly toward the gate, willing myself not to turn around again.

Just breathe. Just breathe. I keep repeating this to myself over and over in my head. *Just breathe. Just breathe.* I've made it out of the backyard and onto the driveway safely hidden by the fence. I stop and bend over. My stomach is twisting, I feel like I'm going to vomit right here on the driveway. Since I haven't eaten in three days, it appears I'll just dry heave here instead.

Just breathe for fuck sake. I feel like I got the wind knocked out of me. I try to catch my breath as my stomach coils.

As I stand up, there is a violent crash and glass breaking, along with raised voices, and seconds later, more glass breaking. Walking as fast as my legs will take me, I cross the street. Stepping onto my front patio, I turn around to look one last time across the street to the house where every good memory of my childhood resides.

Opening my front door, I step in and shut the world out again. Collapsing onto my couch, I curl myself into a ball and cry. I have no reason to be mad at Gabe. I pushed him away. I broke up with him. But it killed me to see him hugging Heather, and it hurt me to know he could move on so quickly. The vision of him hugging her is burned into my memory as I try to fall asleep.

For hours, I lie on my couch, whispering words to Gabe that he'll never hear. How much I love him, how much he deserves to be happy, and how proud I am of him. Words he'll never hear because I'm too weak to talk to him, and I pushed him into the arms of another woman. Sleep finally finds me as I feel the last tear roll down my face.

CHAPTER TWENTY-FOUR

-Gabe-

"What did she say?"

My heart is going to beat out of my fucking chest. I can literally feel it bouncing off the walls of my ribs. I saw the look of pain, of utter disgust, on her face when she saw me hugging Heather. *Fuck.* I couldn't hear what she was saying to Luke or to Ava, but she was crying. I tried to move closer, to hear her voice, but before I even had time to think, she was gone.

"God dammit, what the fuck did she say?" I yell this time.

"She's leaving," Ava chokes in between sobs, tears still falling down her face.

"What do you mean she's leaving? Where is she going?"

"Out East. That's all she said, out East," Ava cries, her eyes glistening with tears.

In this moment, every ounce of self-control I've ever had vanishes. I take my beer bottle and, as hard I can, toss it at the side of the brick garage. I've never seen glass explode and shatter like that green beer bottle did. People near me duck, and back away. I'm like an out of control animal. My heart is beating violently, and rage courses through me.

I grab another beer bottle that's sitting on the table and throw it against the garage, shattering that bottle as well. Just as I'm looking for a third one, Luke grabs my arm and pulls me away from the table. Everyone is yelling at me to calm down. *Calm down?* The only person I have ever truly loved is moving out East, wherever the fuck that is, and I'm supposed to just calm down?

Luke now has me in a bear hug so that I can't destroy anything else, and Ava is holding onto my arm. "Please, stop," she cries.

I'm breathing so fast and so shallow that I feel like I could pass out. My head is dizzy, mostly from rage, and I'm sure the beer hasn't helped. Feeling my chest rising and falling with every sharp breath I take, Luke continues to hold me in this position for a couple of minutes while my mind has time to absorb everything that just happened. As my breathing settles, Luke lessens his grip on me until he lets me go altogether.

"Sorry everyone," I say, pulling away from the small group that is now watching me as I walk straight to the patio door. Sliding it open, I move quickly through the house and up to my room, the room I don't stay in anymore. Shutting my door, I lock it and sit down at the only thing left in this room, my wooden desk. Leaning forward, I drop my head into my hands and fight to control my emotions. I can't believe she's leaving. She's really leaving. A million thoughts are racing through my head. I know she won't talk to me, or listen to me, but I have so much to say and so much to tell her before she leaves.

My laptop is at Luke's apartment, but I won't let her leave without telling her exactly how I feel. Opening the desk drawer, I pull out some paper and a pen. Pushing the stacks of notebooks aside, I start writing. She may be leaving, but she will never be able to run from my heart.

Chapter Twenty-Five

~Jess~

"Jess, I know you think this is a good idea, and I promised you that I wouldn't tell anyone where you're going, but are you *really* sure this is what you want to do?" Dad asks quietly. I stare at him and all I see in his eyes is regret. I don't want to regret my life.

"Dad, I have to do this. I have to move forward, and I can't do that here. There is too much pain here. I'm suffocating," I say, my voice void of any emotion.

Dad nods his head slowly in agreement. "You going to go say goodbye?" he asks, shifting his head back in the direction of the Garcia house across the street. My eyes sting with the tears forming in my eyes, and the large lump in my throat will barely allow me to talk.

"I did last night." I think about Gabe in Heather's arms, the yelling, and the breaking bottles. "It didn't go so well."

With a deep sigh, Dad walks toward me and pulls me into a tight hug. I can't remember the last time he touched me, let alone hugged me. Dad doesn't show his emotions; he's the master of disguise when it comes to displaying any emotion. I snuggle my head into the crook of his neck and let the man, the father I barely know, hold me and comfort me for the first time in fourteen years. He didn't hug me after I was raped. He didn't hold me when I was young and sick with a fever, but today, I let him hug me, and I try to bury the anger I have toward him and simply find comfort in his arms.

The hug is warm and caring and loving, and exactly what I need from him. This is confirmation that after everything I've been through in the last eight weeks, that he does love me and supports me and my decision. Dad pulls out of our embrace first, grabbing both of my cheeks like I'm a little girl again. Raising my head so that I'm looking at him in the eyes, he says, "I'm so proud of you. You are the strongest person I know. I mean that. I'm so blessed that you are my daughter. Your mom would be so…" He pauses while collecting his thoughts. "…so proud of you. You remind me so much of her, Jess. Your mannerisms, your laugh, even the way you walk. You are exactly like her." His voice breaks.

This is progress for him. In fourteen years, he has never talked to me about her. When I was young, I would ask him questions, and he always found a way to distract me and not talk about her. Wrapping his arm around my shoulder, he guides me to my car, giving firm instructions to call every three hours from the road and every time I stop for gas. Giving him one last hug, I slide into the driver's seat and buckle my seatbelt.

Backing out of the driveway, I will myself not to look in the rearview mirror at the house across the street, the house that holds my heart. But I do. Out of my side mirror, I see him sitting on his front step. His head is hanging, and his arms are resting on his knees. With a deep breath, I put the car in drive, wave to my dad, and head east, hoping for the strength and sanity to start over while a small piece of my heart dies as I see Gabe grow smaller in my rearview mirror.

Exhaustion does not even begin to explain what I'm feeling. I just spent three days driving from coast to coast, literally— Pacific Ocean to Atlantic Ocean. Arriving in Wilmington, North Carolina, I head straight to the TV station where I will be interning. I am meeting my new boss, Kevin, for the first time. He is renting his small, mostly furnished condo to me. Kevin is also the General Manager of the TV station where I will be spending most of my time, working and building my resume.

The TV station is a small local affiliate. This means I'll be working long days for no pay, but walking away with a shit-ton of experience. I won't be just serving coffee and answering phones. I'm actually welcoming the long hours as a form of distraction, a mental health break from the chaos that is consuming my head.

Pulling into the parking lot of WXZI, I pull into the first open spot marked "visitor." Shifting my SUV into park, I roll up the window and flip my visor down. Taking a long look at myself in the mirror, I assess the damage. Fortunately, I travel well. I don't look awful, just tired.

I grab my purse and pull out my lip-gloss, smoothing it over my lips. I tussle my hair to give it a little body and decide that this is as good as it's going to get for a Tuesday afternoon.

I open my car door and slide out. My legs are stiff from the last six hours of driving, so I stop to stretch a bit. As I make my way towards the large glass doors of the station, I find the main doors are locked. Noticing a small callbox on the brick to the right of the entrance, I push the button, and a man answers, "WXZI, how can I help you?"

I take a quick breath and announce, "This is Jessica Harper. I'm here to see Kevin Lincoln. He's expecting me."

There is a moment of silence, and I'm wondering if I've been disconnected from the man in the box, when I hear, "I'll buzz you right in, Ms. Harper." Just then, I hear the doors click and buzzing coming from the callbox.

Pulling the doors open into a small lobby, I step inside, noticing a main desk, but no one is behind it. Standing there for a minute, I take in my surroundings. There are plush, leather chairs in the lobby, along with small side tables and lots of green plants. It's a modern lobby for such a small station, and I'm impressed with what I've seen so far. Just then, a wooden door to the left of the lobby opens, and a man in his late forties or early fifties enters the lobby quickly. I smile and offer my hand as he does at the same time.

"I'm Jessica Harper," I say with a big smile.

"I'm Kevin Lincoln."

"Nice to meet you," I say with a firm handshake.

"Likewise, Jessica. I've got about ten minutes before I need to be back in the studio, but let me get you the keys to the condo and show you your desk."

I'm thankful that I'm getting a short tour of the station. Kevin has agreed to let me start next Monday to give me a few days to get settled at the condo and get acclimated to my new city.

"Here is where you'll be sitting." Kevin points to an empty gray desk. There is nothing except a black multi-line phone and notepad on the desk. "We'll get you all set up on

Monday. I have a computer coming, and we'll get you some supplies."

Glancing around the small newsroom, I notice there are several empty desks, but most are full of computers and notepads and personal pictures. For the first time in months, my stomach does a little flip, and I feel butterflies of excitement. As we walk through the newsroom to the large corner office, which is Kevin's, I stop in the doorway. Kevin walks to his desk and grabs an envelope. As he's walking back to me, he's talking at the same time. "I'll introduce you to everyone on Monday morning. Be here at eight thirty sharp."

As Kevin hands me the envelope, he starts going over the contents. "The keys to the condo are in there, along with the address. It's right on the beach. You'll love it. Call me if you have any questions once you get there. Oh, and your badge for the office is in there. Don't lose it. It will get you in the front doors at all hours. Most of the time, we don't have a receptionist. Oh, and Janet asked me to give you a phone number. It's on the yellow sticky note inside the envelope."

Kevin looks down at his desk as he's saying that. Janet is my academic advisor and Kevin's sister. She is also the person who pulled off this internship in record time. I nod my head at Kevin and give him a tight-lipped smile.

"Kevin, thank you for giving me a chance. I know that I'm a liability and have no experience, so I appreciate your kindness." Kevin nods politely at me, and I turn to make my way out of his office.

"See you Monday," I say, flashing him a smile, hoping he'll believe how grateful I truly am.

"See you Monday," he replies with a small sigh.

CHAPTER TWENTY-SIX

-Gabe-

After finishing my letter, I seal the envelope and walk across the street to Jess' house. I see Chief's truck is gone, so I can only assume he is at the station. As I stand on the front porch, my mind races while I talk myself in and out of giving her this letter. My heart gets the better of me, and I reach into the hanging flowerpot and find the spare key.

Inserting the key into the front door, I turn the doorknob and push the door open quietly. There are no lights on in the house. Closing the door behind me, I use the backlight from my phone to search out Jess' purse.

Seeing her purse on the counter, I cross the living room floor to the granite island that separates the kitchen from the living room. I open her bag and push the letter to the bottom. I set her wallet, keys, and sunglasses on top of the letter and close her bag. Standing there, my eyes have adjusted to the darkness, and I glance around the empty living room and down the hall that leads to her room.

Before I even have time to think, my feet are quietly shuffling down the hallway. Her bedroom door is cracked open. Pushing the door open slightly, I stick my head in. The blinds are open and, the moon lights up her room. My beautiful girl lies on top of her comforter, curled so tightly in the fetal position that her forehead is almost resting on her knees, and her arms are wrapped around her legs. I can hear her small, shallow breaths, telling me she is asleep.

Crossing her bedroom floor, I see a few small boxes resting at the foot of her bed. Most of her room has been packed up with only a few pictures remaining on a bulletin board above her desk. I gently pull the blanket from the bottom of her bed and place it over her curled up body. Watching her sleep was one of my favorite things to do; the look of contentment on her face, the way her lips twitch when she dreams. I'd lie with her wrapped in my arms, and watch her sleep for hours. Those memories now nearly kill me as I lie in my cold bed alone every night. Leaning down, I brush her soft brown hair gently on the pillow and softly plant one last kiss on top of her head as I whisper, "I love you," one last time.

Closing the door behind me, I lock it and place the hidden key back in the planter. The back of my eyes sting with the tears that I've been fighting back as I walk away from her house for the last time. Ava is sitting on our front steps, waiting for me, all bundled up with a blanket wrapped around her.

"What are you doing up?" I ask her quietly, knowing that it's well past two o'clock in the morning.

"I came to your room to talk to you and to see how you were, but you were gone. I knew you could have only gone one place, so I waited for you," she answers quietly.

Exhaling a deep breath, I stand with my hands tucked into my pockets. I have been so wrapped up in my own emotions that I forgot that Ava is losing her best friend when Jess leaves tomorrow.

"How are you holding up?" I ask as Ava shrugs underneath the blanket she's wrapped in.

"I just wish she would talk to me, that's all. I just want to understand why she's leaving and where she's going," she says.

"Me too, Ava. Me too."

"What were you doing over there?"

"I stuck a letter in her purse."

"You broke into her house to put a letter in her purse?"

"I didn't break in, Ava. I wanted to put it in her car, but she locked the door. So I used the spare key and let myself in so I could put it in her purse."

"That's breaking in."

I can't help but laugh a little at my sister.

"Sit down." She pats the concrete steps of our front patio. She offers me part of her blanket, but I shake my head no.

Ava and I sit for hours, watching the house across the street for any signs of movement. The morning sun is just about to rise when Ava stands up and hands me her blanket.

"I need to go inside," she whispers.

"Why?"

"I can't watch her leave." Her eyes are full of unshed tears. I nod my head as she quietly opens the front door and leaves me alone on the steps. I continue to sit and watch for another half hour or so when Chief's truck pulls into the driveway. As he's getting out of his truck, the front door opens, and Jess steps outside. She walks to the end of the driveway, her purse slung over her shoulder and her car keys in her hand.

I feel bad watching them talk, even though I don't know what's being said. I'm just glad I finally see Chief hug Jess. I can't remember him ever hugging her—hell, I don't remember him ever touching her. He walks Jess to her car and opens the door for her. My heart falls to my stomach when I see her slide into the driver's seat.

"Don't go," I whisper. "Love me enough to stay."

I see a few more words exchanged between Jess and Chief, and then her car backs slowly out of the driveway. Chief stands watching Jess; his shoulders slumped forward with a small, straight smile on his face. I can't watch as she drives away. My head falls, and my chest constricts. Tears are threatening to spill out of my eyes as I focus on the cement stairs on which I'm sitting, while the SUV that has my heart is driving away.

I heard her car pull away about fifteen minutes ago, yet here I sit. Hoping that this is a dream, and that when I wake up, her SUV will be sitting in her driveway where she's parked it every day since Chief bought it for her. Standing up, I glance across the street to her house one last time before opening the front door to my house. Ava is sitting on the couch, staring out the front window with Mom and Dad on each side of her. Everyone's eyes shift to me as I enter. I swallow hard, and force out the only two words that I know I can speak in this moment. "She's gone."

CHAPTER TWENTY-SEVEN

~Jess~

The sun seeps through the sheer white curtains that hang over the floor to ceiling windows in the condo I'm renting. The entire wall of the master bedroom is one giant window with a sliding glass door in the middle that opens to let in the fresh air off the Atlantic Ocean. Stepping out of bed, I walk over to the floor-length curtains and pull them all the way open. The sun is bright and high in the sky and is reflecting off of the small waves of the ocean.

Opening the sliding glass door, I step out onto the patio and take a seat in a tall, wrought iron chair that is part of a bistro set on the small patio. Closing my eyes, I breathe deeply for what seems like the first time in weeks. I feel the air surge deep into my lungs, and I can almost taste the salt in the heavy, humid air. I love the smell of the water and the sand. My mind wanders to all of the errands I need to get done today. My short-lived reprieve on the patio is over when I realize that the better part of my day will be spent getting shit done.

Closing the patio door behind me, I look around the mess that is my new room. Aside from all the boxes and my large suitcase, the room is modern and decorated gorgeously. There is a large king-size bed that is centered on the main wall. The walls are painted light cream, and the deep, rich purple bedding is made of raw silk. The dark hardwood floors are covered by a cream throw rug that the bed sits on. I tackle making the bed first. I'm a creature of routine. Making my bed was always the first thing I did at home, and it will be the first thing I do here too.

Tucking the sheets, and pulling the comforter up the large bed, I think about Gabe and how much he'd love this room. This room reminds me of the weekend we spent in Santa Barbara and how we loved to stand on the patio and watch the ocean. Thoughts of him are never far from me. I miss his smile, his hugs, and his touch. I miss the comfort that was *us*. His gorgeous face is burned into my memory.

I know I need to let my thoughts of him go, but my first night in a new city, in a new home, I needed a piece of him with me. I wore his navy blue Santa Ruiz Fire Department issued t-shirt. I always wore one of his t-shirts to bed, and I somehow inherited this particular one. It was a piece of home, a piece of my heart, and I needed to wear it last night.

Walking down the stairs, I deposit myself into the modern living room. Kevin has set me up well in this gorgeous condo. I circle the breakfast bar that separates the kitchen from the family room and find my way to the coffee pot that is seated on the counter next to the refrigerator. Rummaging through the pantry, I find the coffee filters and a package of Dunkin' Donuts ground coffee, and I remind myself to thank Kevin for supplying with me the essentials.

Preparing the automatic coffee maker, I turn it on and run up the stairs to quickly shower. Pulling the t-shirt over my head, I set it on the granite bathroom countertops. I step into the gorgeous tiled master shower and let the hot water pelt my skin. I finish quickly and wrap myself in an oversized bath towel, hand drying my hair with another towel.

My clothes are still in my suitcase, except for the dirty ones discarded in a pile on the bathroom counter, so I stay wrapped in my towel and traipse back downstairs. The coffee is done brewing, and I grab an oversized mug, *just my style*, and fill it up. I check the refrigerator for creamer, and find none. *Dammit*. Black it is today.

Sitting down at the breakfast bar, with my giant mug of coffee, I look around the lonely condo. Or maybe it's me that's lonely. But isn't that what I wanted? To run? To escape? To start over? To be alone?

Knock, knock, knock...

Jumping from the barstool, I realize I am still wrapped in a towel. *Shit!*

"Um, give me just a minute," I shout at the door, taking the stairs two at a time. I realize as I'm at the top of the stairs that there is a glass panel in the center of the door, and whoever is outside probably saw me running up the stairs. Tossing the towel to the floor, I run into the bathroom and grab Gabe's t-shirt off of the counter, tossing it back on, I grab my dirty khaki shorts off the floor and pull them on too, buttoning them as I'm running back down the stairs.

Opening the condo door, there are two police officers standing there.

"Can I help you?" I say as I try to remain calm, but wonder why the hell there are two policemen at my door.

"Miss..." the tall, sandy brown haired officer drawls. "Ms. Garcia?" he says questioningly, looking at my shirt with the name across my upper chest.

Throwing my hand across the name, I shake my head at him. "No, I'm Harper. Jessica Harper."

"Do you own that white Acura SUV with California plates parked in the spot marked 101?"

"Yes, is there a problem? This is my condo, and that's the spot that is registered to this condo," I say accusingly.

"No problem. We were patrolling the parking lot late last night and noticed you left the interior light on. Wanted to let you know before it drained your battery."

"Are you serious?" I actually laugh at the two of them. In California, the police have obviously more pressing matters than alerting idiots that they left interior lights on in their car. I'm still chuckling as I walk to my purse that is on the small kitchen table. Reaching in, I grab my keys and walk back to the door. Slipping on my flip-flops, I step outside the condo and onto the front walkway that leads down to the parking lot.

Closing my door to the condo, I see that the second officer who was standing at my door is now gone and most likely back in the patrol car. "I'm Officer Christianson. Sorry to have disturbed you, Ms. Harper." He's smirking. That asshole has a smirk on his face; his gorgeous, chiseled face. I know I shouldn't be looking at him like that, and I feel guilty for doing it, but he is striking.

"You didn't disturb me. You just caught me off guard," I reply, walking as fast as I can away from this beautiful stranger. Using the key fob, I unlock the doors and open the driver's side front door. I reach in and turn the switch to shut off the inside light. Officer Christianson found his way right up to my open door and planted himself between the open door and the body of the car, trapping me between him and the interior of my car. "How did you even see that light on?" I question him.

Turning around and narrowing my eyes on him. He shakes his head slightly, chuckling at me.

"Saw it last night. We didn't want to wake the owner, ahem, you, up at three o'clock in the morning when we first saw it, so we stopped by on our way back to the station at the end of our shift, which is right now."

God, I feel stupid.

"Well, um, thank you...officer..."

"Christianson, Landon Christianson." He reaches out his hand to shake mine. The distance between us is small, but I offer him my hand and slide it into his. I notice right away how large his hands are and how firm his handshake is. Holding onto my hand a bit longer than a stranger shaking hands should, I gently tug my hand out of his and place it back to my side.

My eyes focus not on his hands, but on the muscles of his forearm. This guy is built. Not big, but defined. You can see every ridge of muscle in his arms. Following the length of his arm, I notice a tattoo that starts at his elbow, and just peeks out from under the sleeve of his uniform. I'm curious what it is and how far it goes up. I swallow tightly, making eye contact with those piercing blue eyes again.

Landon tilts his head slightly at me. The corners of his lips turn just slightly upward. *Shit.* He noticed me checking him out. "You just move here?" he asks.

"Yep. Yesterday," I say, pushing past him as I walk away from those blue eyes and that dangerous smile.

Standing with his hands on his hips, showing off his well-defined arms, Landon flashes me a sexy smile. "Well, welcome to Wilmington, Jessica. Jessica Harper." God, that man is sinful, every last inch of him.

"Thanks," I mutter to myself, walking back to my condo. I think I'm going to like Wilmington.

CHAPTER TWENTY-EIGHT

-LANDON-

As I slide into the passenger seat of our patrol car, my partner, Matt, looks at me and shakes his head. "She's not your type, man; leave that one alone."

"You never know, bro. She may like what I have to offer."

Matt knows about me, about my preferences. I like to be in control. I like it how I want it and when I want it. And right now, I want Jessica. Jessica Harper from California.

"She's young; you saw her. Don't go there, Landon."

"She's of age."

"Really? That's all you care about? She's of age? So you'll fuck her a few times and not worry about it because she's of age?"

"Uh, yeah. That's what I do."

"You're a real asshole sometimes, you know that?"

"Tell me something I don't know, Matty."

Pulling out of the parking lot of her condo complex, I can't help but wonder how in the hell Matt ever saw that damn overhead light on in her car. When I ran her plates, and the picture of her on her driver's record flashed across my screen,

I saw something I needed to have. Something in her eyes, in her small smile, called to me. Jessica Louise Harper would be mine.

"Want to grab breakfast before we head home?" Matt asks.

Looking out my window, I lose myself in thoughts of Jessica. I can't shake her round green eyes, her long, tan legs, and the way her hips swayed when she walked towards her car.

"Sure, let's grab breakfast."

There is silence as Matt drives us the few miles back to our station. Pulling into the side parking lot, Matt rolls down his window and punches the code into the key pad that opens the security gate where we park our patrol cars. As he pulls into our assigned spot, I pop the laptop out of the docking station and open my door.

Matt hollers over the top of the patrol car. "Landon, let this one go."

Two words I've never spoken before roll off my tongue. "I can't."

CHAPTER TWENTY-NINE

-Gabe-

"Dude, are you even fucking listening to me?" Luke spits out.

"Shut the fuck up. Just spot me," I respond. Working out used to be the one thing that would help me clear my mind, get my shit straight. Now, I can't even focus on lifting the weights that are hovering over my head. I let them fall back onto the bench, and I grunt in frustration. Luke shakes his head at me and walks away. "What?" I yell out in frustration. Luke keeps walking towards the locker room, away from my outburst.

"Fuck!" I scream, soliciting head turns and dirty looks from the other gym members around me. I grab my water bottle and head to the locker room too. Jess has been gone for four days. Four fucking days and I still haven't heard from her, not that I expected to, but I just want to know she's safe. I need to know she's happy. I need to know something about her, anything. I toss my water bottle at the row of lockers directly in front of me. The bottle bounces off and rolls around the floor.

Luke walks around the corner from the showers with his gym bag hanging off of his shoulder just as I'm entering. He looks me up and down as he quietly speaks. "Just go get her. Bring her home."

I lower my eyes to the floor. "I can't. She's been gone four days, Luke. Only four days, and I don't even know where she is." Pushing past him, I move farther into the locker room and open my locker. Grabbing my gym bag and car keys, I punch the locker door closed, causing an obnoxious bang that echoes off the tile floors of the locker room. I make no effort at acknowledging anyone at the gym on my way out to my truck. I just want to get the hell out of here, and I just want to get my life back. I want Jess back.

Walking to my truck, I remember all of the promises we made to each other, all the plans we made for our future. I listened to everything she ever said, everything she mentioned she wanted. I was going to give her everything. She was my entire fucking world, she still is. I fear now that she is gone for good, and I will never get her back. I want to fucking kill someone, and I will, when I fucking find him. Just then my fist connects with the side window of my truck. That will be that motherfucker's face when they find him.

Chapter Thirty

~Jess~

Monday morning comes all too soon. I'm still getting settled at the condo and unpacking boxes. The last boxes that Dad shipped arrived Saturday. I've found the grocery store and Target—the essentials, so I'm happy. Wearing capri-length black pants and a fitted black and white polka-dot blouse, I throw on a red chunky necklace, matching red earrings and bracelet, and red ballet flats. Since I know I'll be on my feet all day, I opt for comfort and fashion. Pouring half a pot of coffee into my large travel mug, I stir in some creamer and screw on the lid. Grabbing my purse off the counter and a stack of paperwork and bills that I need to sort through, I head out the door and to the first day of my internship.

Using the badge Kevin gave me, I let myself through the main doors of WXZI and move quickly down the hall that leads to the newsroom in the back of the building that houses all of the cubicles and offices for the reporters and other staff. I'm fifteen minutes early. Figures; I'm always early. I hang my black sweater on the back of the chair that is at my desk and set my purse and coffee mug down. There are a few people in offices, but no one notices me.

Walking toward Kevin's office, I see him hunched over his desk, reading a newspaper. I knock lightly on the doorframe of his door, causing him to startle and raise his head. "Hi, Jessica. Ready to work?"

"Ready," I reply enthusiastically.

Kevin leads me out of his office, into the newsroom, walking past my desk and into another office that sits directly across the floor from his. "Jessica, this is Elaine Winters. Elaine is our daytime News Director, and you'll be working primarily with her. Elaine, this is Jessica Harper, your newest intern." I reach out to shake Elaine's hand, and she stands up. She's thin, as in looks like she hasn't eaten in a year thin, and her hands are cold, bony, and frail. I'm afraid I'm going to crush her fingers if I squeeze too hard.

"Nice to meet you, Jessica." She smiles politely.

"Thank you; it's nice to meet you too," I respond. Elaine is short. I mean everyone is short compared to me, but Elaine is really short. She maybe stands right at five feet.

"Well, then, let's not pussy-foot around. Let's get you set up so you can work!" Elaine exclaims. She may be small, but I can tell she's fierce. I know I'm going to like her. I can't help but smile as she's shuffling papers around her desk and grabbing pens. I need good energy around me. Kevin shoots me an expression that says "good luck" and wanders out of her office.

"Tell me you like coffee, Jessica, or you can't work for me," Elaine jokingly says.

"Can't live without it."

"Good. Initiation starts now. We're going down the road to my favorite little coffee shop. You've got a five-minute car ride to tell me everything I need to know about you. Go."

Holy shit, this woman is nuts.

"Well, I'm nineteen years old."

"Whoa, wait. What? Nineteen years old. Are you kidding me?"

"No, I…uh…completed almost two year's worth of undergraduate classes while I was in high school. I didn't even know I was so far ahead."

She cuts me off mid-sentence. "So you're an overachiever?"

"Not sure I'd say an overachiever, but maybe a maximizer; is that even a word?" I say, shrugging.

"Sounds like a vibrator. No, you're an overachiever. I like you already, Jessie. Can I call you Jessie?"

"I prefer Jessica," I say, almost afraid to correct her. Maybe I should just let her call me Jessie, except I fucking hate Jessie. Dad is the only one allowed to call me Jessie.

"Jessica it is."

Before I even realize it, we'd gotten in her black BMW 350 and are racing through the side streets of Wilmington. I know I have about two minutes to tell her everything she needs to know about me, and I do the Cliffs Notes version, excluding why I left California and the man who will always have my heart. Pulling into the parking lot of a small, local coffee shop, Elaine turns the steering wheel sharp and squeezes into the tiniest of parking spots. This woman talks and drives like she's on speed.

Before I can even exit Elaine's car, I notice she is already speed walking to the front door of the coffee shop. "How do you like your coffee, Jessica?" she yells over her shoulder. I can hardly catch up to this ball of fire, and her legs are half my size.

"Black with room for some creamer," I reply.

"Black, huh? Just how I like my car, my men, and my coffee," she says without missing a beat. I burst out laughing. I retract my earlier thoughts; I'm not just going to like Elaine, I'm going to love this woman. Big.

I spend the rest of the day with some guy from IT. He's been installing my computer for at least two hours, getting me access to printers, systems, and programs I'll need for my internship. I'm starving, but I don't know how much longer this dipshit is going to be, so I just sit here, watching him, like I have for the last two hours.

I've raided the supply closet and set myself up with notepads, pens, scissors, a stapler, and an endless supply of sticky notes. I love sticky notes, as in have an obsession with sticky notes, all the sizes and colors. I catch myself, for the first time, feeling a little bit normal, a little less sad, and a small smile creeps across my face.

"What'cha smiling at?" I hear a strong Southern drawl. Turning in my chair, I find the cutest blonde-haired, blue-eyed girl smiling back at me. "I'm Lindsay, the other intern," she clarifies. "I've been here just a few weeks. What's your name?" Her accent is thick. I like it.

"I'm Jessica. Nice to meet you, Lindsay."

"Got any lunch plans?" she asks.

"No, and I'm starving. What's good to eat around here?" I ask, grabbing my purse off of my desk. Lindsay's cube is directly next to mine, and she stops to grab her clutch and car keys.

"There is a small deli across the street. They have great salads and sandwiches. Or there's Bar-B-Que." She wrinkles her nose. I take it Bar-B-Que isn't her thing.

"A salad sounds great," I say, eliciting a smile from Lindsay.

"Well, then, let's go."

To say lunch was a whirlwind would be an understatement. Lindsay talked my ear off, but I actually enjoyed listening to her. She's from here, born and raised. She went to college in Tennessee and graduated a semester early, this past December. She claims that Tennessee is where she got her Southern accent. *Right.* I love her spicy personality. She reminds me a lot of myself, not long ago. I want to be spicy again. I want to be fun and friendly and eager. We exchanged phone numbers, and I actually consider Lindsay to be my first friend in North Carolina.

I loved hearing all about her, but the best part was that I didn't have to talk about myself. I was going to have to do enough of that Friday night when I meet with Dr. Peterson, my therapist, for the first time. My computer is finally all set up, and I have a phone now too. Glancing at the time, I shut down my computer and walk to Kevin's office.

Looking up from his desk as I approach his door, Kevin gives me a warm smile. "So how was the first day?"

"It was really good." I catch myself smiling again. "Everyone has been very welcoming. I can't wait to get started tomorrow now that I have a computer and a phone." I think about the stack of notes Elaine had left on my desk while Lindsay and I were at lunch. I have a lot of research to do tomorrow.

"I'm glad to hear it. Have a great night, and we'll see you tomorrow morning."

Offering a slight wave, I move back through the newsroom to head to Elaine's office, but her light is already off. I remember our morning coffee and chuckle to myself. Grabbing my purse and keys, I would call my first day a success.

CHAPTER THIRTY-ONE

-Gabe-

Restless doesn't begin to describe me right now. With my hand in a cast, thanks to my shitty temper, I now have a broken driver's side truck window and a broken right hand. Being a firefighter requires the use of two functioning hands, so I cannot work for the next five, maybe six, weeks. So now, I get to sit on my ass and think. Fucking perfect.

After having my window fixed, I find myself driving around Santa Ruiz endlessly. I don't know where I'm going or why. I just drive. For the first time since she left, I might understand why she left. Everywhere I go, there is something to remind me of her. I wonder if that's why she left, because she was assaulted with memories of us and her attack everywhere she went. Assault. That's what fucking tore us apart. Everything was perfect until then.

Pulling into the firehouse, I park and spend the next few minutes just sitting in my truck. Time escapes me most days. I am numb to the world that is moving around me. I lock my truck door and walk into the bay, where I see the two fire trucks and the ambulance that our station uses.

Sitting down on the large leather sectional couch that is in the dayroom of the firehouse, I stare blankly at the TV that is looping infomercials over and over. The guys just left to go on a call, and Chief is in his office. Chief provides weekly updates on Jess' case; he knows I'm still interested, even though I don't ask. He communicates frequently with the detectives and has promised to tell me if there are any developments, but we've yet to hear anything. Beyond work and our infrequent talks, he doesn't speak to me about her, and I don't ask.

She's been gone for six days, twelve hours, and thirty-seven minutes. I wonder if I'll ever stop counting. At times, I feel like I'm losing my mind, and I question if I'll ever be able to truly let her go as she asked me to do. I don't even know why I'm here at the firehouse, since I can't work. Grabbing my sweatshirt, I pull my truck keys out of the pocket of my hoodie and kick open the back door.

As I slip the keys into the ignition, I hear a soft knock on my driver's side window. Luke is standing there and he motions for me to roll down my window. When I push the button, the window slowly falls, and Luke takes a step closer to the truck, resting his forearms on the door. "How's the hand?"

"Sore," I answer solemnly.

"Hey, uh, Dad called. He said you were thinking about looking at a house? You know you can stay with me for as long as you want." Luke's voice sounds almost hurt, as if my desire to move is because of him, which it's not.

"Yeah. Dad found a great house down the road. Remember Old Man Johnson? It's his old house, a foreclosure, and the price is a steal, so I'm going to make an offer on it. He said it needs a lot of work, but he's willing to help me do it once my hand heals." Luke looks at me intently, trying to read through the words I'm speaking.

He nods his head as he listens to me explain my reasoning, or better yet, excuses for buying this house. Luke knows why I'm trying to buy this damn house—because it's what I was going to do for *her*. It was what I was trying to do for *us*. It was why I was busting my ass working sixty plus hours a week for the last few months, to save for the down payment. It's why I fucking left her that night, and she ran alone. It's my way of holding onto some piece of what I had and wanted with her.

"Let me know if you want any help, you know, working on the house," he offers with a stiff smile.

"Thanks, man. Catch ya at home in the morning," I say, shifting my truck into reverse and leaving the firehouse. Luke stands there with his hands tucked into the front pocket of his hoodie and watches me pull out of the parking lot.

I'm edgy and irritable while looking at the house. I'm glad I came alone. My stomach is in knots as I walk from room to room, surveying the condition and what needs to be done. What kills me is that this house is perfect, would be perfect, if she were here. This bungalow is bigger than most on our street. It's four bedrooms and two baths, with a huge kitchen and large living area. Every room I walk in, I envision what Jess would say or point out. I love this house, or maybe I'm in love with the idea of what this house should be.

Chapter Thirty-Two

-LANDON-

"Faster," I tell myself. "Push harder."

I run as fast as my legs will carry me. My lungs are burning, sweat is running down my face and into my eyes, making it hard to see, but I push myself hard these last few miles. I never enjoyed running until we started training in the police academy. I enjoy physical pain. Not excruciating pain, but I enjoy stretching my body and mind to their furthest limits.

Slowing to a walk, I wait for the rest of the group to catch up to me. I've been running with this group for about six months. Some people join the group to meet people; I joined so that I could push myself harder and run faster than all these assholes. I'm competitive and I hate losing.

Chuckling to myself, I realize the point of joining a running club is actually to run with other people, and yet I've left these people a half mile behind me. Pulling the Harley Davidson key from the chain around my neck, I insert the key and flip the switch. I push the starter, and turn the throttle, and let my Night Train roar to life. This motorcycle is my pride and joy. It's black on black, and loud as hell with its

Samson boneshaker exhaust pipes. Every woman that sees my bike wets herself. I pull the throttle and spit gravel behind me as I take off toward home.

I park my baby in the garage and shut her off, hanging my helmet from the handlebars. My sister's car is in the driveway. She must have just gotten home from work. Even though she's my little sister, four years younger than I am, we get along fine. She's been living with me since she graduated from college, but I've always taken care of her. Opening the door from the garage that leads into my kitchen, I hang my key on the hook that is on the wall next to the door and kick off my tennis shoes.

I shrug off my gray sleeveless shirt and bunch it into my hands as I walk to my bedroom, closing the door behind me. Turning the shower on, I remove the rest of my clothes, tossing them into the black wicker hamper that stands at the corner of my bathroom and step into my tiled shower. I adjust the showerhead and place my head directly into the stream of warm water, washing away the dirt and sweat from my run. I grip the handle and adjust the water temperature so that it's as hot as my skin can handle.

The water feels good and helps relax my tense muscles. Closing my eyes, my mind instantly wanders back to Jessica. It's been six days since I met her, and I need to devise a plan to see her again, to talk to her, to make her mine. I shampoo my hair and finish my shower. After I dry off, I wrap a black towel around my waist, tucking in the corner so that it stays in place, low on my hips. Stepping into the walk-in closet that is attached to my master bathroom, I pull down a pair of black jeans and a gray button-down dress shirt. I layer a white t-shirt underneath and roll the sleeves.

I toss some gel in my short hair; the style is messy, and it takes me just a few minutes to get ready. I opt not to shave tonight, leaving my face a bit scruffy, as it's been a full day since it's seen a razor. I'm just going to dinner with my sister, and she doesn't care that I haven't shaved.

"Laaaannnnddooonnn," I hear her yell for me from the living room.

I open my bedroom door and head down the hallway and into the living room where she's laid out on the couch, still in her work clothes with her feet propped up on the arm of the large, brown leather sectional couch.

"Make yourself comfortable, why don't you," I grumble. I like having my sister here, but I love giving her a hard time.

"Looks like I already have, doesn't it?" she fires back, causing me to stifle a laugh. She's a firecracker. We are definitely from the same bloodlines. Neither of us will take shit from anyone. I love that she's feisty. I worry less about her every day.

"Ready?"

"Ready as I'll ever be," she shoots back. "Oh, I invited a friend. Don't know if she'll come, but heads up in case she does."

"She better be hot," I grumble, knowing I sound like a complete asshole.

"She's stunning," my sister tosses over her shoulder as we're walking out the door.

CHAPTER THIRTY-THREE

~Jess~

I made it through my first week at the news station. To say I'm exhausted would be an understatement. Most of my time was spent learning the ins and outs of the news business. I spend hours every day watching news feeds, assisting reporters with research, listening to scanners, and even learning how to edit. I've filled two entire notebooks with chicken scratch, tips, and how-tos. I know this experience will prove to be invaluable.

It's only four o'clock, and I have my first appointment with Dr. Peterson at five. Shutting down my computer, I stand and lean over the short cube wall that separates my cubicle from Lindsay's.

"Hey, I have to take off a bit early today. Have a great weekend. I'll see you on Monday, right?"

"Like hell I'll see you Monday. Girl, you're coming to dinner with me tonight. No way are you spending the weekend alone. Remember, I am your only friend in Wilmington." She smiles and bats her eyes.

"I don't know if I'll be good company tonight, Linds. I have an appointment, and I'm, uh…"

Jumping up from her chair, Lindsay cuts me off mid-sentence. "Just come to dinner. It's just dinner. And regardless if you're good company or not, I don't want you to spend your first Friday night in Wilmington alone."

"It's not my first Friday in Wilmington," I remind her as I smile at my sweet new friend. "Plus, being alone is okay, you know."

"No, it's not. I'll text you the address of the restaurant. Be there," she says, flashing me a huge smile.

Grabbing my purse, I just shake my head and smile at Lindsay. "Bye, Linds," I say over my shoulder.

"See your sweet ass tonight, sister!" she yells back over hers. All I can do is laugh.

I pull into the parking lot of the small single-story office building. My stomach is in knots and and my hands are sweating. With a deep breath, I close my eyes and let my head fall back against the headrest in my car. I tell myself just to breathe. *Take three deep breaths. Three deep breaths.* I repeat this to myself over and over. Reaching for the door handle, I pull the latch and push the door open. With a step out onto the black asphalt, I place both feet on the ground and will myself to take the small steps to the front door of the office building. *Three deep breaths.*

Step by step, I get there. My heart is racing, and my stomach knots tighten some more. I can almost taste the bile that is trying to make its way up my esophagus. I want to throw up, but the dry lump in my throat won't let me. Tugging the door open, I step inside to the cool air-conditioned office.

It's quiet, and there is a small front desk with a stack of clipboards. There is a note instructing clients to fill out the paperwork attached to the clipboard, so that is what I do.

Taking a seat in a chair in the far corner of the waiting room, I start answering all of the questions on the intake sheet. I question if I should answer them honestly or lie. Lying seems easier right now, but I know she'll see right through my lies, so I answer them honestly. As I sign my signature on the last page, the office door that is adjacent to the waiting room opens. Out of the office walks a middle-aged woman with light brown hair and dark eyes. She steps out and looks around the waiting room.

"Are you Jessica Harper?"

"Hi. Yes," I barely announce, standing up to meet her. My mouth is still dry, and my hands are shaking. I'm a ball of nerves.

"Come into my office, Jessica. I'm Dr. Peterson." She reaches out her hand to shake mine, and I take it, shaking back before we walk into the small office. The office is modern and bright with a small loveseat and two larger plush chairs, all cream colored. She has an entire wall of books, and every shelf is full.

"Take a seat wherever you'll be comfortable, Jessica." Nodding my head at her, I take a seat in one of the plush cream chairs across from the chair in which she sits. We're facing each other with no barriers between us. Dr. Peterson is flipping through all the paperwork I've filled out, stopping to read more thoroughly on a couple of different pages.

"So, Jessica, tell me what brings you here."

I stare at Dr. Peterson for what feels like a solid minute and look down at my hands, which are folded in my lap. My fingers are twitching from the nerves with which I am overcome. Feeling the tears I was holding in start to roll down my cheeks, I swipe a few away, wiping my hands on my pants. I can barely speak the words forming on my lips due to the giant lump in my dry throat that won't go away.

"I'm starting over. I'm scared and angry and lost and sad and hurt and afraid. And I'm worried that if you don't help me, I may not be able to move forward," I say. My voice is not even recognizable, as it's overcome with emotion. I haven't said those words to anyone before, including myself.

Taking a deep breath, I wait for her reaction, or next question, or anything. I want her to say something. Looking at the intake paperwork I filled out, she quietly sets down her notebook and pen and just looks at me. She looks at me like she doesn't even know where to start. I officially feel like a fucking hot mess. Maybe I'm unfixable.

Glancing at the clock on the wall, she says, "Tell me about *you*, Jessica. Tell me everything that led to you walking through my door."

A small, sarcastic laugh slips out of my mouth. Does she have four fucking hours on a Friday night? Because I'm pretty sure that's how long it will take to tell her my story without her asking any additional questions. She saw my intake sheet. She saw what I wrote. She saw how damaged I am.

Reaching into my purse, I grab the bottle of water I brought with me from work. Taking a small drink of water to alleviate the dryness in my throat, I place the cap back on and set it down. Grabbing a tissue from her side table, I wipe my cheeks and take a deep breath. Closing my eyes for a few seconds, I will myself to open them and look at Dr. Peterson.

It is here that I will begin to unravel the insanity of my life. It is here where I hope to get control of everything that I seem to have lost. It is here where I hope to find a shred of hope, the beginning of a new chapter for myself. With tears falling down my cheeks, I begin talking. Reaching up to my neck, I twirl the ring I've been wearing on my white gold chain since I left California, willing it to give me the strength I need to get through the next hour.

Opening my car door, I slide into my seat and place my head on the steering wheel. My head is throbbing from crying and talking and reliving details of my life that I've never shared with anyone. I'm mentally exhausted and drained, and closing my eyes feels good. A soft *beep...beep...beep* from inside my purse catches my attention. Raising my head, I sit back up and reach into my purse to pull out my phone.

Hi Doll! At Finn's, 120 Main Street.

There is no way I'm getting out of this, but dinner with a chipper Lindsay is not what I want to do tonight. Flipping down the visor, I open the mirror, and the lights illuminate my almost dark car. I have dark circles under my eyes, and most of my make-up has been wiped away from the hour of crying that I just did in Dr. Peterson's office.

Reaching into my purse, I pull out a compact and brush some light powder over my face. I toss the compact into my purse, grab a tube of lipstick, and dab some on my lips. My cheeks are still red and splotchy from crying, and it takes forever for that to disappear. Hopefully the restaurant is dark, and Lindsay won't notice I've been crying.

Driving to Finn's, I recall the past hour, and even though it was hard to admit and say much of what I told Dr. Peterson, there was also something liberating about it. A small weight was lifted off of my shoulders and, for the first time, I feel a glimpse of hope; a feeling that I *might* make it through this.

Opening the door to Finn's pub, I glance around the crowds of people. The bar is full, and every booth and table is occupied. There are small groups of people gathered around talking, drinking, and letting go on a Friday night. When I see Lindsay flailing her arms from a booth in the far corner, I wave in acknowledgement, and I move through the groups of people, zigzagging through the tables. The booths are tall and a small pub light hangs over each booth, casting a muted light into each booth. Circling the last table, I'm almost to Lindsay's booth when she jumps up and greets me with a giant hug.

"I'm so glad you came!"

"Me too," I admit, pulling out of her over-eager hug.

Before I even look into the booth, I hear my name. "Jessica?"

"Officer…"

"Landon," he says with a huge smile on his face. "Have a seat."

Shit. I'm pretty sure my heart just stopped.

CHAPTER THIRTY-FOUR

-LANDON-

"So how the fuck do you two know each other?" I ask in between sips of my beer, looking back and forth between Lindsay and Jess.

"Jesus, don't be such a dick. And I should be the one asking, how do *you two* know each other?" Lindsay tosses back, looking between Jessica and me. Jessica looks pale and she is fidgeting with her hands. I make her nervous. Good. She was so confident the other day, but now I see I have an effect on her. Fucking perfect. Jessica slides into the booth next to Lindsay.

"Well, I met Jessica last week. Seems our little California girl left the lights on in her car. Matt spotted it while we were patrolling her parking lot." Jessica doesn't make eye contact with me, but she glances at Lindsay and offers a straight, short smile.

"So that's it?" Lindsay asks.

"That's it," Jessica says firmly.

Our waiter makes an appearance and takes orders for drinks.

"What'll it be, Jessica?" I ask, hanging on the "s" in her name. Looking at me, before turning to the waiter, she answers to him, not me.

"Just a Diet Coke, please."

"Diet Coke? It's Friday night; let loose, live a little," I command. Our waiter pauses for a second to see if she's going to change her drink order.

"Diet Coke is fine. Thank you," she responds again as our waiter walks away. Before I can even give her shit about drinking a Diet Coke, she snaps her head at me and snarls viciously, "I'm only nineteen years old. Diet Coke is fine. And don't you fucking tell me to live a little. You know nothing about me. Understand, pretty boy?"

Jesus H. Christ. Jessica is a feisty one, and she's only nineteen. *Holy shit*. Why didn't I notice this when I ran her plates?

"Got it," I reply, taking a long drink of my beer. Lindsay lifts her eyebrows at me and smirks, letting me know that Jessica has clearly put me in my place. I don't let women put me in my place.

"Looks like you two have worked this out. Now let's figure out what we're having for dinner," Lindsay says, smiling and looking back and forth between Jessica and me.

Lindsay and Jessica make small talk across the table from me, pointing at different things on the menu while I spend the next few minutes intently studying Jessica. There is something different about her today. She looks sad, her eyes have lost some of the glimmer I saw in them last weekend, and it clearly looks like she's been crying.

Lindsay shoots me a look from across the table again, which clearly says "play it cool," and I nod in acknowledgment of her unspoken message to me. After we order dinner, we keep the conversation light and friendly. Jessica seems to have calmed down a bit and even laughs at something Lindsay whispers to her. I have a hard time paying attention to the conversation that is happening across the table, as I'm drawn into Jessica, just watching her, studying her.

"So, you moved all the way from California to work at a TV station in Wilmington, North Carolina, huh?" I say, trying to steer the conversation back to Jessica. I want to learn more about her. I need to learn more.

"Yep."

Okay, then, she's not going to throw me a bone here. I will fucking dig the information out of her if it kills me.

"Why North Carolina?"

"Why not?"

"Why not stay in California?"

"What's wrong with North Carolina?"

"I didn't say anything was wrong with North Carolina. I just don't understand why you moved across the country at nineteen years old for an internship."

Lindsay's eyes are darting back and forth between us like she's watching a tennis match. There is tension in the air, but not aggressive tension. I can hold my own with her, and she is clearly holding her own with me. Neither of us will back down. I'm really going to like this girl.

"Sometimes you just need a change," she says quietly, dropping her eyes from mine.

"Explain."

"I don't have to."

She's not telling me the whole story, but I'll get it out of her eventually. I always do. That's why I'm a cop. I can dig and find shit out without people even knowing they've really told me. Thinking about how stubborn Jessica is, I inhale sharply,

"No, you don't have to, but I'd like to know more about you." Those words stop her suddenly. Her eyes widen, and I can hear her breath hitch.

"Why?"

"Why not?" I smile cunningly at her. I can tell what I've said has an effect on her. Good. I will break her down. It's what I do best.

Lindsay's had enough of our bantering back and forth. Grabbing her purse, she jumps up from the table. "Excuse me while you two play your little game of cat and mouse, but I need to pee."

Jessica laughs at Lindsay's reference, sliding out of the booth to let Lindsay out. Sliding back in, she grabs her Diet Coke and puts the straw to her mouth, wrapping her pink lips around the white straw. My eyes won't leave her full lips. I envision what they taste like and feel like pressed against mine as I suck on her bottom lip. Releasing the straw, I catch the slightest glimpse of her tongue as it passes over her bottom lip, and I'm instantly hard. I want that tongue in my mouth and all over my body. I want to feel her lips pressed up against mine. I want to taste her; all of her.

Leaning forward across the table, closing the space between us, I whisper, "Tell me more about you, Jessica."

As she sets her drink down on the table, I see her hand shaking slightly. I love knowing that I get to her. Taking a deep breath, she opens her mouth to say something, but then pauses, pressing her lips together. I can tell she's thinking about what to say, struggling to find the words.

"Tell me," I whisper again, leaning in a little closer just as she leans back slightly.

Offering me a half-hearted smile, she inhales. Raising her shoulders slightly, she begins, "I'm nineteen. I guess we've established that already, huh?" She giggles nervously. "I'm from Santa Ruiz, California. It's in Orange County. I spent most of my life in California. I moved there from Iowa when I was four, after my mom died." She stops here, and I can tell she's momentarily lost in thought. I wonder to myself how her mom died and if she remembers her. I want to ask, but it's too soon to ask those personal questions. Her eyes focus intently on Lindsay's half-full glass of white wine on the table. Shaking her head lightly, Jessica continues.

"I took dual-enrollment classes for most of my junior and senior years of high school. That's where you take AP classes and get college credit at the same time."

I nod in understanding while raising my glass of beer to take a drink. She's fucking sexy as hell and smart—and dangerous. This could be the total package. I try to contain my smile, but she notices and narrows her eyes at me. I raise my eyebrows, a gesture urging her to continue on with her story. She either doesn't get it, or is pissed.

"Continue," I say.

"Well, I'm technically a first-year college student, a freshman, but this is where it gets complicated. My academic advisor called me in a panic right before Christmas break. With the amount of college credits that I earned taking dual-enrollment courses, plus a full credit load my first semester of college, I'm actually, technically closing in on finishing my sophomore year of college, credit wise." She takes a deep breath, and lowers her eyes to the table.

"Holy shit," I reply.

Shocked at my response, she looks back up at me. "I know. It came as quite a shock to me too. Since I will be so close to completing my sophomore year, the requirements for my Broadcast Journalism degree required an internship. Since they are hard to come by, she suggested I not wait until next year, so I jumped at this opportunity. It just so happens to be across the country. So, um…here I am." A small smile creeps across her face. She's so fucking beautiful when she smiles.

"Well, smarty pants, tell me about your family," I prod her for more personal information. I need to know more about her, aside from the fact that she's brilliant and sexy, and mine. Shit, not yet, but she will be.

Relaxing into our conversation a bit more, she smiles as she continues. "Well, it's just me and my dad. He never remarried after my mom died. Honestly, our relationship is weird. I rarely see him. He's a firefighter." Jessica stops here and takes another sip of her Diet Coke. Twirling the straw with her fingers, her eyes gloss over slightly. "Actually, he's the Fire Chief for the City of Santa Ruiz. He pretty much spends every free second at work. It's how he coped with my mom's death. He poured his life into his work." Her eyes drop again. I notice she does this when something's bothering her, or she's thinking deeply.

I swallow hard. I understood the meaning behind those words all too well. Her dad put his job before her. What a fucker. Changing topics, I ask, "Boyfriend?"

"Um. No." A quiet sigh escapes from between her perfect pink lips. Her shoulders sink slightly, almost falling in defeat. "Not anymore," she says, reaching for her drink again. She takes a long sip from the straw and sets the cup down again, not making eye contact with me. She's suddenly quiet, so I will ask questions, and hopefully she'll answer.

"You said your last name is Harper, right?" Finally making eye contact again, she smiles slightly.

"Yes, very perceptive."

"It's my job to be perceptive." I smile back at her. "Then who's Garcia?" I ask inquisitively.

She actually quietly gasps at that question, and I see her back straighten. I've struck a nerve; I can tell by the way she shifts in her seat and fidgets with her hands. *Who the fuck is Garcia?*

"How do you know about the Garcias?" she asks, eyeing me closely.

"What?" Now I'm confused. I'm asking about a Garcia, singular, not plural. "I was asking who Garcia was, not who the Garcias were," I clarify.

Her concerned look remains planted on her face, and I can tell she's not going to offer up information on Garcia easily. "The day Matt and I came to your condo to tell you about your car light, you were wearing a Santa Ruiz Fire Department shirt that said 'Garcia' on the front." She nods in recognition, closing her eyes and holding them closed for a few seconds.

"That's the ex," she says quietly. "Can we talk about you now?" she asks, looking uncomfortable.

I don't want to talk about me. There is so much more I need to know about her. We've just scratched the surface, but I'll play her game for now.

"Sure. What do you want to know, Jessica?" I ask coyly. She hears the innuendo in my question and the tone of my voice.

Rolling her eyes at me, she asks, "How old are you?"

"Twenty-eight," I answer honestly.

Jessica's eyes widen.

"What? Does twenty-eight scare you?" I say with a low voice.

"Why would twenty-eight scare me?" she snaps back at me, trying to seem unaffected.

"Next question," I say. I want to continue getting to know her, not piss her off, so it's best if we move on. "What made you want to become a police officer?"

Fuck. Loaded question. Do I go with the real reason or the safe explanation? I'll go safe, for now. "Our dad was a police officer, and my uncle was too. It's all I've ever known. From the time I can remember, it was always something I wanted to do."

A small smile spreads across her face. "I like that answer," she says shyly.

"Good," I reply. "What else do you want to know?"

"Have you ever been shot at?"

"Once."

"Do you ever get scared?"

"Nah, not really."

"What's your favorite part of being a police officer?"

"Handcuffs." God, the expression on her face is priceless. She squirms.

"Handcuffs? Did you say handcuffs?" she spits out. I realize I may have just scared the shit out of her.

Squinting my eyes at her, I lean in against the table again. "There's something about restraining people that really gets me excited." *Fuck if that isn't true.*

She doesn't seem amused. In an almost mocking tone, she says, "You get excited handcuffing bad guys and tossing them in the back of your car?" *No, I get excited handcuffing women to my bed and fucking them senseless.*

"Yep." I keep my answer short. "Jesus, I'm kidding. I love helping people. That's what I love most about my job."

Rolling my eyes at her, I shake my head in amusement at how worked up she gets. "But I like handcuffs too," I quip.

Silence fills the air between us for a few seconds as Lindsay strides back up. "At least you two didn't kill each other while I was gone."

Neither Jessica nor I respond to her remark. Just as Lindsay is getting settled back in at the table, our waiter reappears.

"Anything else I can get for y'all tonight?" We all glance back and forth to each other. Jessica shakes her head lightly, and Lindsay shrugs her shoulders.

"No, I think we're all set," I respond, wishing that one of the girls had wanted another drink. I'm not ready to let Jessica go home yet. I have a million more questions for her. I need to get inside that head of hers...and those pants. Reaching for the bill at the same time, Jessica's hand just beats mine to it. I grab her hand firmly, holding it in place. "I'm picking this up."

"Landon, you don't have to do that. I can pay for myself," Jessica counters.

Lindsay pipes in, "It's not worth arguing about with him, Jessica. A little tip about my brother: you won't win an argument with him. Just let him pay the bill."

She releases the bill, but I continue my gentle grip on her hand. It's soft and delicate, and I'm not ready to let go.

"Ah, okay. Thanks. You really don't have to pay for me." She's trying to pull her hand out of mine, but I still won't let go.

"I know I don't, but I want to."

A small smile creeps across my face. She drops her eyes from mine, and I finally release her hand. Reaching into her purse, I see she's rifling around.

"Lose something?" I ask. "You could fit a small child in that bag." Her purse is huge and seemingly full of stuff.

She laughs and shrugs "I like big purses; what can I say?" She has the cutest laugh. Pulling papers out of her purse and setting them on the table, she removes her wallet, a case with sunglasses, and a small make-up bag. Shit, her bag is a never-ending pit.

"Ah ha! Found them," she says, jingling the keys in her hand. She starts placing the contents of her bag from the table back into her purse. All of a sudden, she freezes and all the color drains from her face. Her smile is gone and her eyes are glossy. She's holding a plain white envelope in her perfectly manicured fingers. Shoving the last of her contents into her bag, she turns quickly to Lindsay. "I really have to go. Thank you for inviting me to dinner. And Landon, thank you for paying. I, ah, um, really have to get home now."

Without another word, she slides out of the booth, offers a tight smile to Lindsay, and a small wave to me, then hurries out of the pub. Her pace is fast and she's gripping the white envelope in her hand along with her car keys.

"What just happened?" Lindsay asks me, looking confused.

"Hell if I know. She looked at that envelope in her hand and it was like she saw a ghost." I recall the look on her face, and it was a combination of sadness and fear.

"I'll ask her on Monday. Thanks for dinner, Lan. Let's go."

Chapter Thirty-Five

~Jess~

My heart is racing. My feet can't keep up with how fast my body wants to get me to my car. I'd recognize that handwriting anywhere. How? When did that envelope get into my purse? My mind is consumed with thoughts of what's in that envelope. Clutching it to my chest the entire drive home, I'm so distracted with thoughts that I don't even know how I made it back to my condo. I sit in my parking spot for a minute, just holding the envelope, staring at the script "Jess" that's written on the front. I even smelled the envelope to see if I could smell him.

Fumbling with my keys, I somehow make it into my condo and toss my purse onto the kitchen table. Flipping on lights all over the kitchen and living room, I sit down on the couch, still clutching the letter. I stare at it. I want to open it, yet I'm so afraid of what the words on the inside will do to me. Since I told Gabe that day in my living room to let me go, he has. But right now, I want him here. I want to hear him tell me that he loves me, that we'll be okay, even though I know in my heart we won't.

When I slide my finger under the sealed flap of the envelope, it tears open, and I pull the folded letter out. Taking a deep breath, I tremble slightly at the sight of his handwriting. Unfolding the letter completely, I begin reading.

Jess,

These weeks of silence have damn near killed me. I can't focus, and I can't sleep. I can't think about anything but you. My days always began and ended with you, and I have been lost for weeks. I know that you asked me to let you go, but please just let me know that you are safe, that you are okay. Tell me something, Jess, anything. Communicate with me, talk to me.

For the rest of my life, I will live with the guilt of knowing that I couldn't do the one thing I promised you I would do: take care of you and keep you safe. Every single day, I regret leaving you that night. From the bottom of my heart, I am sorry. I will never get over the fact that I failed you. I failed you. None of this was your fault. Please know that.

I know you don't want to be found, you made that clear. Wherever it is you are headed, I hope that happiness and peace await you. You are truly the strongest, most amazing woman I have ever met. I have no doubt that your future holds much success in whatever you choose to do.

No matter where the roads in our lives lead us, you will always be the love of my life, the one person who touched my soul, and the one person I will never forget. I will never get over you Jessica Louise Harper. Always

*know that there is one person in this world that loves you
forever.*

My love always,
Gabe

I can't stop the sobs wracking through my body, or turn
the tears off. Undoubtedly, I love Gabe. But I love him
enough to know that he deserves better than the damaged
goods that is me, Jessica Harper. I know in my heart that I will
never, ever get over him. There are some people who own a
piece of your heart, your soul. For me, that is Gabe.

Folding the letter, I toss it onto the end table. Curling
into a ball on the couch, I pull my knees to my chest and cry. I
cry uncontrollable tears, and I punch the pillows of the couch.
I yell and punch and cry. I have no idea how I ended up on the
floor. I must have rolled off the couch, but I'm tossing pillows
at the couch and punching the cushions. I actually wonder to
myself if I'm having a nervous breakdown. I reach to the letter
again and run my fingers over the handwriting. Maybe if I
touch it, I will feel him. Out of nowhere, there is a sudden,
loud knocking on my door.

"Jessica, open this door now, or I will break the fucking
door down." I recognize the voice as Landon's.

"Go away, Landon. I'm fine."

"Open this goddamn door, right now, or I swear on my
father's grave, I will kick the fucking door in."

Shit. I don't need to explain to Kevin how some cop I
barely know kicked in his door.

"Hold on."

Walking to the door, I wipe the tears from my face and
take a deep breath, trying to calm myself down, but I realize
there is no cleaning up this mess. I am a mess. Turning the

deadbolt, I hear it click. Before I even have my hand on the handle to open the door, Landon bursts through the door and pulls me into his chest tightly. He has a gun in his hand, and his eyes are searching the condo.

"Jesus Christ, put the gun down. There is no one here but me," I snap, trying to pull away from him.

He doesn't loosen his grip on me and he won't let me pull back away from him. Actually, he pulls me in tighter after holstering his gun somewhere along his back.

"I heard you screaming. What happened?" His voice is full of concern. He's rubbing circles on my back and I realize that I've got my arms securely wrapped around him. My face is pressed against his firm chest and, if I tilt my head up slightly, I could press my lips to his neck.

"Nothing happened." Tugging, I'm able to pull away from him this time, but his hands are still grasping my upper arms, holding me closely. I duck my head slightly when I catch his eyes searching my tear-streaked face.

"Besides, what are you doing here anyway?"

"I could tell when you left dinner you were upset. I wanted to make sure you made it home okay. I was worried about you."

"Worried about me? So you followed me home?"

"I didn't follow you home, Jess." My heart sinks. He just called me "Jess." No one has ever called me "Jess" except for Ava or Gabe. I won't correct him, not right now anyway. "I dropped Lindsay off at the house, and the more I thought about how you left the pub and looked upset, the more worried I became. I just wanted to stop by and make sure you got home okay."

"Well, I'm home, and safe, so you can leave now." I know that those words came out snotty. I can only imagine what I look like. I can feel how swollen my eyes are and I'm all stuffy from crying. I can hear it in my voice. I just want him to leave.

"Why were you crying, Jess?" He said it again. The way my name rolls of his tongue sends a shiver up my spine. "I'm not leaving until you talk to me, and I know that you are really all right." And just like that, he throws himself down on the couch that is covered in my tears. Releasing a deep sigh, I ask him to leave once again.

"Not happening, baby girl. Take a seat and let's talk."

"Did you just call me 'baby girl'?" I force a smile and roll my eyes at him. This guy has some serious balls, and now he has a pet name for me? Walking over toward the couch, I stand firmly in front of him, crossing my arms across my chest. He tips his head back slightly to look up at me. As he tilts his head to the side, the corners of his mouth curl up, and a small grin falls over his lips.

"Please, everything is fine. I was just upset, and I needed to cry it out. It's out, and I'd really like you to leave now."

Placing his foot over and onto his opposite knee, he leans back further on the couch, making himself comfortable. Patting the cushion next to him, he looks back up at me. "Sit down."

I contemplate for a few seconds before I sit down, making sure that there is plenty of room between us. I figure, if I can talk to him for a few minutes, he'll be satisfied, and I can get him to leave so I can go to bed and finish my mini breakdown.

"Happy now?" I ask angrily.

"Not yet. Tell me why you were crying."

"It's personal. Please, just let it be."

"I can't just 'let it be.'" His voice is full of intensity, and his eyes are a deeper shade of blue. I can't deny how good-looking he is, and my pulse quickens just a little bit. Swallowing hard, I glance at the letter on the end table and then look back to him. He notices where I was looking and turns his head to look at the letter.

"Is that what upset you at the restaurant?"

Nodding my head slowly, I can feel my lip quivering. "Yes. I found a letter in my purse that I didn't know was there. I recognized the handwriting, and I just needed to leave. I wanted...needed to be alone when I read it."

"Who's it from?"

"Does it matter? Jesus, you're being really nosy."

"Who's it from?" He sits up straighter and, suddenly, I'm wondering if he's going to reach for the letter.

"Gabe," is all I respond.

"Ex?"

"Yep."

"Is that why you left California?"

"Partially."

I can feel the stinging of the tears behind my eyes again. My heartbeat picks up even more. I can feel my pulse in my neck and my throat is dry.

"What other reasons?"

The tears I'm fighting to hold in are suddenly falling down my cheeks. My eyes are turned down, looking at my hands, which are folded in my lap. The tears that have fallen have sprinkled my folded hands. I watch a stray tear roll off the top of my hand, over my knuckle, and fall into my lap. Suddenly, there is a gentle finger wiping another falling tear. Looking up, I see that Landon has shifted himself considerably closer to me. He is holding his hand just near my cheek.

Stilling himself, he looks at me as if asking permission to continue wiping my tears.

When I don't respond, he takes another swipe at my cheek with his long, gentle fingers, but this time, after he wipes my tears, he rests his palm on my face. Tilting my head, I let my cheek fall into his hand. As I close my eyes, more tears continue to spill down my face. I gasp for air and my chest heaves with sobs. Pulling me into him, he wraps me in his arms, squeezing me gently, and I cry. I release the emotions I've kept locked inside, but mostly, I cry for Gabe.

"Talk to me," he whispers.

"I can't."

"I want you to trust me," he whispers.

"I don't trust anybody." I pause to swallow. "Including myself."

There are no other words spoken between us as I lie in Landon's arms, but no words are necessary. I find solace in the comfort and safety of his arms. I close my eyes and soak in the contentment of lying with him.

Opening my eyes, I realize that I'm lying on top of Landon and that he is asleep underneath me. I raise my head slowly and pull myself off of him. I stand for a few moments above him, and notice how peaceful he looks, and I am conflicted with whether I should wake him or not.

The large clock that hangs on the wall in the kitchen tells me it's three in the morning. There is no way I'm going to wake him at this hour to send him home. I grab the soft, teal blue blanket that hangs over the back of the couch. Opening it, I lay it as gently as I can over him, hoping I don't wake him.

Leaning over him, I can't help but look at his beautiful face. His sharp jaw line is covered in a five o'clock shadow. It's the perfect amount of facial hair to give his face, that rugged "bad boy" look. His full lips are slightly parted and perfectly shaped. I can't help but think about how handsome this man who is lying on my couch is.

I take the steps upstairs to my bedroom quietly, so as not to wake him. Lying in bed, I see the words from Gabe's letter running through my mind. Silent tears slide from my eyes and down into my hair. I miss him more than I ever thought possible. Even with the handsome stranger asleep on my couch downstairs, I know it's Gabe who still holds my heart.

Chapter Thirty-Six

-Landon-

Reaching my arms above my head, I stretch and roll onto my side, filling the entire length of the couch I'm lying on. The littlest hint of sun is peeking through the wooden shutters. Looking at the blanket that has been carefully laid on top of me, I have to assume she was okay with me staying here. Propping the throw pillow under my head, I wonder when she finally woke up last night and moved to her room. Falling asleep with her on my chest was amazing.

I can still smell a light hint of her perfume on my shirt, and it reminds me of holding her last night. She felt perfect lying in my arms and across my body. It was so hard to hear and see her cry, but listening to her breathing settle as she calmed down in my arms, and the slight whisper of her breaths as she fell asleep on top of me, caused an emotion in me to surface that I rarely see—compassion.

I see that folded letter lying on the table in front of me, the one that clearly upset her. It would be so easy to reach over and read it and, for a minute, I contemplate doing just that. Turning my head, I glance up the stairs and see that there is a door that is slightly cracked, and I wonder if that is where she is.

Sitting up, I decide not to read her letter. I want her to tell me, in her own words, with her sweet voice, what happened. Pushing myself off the couch, I wonder if I should just leave before she wakes up, but something inside of me won't let me leave just yet. There is a pull, a desire I've never felt before. I *need* to see her.

Quietly taking the stairs, I find the door that's cracked slightly open and peek inside. There, on the large bed, she lies on her side. A purple comforter is pulled up to her chest, her arms securely holding it in place. Her long dark hair has been pulled high into a ponytail, and she looks so peaceful as she sleeps. Her face has returned to its olive tone and is no longer covered in red patches from crying.

I know it must have been late when she came to bed, but I want to talk to her. She is lying on the right side of the bed, and there is just enough room to slide onto the left side of the bed without touching her. I realize this is brazen of me to just slide into bed with her, but I'm not going to touch her, yet.

Walking across the wooden floor, I gently lower myself onto the bed. I don't pull the covers back; I lie on top, and pull the blanket that is at the foot of the bed over me. I'm propped on my left side, watching her sleep, and I can hear her steady breaths telling me she's sound asleep. My presence hasn't disturbed her yet.

I lie here for almost an hour. I watch the minutes change on the clock, wanting so badly to reach out a few short inches to touch her. I can almost feel how soft the skin on her arm is as my hand hovers over where I want to run my fingers. It would be so easy to lean in and press a kiss to her forehead or her cheek. She rolls slowly to her back and throws her arm up over her head, causing the comforter to drop to her waist. She's wearing a light gray tank top that her large breasts are almost spilling out of. I'm instantly hard as I think about taking each of her nipples in my mouth, running my tongue around each hard bud. Fuck. She's not ready for that yet, I remind myself.

Unsettled in her new position, she keeps moving her legs. I can tell she's either not comfortable or she's beginning to wake. Leaning toward her, I whisper in her ear, "Good morning, baby girl." With no warning, she sits straight up and screams.

"Jesus Christ, Jess. It's just me. Calm down." Her hands are covering her face, and she's now breathing erratically, almost hyperventilating. Pulling her hands down, she glares at me, her eyes narrowed, her lips pursed, and she looks ready to kill.

"You can't just climb into my bed and think that I'm not going to freak the fuck out."

"Did you just say 'freak the fuck out?'?" I actually laugh.

"It's not funny. I'm serious."

She's so cute. Her ponytail is a mess, and she pulls the comforter up higher over her chest to cover herself.

"I'm sorry," I say sincerely. "I woke up downstairs and wanted to make sure you made it to bed." I realize I'm smirking as I say this. "So I peeked in your room, and you were curled up on your side of the bed, so I just laid down next to you. No harm intended." I raise both of my hands to show I'm sincere.

Throwing herself back onto her pillow, hard, she grumbles and pauses before she speaks. "I appreciate you checking on me last night, and I appreciate you checking on me this morning, but you can't check up on me all the time. I don't *need* you." The last sentence comes out as a whisper. Those four words she just spoke—"I don't need you"—hurt. She does need me; she just doesn't know it yet.

It is rare that I am speechless or hurt, but I am both. She continues to lie there with her eyes fixed on the ceiling and her arm laid across her chest with her hand over her heart. I can see her pulse in her neck beating rapidly.

"Why are you afraid of me?" I know this is a loaded question. Shit, I'm nine years older than her. I'm pushy, aggressive, and have intentionally gone out of my way to make her uncomfortable.

"I'm not," she whispers.

"Look at me," I order. My tone is more aggressive with her. Slowly, she turns her head to look at me, and her beautiful green eyes fix on mine. My pulse quickens as I reach out to run the front of my hand over her cheek. She closes her eyes when my fingers brush over her cheek and she swallows hard.

"I know you don't need me, but what if I need you? I wish you would give me the chance just to know you," I stammer. I'm not a man that spills my heart out to women often, or ever, but there is something about the innocence of her that makes it easy to just put my thoughts out there. She stares at me with no emotion on her face.

"What are you thinking?"

She doesn't say anything as she blinks her eyes slowly.

"Please tell me what you're thinking."

She pulls her bottom lip into her mouth and gently tugs at it with her teeth. I can't take my eyes off of her mouth. Leaning in to her, I'm so close I can smell the remnants of the perfume she wore last night, along with the sweet feminine smell of her skin. Our noses are within centimeters of each other. I can feel her breath on my lips. I hover my mouth over hers, and her eyes open wider. *She wants me to kiss her.*

I never make a move to kiss her, but our eyes hold each other's. I whisper, "Will you trust me?" She shakes her head no and closes her eyes again. "Why?"

"I don't trust anyone." Those words tear me apart. She slowly opens her eyes, and I see her chin quivering lightly. Instead of pressing my lips to hers, I lower my mouth to her forehead and give her the lightest kiss. With my lips on her forehead, I can feel her body trembling, and her breathing is quick and shallow. She's fucking afraid of me, and I have to prove to her, and myself, that I'm not going to fuck her and leave her. I won't be *that* guy with her.

Pushing myself up quickly, I hop off the bed. "Get up and get dressed. Meet me downstairs in fifteen minutes."

She looks at me like I've lost my mind. "Why?"

"We're going to breakfast."

"There is no way I'll be ready in fifteen minutes." Her lips pucker out like she's pouting.

"You're beautiful. Just throw some clothes on and brush your teeth. We're leaving in fourteen minutes now." I flash her a big smile. Pushing the thick purple comforter off of her, she pulls her long, tan legs out and hangs them over the side of the bed.

Turning to leave her room, I mutter over my shoulder, "Thirteen minutes now, baby girl. Hurry up."

As I'm closing her door behind me, I hear the pitter patter of her feet run across her bedroom floor. Waiting for her downstairs, I eye the letter on her table again. Whatever is written on that piece of paper is the source of much pain for her. Just as I'm reaching for the letter, I hear her door open upstairs. She comes bouncing down the stairs in a pair of worn jeans that have small rips on the front thighs and a tight green tank top. Her wavy hair is piled on top of her head where a few loose strands have fallen out. She grabs her purse off the counter and slings it over her shoulder.

"You're not going to need that." I smile and point to her purse. She looks at me and scrunches her forehead, looking perplexed.

"I need my purse if we're leaving."

Walking over to her, I slide the purse off her shoulder. "Give me your phone and your ID." Looking at me suspiciously, she pulls her ID out of her wallet and hands it to me along with her cell phone. Sliding both of them into my back pocket, I reach for her hand and lead her to the door.

"Wait, do you have sunglasses?" I stop abruptly at the door.

"Yeah, in my purse. Let me grab them." She releases my hand and walks back to the table. Digging through her purse, she pulls a case out and opens it, sliding a pair of small Ray-Ban aviator sunglasses onto the top of her head.

"Where are we going?"

"It's a surprise. Let's go."

"I hate surprises," she says as a smile spreads across her face. She walks back over to me and I reach for her hand again. This time, she lets me take it. This is a good sign. Closing the door behind us, I lead her down her sidewalk toward my motorcycle that is parked in guest parking. As we cross the black asphalt, she tugs slightly on my hand, trying to pull away from me.

"Oh no, I'm not going anywhere on that." She has now pulled me hard enough that we've come to a complete stop.

"Come on. I promise I'm careful."

She's standing, shifting back and forth between her feet. She's tugging on her bottom lip, and she actually looks scared to death. I watch her contemplate and reach out to grab her other hand. With a small squeeze, I whisper, "Trust me," and press another small kiss to her forehead. I rub both of her upper arms, hoping to calm her nerves. "Trust me, Jess. I won't let anything happen to you. I promise."

"Okay," she whispers, and I actually feel her hands shaking. Nodding at me, she gives me the go-ahead, and I tug her slightly towards my motorcycle. If she's afraid of cycles, I know the sound alone is going to scare the shit out of her. I have to prep her.

"Sit behind me and wrap your arms around my waist." She swallows and nods. "The bike is loud; that's how it's supposed to sound." Inhaling deeply, she nods again. "Jess?" She looks at me, and I grab her chin and hold her head still. "I'm not going to let anything happen to you. Do you understand?" A tight smile crosses her lips.

"Yeah, okay." She laughs. "Let's do this."

I throw my leg over the bike, and she slides on behind me. Wrapping her hands around my waist just as I've instructed her, her feet have found the pegs, and she's pressed her entire torso up against me. I can feel her breasts pressed up against my back, and she has her thighs squeezed tightly around my hips.

"Ready?" I ask.

"Yep."

I turn the key and start my bike. Before she has time to freak out, I take off, slowly. Her grip tightens around my waist. I have no idea where I'm taking her yet, but I have no intention of stopping or letting her off this bike anytime soon.

For the next hour, I drive her through town, north of the city, and back again. I don't care about anything other than the wind in my hair and the sweet body wrapped around me from behind. Pulling into a small diner in downtown Wilmington, I plan to spend the next couple of hours treating her to breakfast and getting to know her better. Pulling into a parking space, I drop the kickstand on my Harley and shut it down. I slide off the bike and help her off. She laughs as she tries to straighten her legs and walk.

"I take it that's your first time on a motorcycle?" When she nods her head, I see a smile form on the corners of her lips.

"Yeah, it was."

"Wasn't so bad, was it?" I nudge her with my elbow as we're nearing the entrance of the diner. I open the door and let her walk in first. Sitting down in a booth, Jess stretches her long legs under the table and puts them on my booth seat between my legs.

"Still sore?" I chuckle.

"Just stretching a bit." I reach my hand under the table and set it on her ankle. She doesn't look up from her menu, but I feel her flinch when my hand touches the bare skin just under her jeans.

"So, what's good here?" she asks.

"They have the best grits in town," I say, sipping the coffee the waitress had just poured.

"Eww…grits." She turns up her nose and whines.

I can't help but laugh. "I grew up on grits, but almost everyone I've met that isn't from the South finds them appalling."

"Yeah, most people in California eat all healthy: yogurt, fruit, and granola. I grew up eating Mexican breakfasts. I miss that," she sighs.

"Mexican?" I question her.

"Yeah." She pauses to open a creamer and dumps it in her coffee. Stirring it with her spoon, she lifts the mug to her lips and takes a sip. I remain quiet, waiting for her to continue.

"When my dad was working, which was damn near every single day, I stayed with our neighbors, the Garcias. They lived across the street and basically raised me." She pauses again, and I notice the sadness in her eyes.

"For almost fourteen years, I spent most of my time there. They really are my family." She's quiet again for a minute, but smiles at a memory.

"So the 'Garcia' from the t-shirt...your ex; that's his family?" She nods her head.

"Do you miss them?" I ask, knowing the answer.

"More than you can imagine," she replies quietly. Our food arrives, and Jess eyes the enormous meal that is set in front of me.

"Holy shit!" she exclaims as the waitress sets the third plate down in front of me. I laugh at her expression. "Hungry much?"

"Actually, I'm starved," I say.

"Apparently," she smirks.

'So tell me about the Garcias," I encourage her, catching her off guard. She stops her fork mid-air, pausing for a minute, before taking the bite of the scrambled eggs on her fork. Setting it down, she takes another drink of coffee and smiles.

"They are everything to me. Everything." Listening to her describe the people she loves warms me.

"But I hurt them when I moved here." She lowers her eyes to the plate of food in front of her.

"How did you hurt them?"

"I really don't want to talk about this." Her eyes are begging me to stop. But I'm persistent.

"How did you hurt them?" I ask again, my tone a bit more firm.

"I told them the night before I left that I was leaving. They don't even know where I'm really at. I told them the East Coast. That's it."

Now I'm confused. "I guess I don't understand. Why didn't you just tell them? I think they would have understood that you needed an internship and that this was available last minute." That is what she told me at Finn's Pub last night.

"The internship is not the only reason I left." She swallows hard. "That's all I'm going to say, okay? Please leave it at that," she begs me.

"Okay." We sit in silence for the next few minutes. I inhale my food, and Jess pushes hers around her plate.

"Not hungry?" I ask.

"Not really."

"You need to eat. You're too skinny, and I like a little meat on my women." That gets her attention.

"I am not your woman!"

I love seeing her flustered.

"I know. Not yet anyway." She shakes her head and humors me with a little laugh. "Eat!" I say, pointing my fork at her plate of food as she takes a bite of toast.

"Thanks." Jess smiles at me.

"For what?" I'm definitely confused.

"For making me get on your motorcycle," she says while a huge smile crosses her face.

"This is just the first of many rides," I say, and yes, the sexual undertones are implied.

CHAPTER THIRTY-SEVEN

-Gabe-

Standing in the front yard staring at my new house is bittersweet. Bitter that it's mine alone—it was always meant for Jess—and sweet that it's the first time I've bought something of this magnitude from the efforts of my hard work. A stack of papers with my signature in at least thirty different places, a cashier's check, and this old place is all mine.

Where everyone else sees an old, rundown bungalow, I see amazing potential. Jess taught me to look past a rundown, weathered exterior and envision what something could be. We used to walk past this place when Old Man Johnson owned it. She used to say, "Look at that wraparound porch; it's gorgeous." Where I saw dingy gray, peeling paint, Jess saw fresh white paint and a hanging porch swing. She'd stop me every time we walked by. "Look at the windows. They add such character to the house. Those shutters are amazing…" I can still hear her voice in my head.

Pulled from my thoughts by the sound of Luke's pick-up truck that just pulled into the driveway, I turn to see my dad and Luke. Now is not the time to be getting sentimental, in front of them. I shove those memories aside and put my game face on.

"All yours?" my dad asks, patting me on the back.

Dangling the keys from my hand, I offer a half-hearted smile. "Sure is."

"Well, let's go check this place out." He grabs the keys from my hand and marches towards the steps that lead up to the wooden wraparound porch. Luke and I follow closely behind him. Opening the large wooden front door, all three of us step inside and stand in silence, taking in the large room that sits in front of us.

"Old Man Johnson never touched this place," I explain, trying to make excuses for its bad condition. Dad is nodding his head. I see his eyes occasionally widen in shock when he sees something that needs work.

"Needs a lot of work," he says, running his foot across the real hardwood floors.

"Inspector said the bones are great; just needs some TLC. But you and I both know I want more than TLC," I say, grinning at my dad. He works magic on homes all over Orange County. My dad has built some of the largest, most beautiful homes from scratch and has done some of the most amazing remodels I've ever seen.

"What are your thoughts?" I know his game; he's asking me what I want, and then I know he'll counter with his recommendations. This is what he does best.

"Honestly, if we're going to do this, we're going to do it right." I walk through the room we're standing in, which is covered in half torn wallpaper, across the old scratched wooden floors, to an opening at the back of the room. "We're taking this place down to the wood studs," I say as I lay out my vision for my new home.

"We're rewiring the electrical in this entire place; I don't need a fire hazard," I say. I've seen one too many electrical fires lately, and I'm not taking that chance with this house. "We're also redoing all of the plumbing in the entire house."

Luke doesn't say a word, but just looks around as I speak, as if trying to see my vision. "I want to upgrade this place, but there are a few things that need to stay to keep its 'charm.'"

"Charm?" Luke laughs at me. It was a word Jess always used. Some things just stick with you, I guess.

"Yes, *charm*," I say. "I'm tearing out the entire kitchen. Everything in there will be brand new. Same goes for both bathrooms." Dad nods and jots notes in a small notebook he has pulled from the pocket of his shirt. "But, I want to leave the hardwood floors throughout the house. Those need to stay and just be refinished."

"*Mijo*, there is a lot of wasted space here. For resale, we should add more closet space and expand the laundry room."

The word "resale" catches me by surprise. "What do you mean 'resale'? I don't plan to sell anytime soon." I see the confusion flash across his face at my words. "This house isn't about money for me. It's not an investment property for me; it's my home."

Dad sighs deeply. "Gabriel, we know why you bought this home. Are you sure you don't want to fix it up, sell it, and double your money? It would put a lot of money in your bank account, and you know…you could buy a condo or something that doesn't demand your attention all the time."

I swallow hard past the lump that has formed in my dry throat. "You think it was a mistake to buy this house?"

"I think it was a wise business decision to buy this house. What I don't think is wise is that every time you walk out that front door, you're going to be smacked right in the face by a house that sits just across the street that holds a shitload of painful memories for you. What if she doesn't come back? What if it never works out? Do you want to look at her bedroom window every time you walk out of your front door? You will never move forward if you see that, if you think about her every single day."

I don't even know what to say. Looking away from my dad, I fix my eyes on one of the huge trees in the backyard that you can see through the large window from the kitchen. Luke has quietly stepped out and removed himself from the kitchen, leaving me alone with Dad. When I shift my gaze back to my dad, he's leaning up against the counter with his arms across his chest and a concerned look on his face. Once I make eye contact with him, he starts to move towards me, placing himself directly in front of me.

"Gabriel," he says in a quiet voice, his tone calm. "You have to let her go. You have to build your life for you. If she is going to come back, she will, but please don't hold onto something that may never happen."

"It's too soon, Dad. I'm not ready to let her go yet."

With a nod of his head, he pats my shoulder and leaves me standing in the kitchen. If my hand hadn't just healed, I'd punch the fucking wall. Instead, I just stare out the kitchen window into the large backyard that is shaded by two large oak trees. I see the flowerbeds that have been taken over by foot-tall weeds and the patio that needs to be redone. Maybe my dad is right.

Locking up, I sit down on the front steps and glance across the street and down two houses to the right. Her bedroom window looks the same from here as it does from my parents' house. Luke steps down off of the porch and onto the stairs, sitting down next to me.

"I heard Dad. It's only been six weeks. You'll know when it's time to let go. Take the time you need. Dad means well. We all love you and just want you to be happy again."

"I know," I reply quietly.

"Let's go, man. Mom made *pozole* for dinner, and I'm starving." Luke stands up and waits for me to join him. *Pozole* is one of my favorite Mexican stews, and I haven't eaten well in weeks. Greeted by the aroma when we get to Mom and Dad's, my mouth starts watering. For the first time in a long time, I'm actually hungry.

"Ah, my boys are here!" Mom exclaims, walking over to both Luke and me, wrapping us in warm hugs. I haven't spent much time over here since Jess left, and I feel guilty for not stopping by more often.

"Sit down. Eat." Mom pulls both Luke and me by our arms towards the kitchen table and pushes us towards the empty chairs. Dad is already sitting at the table, devouring his stew and reading the newspaper. Luke and I settle in and make small talk while Mom is busy bringing over bowls of soup, tortillas, and bread.

"So your dad tells me that the house needs a lot of work," Mom says, looking at me with a raised eyebrow.

"That's an understatement," Luke mutters, shoving a spoonful of *pozole* in his mouth. Narrowing my eyes at him, I turn to Mom.

"Yeah, it needs serious work, but I'm excited about it." Dad has set his newspaper down to join in our conversation.

"Work has been slow lately. We need to get a few permits, but as soon as those are secure, I can have a demo crew over there the next day. We're not changing anything to the structure, correct? Not moving walls or anything?" Dad asks.

"No. I like your idea about expanding the laundry room and adding more closets. But everything else should stay as is."

"Good. I'll submit paperwork to the city first thing on Monday," Dad says, finishing his bowl of soup and leaning back in his chair.

Mom has been eyeing me since Luke and I arrived. "Are you working this weekend?" she asks.

"Yeah. It's my scheduled shift. I picked up some overtime earlier this week now that my hand has healed and I've been cleared to return to work."

Mom nods her head at me. "You work too much, you know. You need to rest. Ava is coming home next weekend, and I hope you're not planning to work while she's here."

"We're both off, Mom," Luke interrupts. "We'll be around when we're not slaving away on Gabe's house." He offers me a sarcastic grin.

Pushing myself away from the table, I stand up and carry my bowl to the sink.

"Leave it, *Mijo*. I'll take care of it when I'm done." Mom smiles at me.

"Sorry to eat and run, Mom, but I'm gonna head back over to the house real quick to make sure it's locked up, and get my truck."

Mom meets me at the door, offering me a hug goodbye. "I'm very proud of you, sweetheart," she whispers.

"Thanks, Ma."

Walking back to my house, my eyes can't help but find their way to Jess' window. I can't tell you the number of times I have sat and stared at her window, wishing she was asleep behind those blinds, curled up in her bed, or sitting at her desk. I just want to know where she is and that she's safe.

Chief's truck is gone, as always, and something inside me pushes me across the street and up the front porch of her house. Pulling the hidden key from its hiding spot in the hanging planter, I insert it into the front door and turn it lightly. Hearing the click, I turn the doorknob and step into the quiet, dark house.

There is no trace of her here anymore, not that I was expecting one. I had just hoped to see a jacket on the couch, a book on the sofa table; anything to remind me she lives, or lived here. I walk the path I've walked so many times to her bedroom. I just need to see her room. I need to feel her presence one last time. The bathroom is empty of anything related to Jess. There are no hair products, brushes, jewelry, or lotions scattered across the counter.

Swallowing hard, I turn the knob to her bedroom door. Stilled by the quietness, I look around at the room that was so full of life, so full of Jess. Taking three long strides across her room, I find myself standing in front of her small desk. There is a large fabric-covered bulletin board hanging above that she has filled with pictures. Many of the pictures have been removed with exception of a few she left behind.

I pull the thumbtack holding the black and white picture of Jess and me sitting on the beach in Santa Barbara. Holding the picture, I'm flooded with memories: Jess on the beach, in the pool, making love to her all over that hotel room. I run my finger over her cheek in the picture, wishing she could feel my touch, wishing I could feel her.

Sitting down on the edge of her bed, staring at the picture, I can't help but hear the words my dad said earlier. "You have to let her go." *Let her go*. No matter how long I continue to love her, there comes a point in time when I will have to accept that she may not love me back. She's been gone for six weeks and she stopped answering text messages long before that, and even my letter went unanswered. I truly believe, even though I want to deny it with every ounce of my being, she is gone and has no intention of coming back. Letting go is the only option I have to maintain my sanity at this point. With one last look at the black and white picture, I stand and pin it back on her board.

Crossing her room, I take a deep breath, hoping I might be able to smell her. I shut the door to her room, let go of the doorknob, and walk back through the living room and out the front door. Walking away from her house is very symbolic for me. Sometimes shutting doors and letting go is the most important step in healing your heart. She shut the door and let go. A small sense of contentment washes over me at this realization; maybe Jess leaving wasn't about me, but maybe it was what she needed to do to heal.

CHAPTER THIRTY-EIGHT

~Jess~

Setting down the handset on my sterile gray desk phone, I catch the time on the digital display: 6:38 p.m. I've been at work since seven this morning. I've been putting in almost sixty hours a week since I started at WXZI, and it doesn't appear it's going to slow down any time soon. I've been squeezing in lunchtime appointments with Dr. Peterson twice a week and feel like I'm making some progress. My stomach growls loudly just as Lindsay's blonde head pops up from over the cubicle wall we share.

"You almost ready to go?" she asks with a little too much energy. Lindsay never tires, never slows down, and at times, her boundless energy is exhausting.

"Do you ever get tired?" I ask, my words dripping with sarcasm.

"Nope, and you're not getting out of this. I don't care how tired you claim to be," she fires back at me.

"Parties aren't really my thing and all…considering I'm only nineteen," I respond, hoping my age will remind her that I'm young and boring, and she should really find friends that she can go out to bars and go clubbing with.

"You'll be twenty next week, and that means you're basically twenty-one."

I actually burst out laughing at her logic. "Yeah, well, the law doesn't see it that way. Ask your brother," I say jokingly.

"Speaking of my brother..." she says, shaking her eyebrows at me.

"Don't. There's nothing there."

"I've been meaning to ask you for weeks what happened when he came to check on you. I've been waiting for you to offer up the goods, but you're holding out on me." Lindsay laughs, tossing her purse over her shoulder. "Plus, you guys have been spending a lot of time together."

"We've gone to a movie and to dinner, once," I snap back at her accusations.

"I think you're forgetting about him bringing you coffee and lunch. And didn't you go to the gym together last week? Those all count as dates."

"You kill me, Linds. Kill Me." I laugh at her.

Reaching down, I shut off my computer monitor and grab my cell phone, stuffing it into the outside pocket of my purse.

"And about that night, there's nothing to tell. He came by, checked on me, and left."

"Right. You can keep lying to me, but I know he stayed with you that night." Lindsay grins at me and rolls her eyes. "Let's go," she says, hooking her arm through mine, dragging my lifeless body out of my cubicle.

"I hate parties," I grumble. "And I'm hungry."

"You love parties and, you know what, maybe if you're lucky, I'll feed you," Lindsay says, squeezing my arm. "Let's do this."

Standing against the wall in the kitchen full of drunk people that I don't know, people I don't care to know, I spy a single French door that must lead to a patio. Slithering through the mass of sweaty bodies that are standing in small groups throughout the house, I excuse myself, bumping into everyone along the way to my escape. There have to be fifty people at this party, and they are all standing between that door and me. In my past life, parties with people I didn't know were fun. It was exciting to meet new people and talk to strangers. Now, I don't give a shit.

Lindsay is across the kitchen, tending to the thirty liquor bottles that have filled up the entire granite island. It's hot and sticky in this house, and everyone reeks of booze, including me. I just need some fresh air. Reaching the door, I open it slightly and squeeze myself out, trying not to draw attention to myself in the process. It's pitch black out on the patio, with the exception of a few landscape lights that light up the bottom of a few trees.

As my eyes adjust to the darkness, I can see there is a large pool that is surrounded by reclining patio chairs. It's unseasonably warm for this time of year in North Carolina, and I'm still not used to the humidity. The air hangs thick, causing my clothes to stick to me. Kicking off my shoes, I walk to the side of the pool and sit down. I slowly dip my toes into the cool water. I let them fall further until the water is midway up my calves.

Kicking my legs slowly, the cool water and the fresh air relax me a bit. Over my shoulder, I look back at the house and watch the party continue. People are talking, laughing, and enjoying themselves. That used to be me. God, I want to be fun again. I lift the red plastic cup to my lips and toss back the remainder of my vodka cranberry. I can feel the effects of the alcohol after tossing back three cups of the sweet concoction.

"Watcha doin', baby girl?"

I hear his voice behind me and I snap my head around to find where he is, but I don't see him.

"Landon, is that you?"

"Better be, unless someone else is calling you 'baby girl.'" He snickers and finally shows himself as he walks toward me.

"What are you doing? You know it's a little creepy, you hanging in a dark backyard by yourself, sneaking up on people," I snap at him.

"Isn't that what you're doing? Sitting out here by yourself."

"Touché, but I'm not sneaking up on anyone."

He crosses the large paved patio and sits down next to me. He's wearing tan cargo shorts and a white button-down shirt with the sleeves rolled up.

"I wasn't outside creeping. See those doors over there?" he says, pointing to the far side of the house, which is pitch black.

"Where? I can't see them," I say as a hiccup escapes me.

"Well, those doors lead to my bedroom. I was in my room and decided to come out here to get some air. Looks like you had the same idea."

I shake my head in agreement. "Yup. I don't do well in large groups of people that I don't know," I quip. At least not anymore, I think to myself.

"Please don't take this the wrong way, but I have to ask." There is a long pause as he contemplates asking me whatever is about to piss me off. "Why are you so pissed at everyone? It's like you have a stick up your ass. You're pissed at the world, Jess."

"I do *not* have a stick up my ass, and I'm not pissed at the world," I protest. Now he's laughing harder.

"Every time I'm with you, there are these moments when you close yourself off. You shut down and become very cold. I just know you'd be so much fun if you just relaxed a little, that's all. I can see it in you."

"See what?" I ask as I contemplate what he's just told me.

"Fun. I see a fun Jess," he answers quietly. I don't respond to him. I used to be fun. I used to be carefree and happy and not so bitter and sad.

"Yeah, maybe," I admit.

"So let's have fun...well, I'm going to have fun," he says, jumping up. "I'll be right back."

Shit. I can only imagine what he's up to. A case of nerves hits me, and my stomach does a small flip, and I'm not sure if it's the nerves or the alcohol that is causing this reaction. Landon disappears into the dark where he had just come from. The utter presence of him makes me entirely too nervous. He's much older than I am, but more than that, he's intimidating in a sexy kind of way. He has a take-charge personality and doesn't mince words or actions. He demands my attention when we're together; he doesn't ask me to do things with him, he demands, or rather, insists.

"Shit. Shit. Shit," I murmur to myself.

"What's that, baby girl?" he says, reappearing and holding a bottle in one hand and a small shot glass in the other.

"Uh, what's that?" I hiss at him.

"Tequila."

"You are a cop. You cannot give me alcohol. Wouldn't that be contributing to the delinquency of a minor?" I razz him.

"Yeah, yeah. Looks like you've already contributed to your own delinquency." He kicks the empty red plastic cup out of the way as he sits down next to me. "Plus, this is for me." He raises and shakes his eyebrows at me. "Oh, and by the way, you're not leaving here tonight." His lips twist into an evil smile.

"I'm not staying here," I fire back at him.

"Yes, you are. You're staying with Lindsay. It's not open for discussion. You've been drinking, Linds has been drinking, everyone at this damn house has been drinking, and I'm about to start as well. You are not leaving here tonight. *Comprende?*" His tone is firm with me. I had forgotten all about Lindsay. *Fuck.*

"By the way, remind me to talk to Lindsay about having parties at my house without talking to me first, will ya?" Oh shit. Lindsay never told him about the party? No wonder he was in his room. He was probably pissed off.

When he sticks his feet in the water next to mine, the bottle of cheap tequila and a shot glass situated between us, my mind wanders back to the day I rode on the back of his motorcycle. My arms around his taut stomach, the smell of his masculine body wash and testosterone all mixed together.

"Couldn't have bought better tequila?" I grumble, looking straight ahead over the pool. That elicits a deep belly laugh from him.

"So you have experience with tequila?" Landon asks coyly.

"Maybe a little," I snicker. "Remember who raised me. Mexicans do not drink shitty tequila," I announce.

We sit in silence for a few minutes. I'm leaning back with my arms extended out behind me, propping me up, and my legs still dangling in the pool water.

Pushing myself up, I reach for the tequila bottle and twist the gold cap off. Lifting the large bottle up, I pour a shot for me. He raises his eyebrows and I can tell he's wondering what in the hell I'm doing. Grabbing the shot glass, I raise it in the air between us. *"Salud,"* I say, and he never takes his eyes off of me.

I toss the fiery liquid to the back of my throat. I've learned that getting it down in one swallow with as little of it touching your tongue is the way to shoot tequila. Shaking my head from side to side in disgust, I let out a small grunt while my body shudders. A small chuckle leaves his lips as he reaches out to rub my arm, which has broken out in goose bumps from a combination of nerves and shitty tequila.

Setting the shot glass down between us, I try to focus on keeping the tequila down in my belly. I continue to slowly kick my legs in the water, and I can feel his eyes trained on me, along with the alcohol burning in my stomach. Hearing him shift, I try to see what he's doing out of the corner of my eye. He's pouring himself a shot, and he raises the glass and salutes me in return. Tossing back the shot, he immediately pours himself another one and tosses the second one back.

I almost gag at the sight of him taking two shots of that shitty tequila, as I can still taste it on the back of my tongue. I don't think I could do another shot of tequila without losing it all over this pool deck.

"Where are your keys?" Landon whispers.

"Seriously? I'm not going to drink and drive. I'll stay with Lindsay, all right. Just relax." I realize how bitchy that just came out.

He obviously doesn't care about my little outburst as a smile tugs at the corners of his mouth, and he nods at me in understanding. Silence fills the air, except for the small laps of water that hit the side of the pool from me fluttering my feet. Landon lies down on the pool deck. With his hands behind his head, he looks up at the sky, feet still hanging in the water.

I'm starting to feel a little fuzzy from the three drinks earlier and the shot of tequila, and I have to use the restroom. Pulling my feet out of the water, and pushing myself to stand up, I search for my flip-flops in the dark.

"Where do you think you're going?" he asks.

"I'm not leaving if that's what you're asking. I have to brave the crowd in there to find the restroom," I say, spotting my flip-flops. Walking over to them, I bend down and line them up so I can slide my wet feet into them. As I right myself, I wobble and step back, catching myself.

"Not so fast, baby girl," he says, jumping to his feet. Moving quickly across the patio, he closes the distance, and instantly wraps his arms around my waist from behind, steadying me. Leaning forward, he rests his chin on my shoulder. I can feel his warm breath on my neck. My pulse quickens, and I take a deep breath, smelling the light scent of his body wash and tequila. Turning his head, I can feel how close his lips are to my ear, and it sends shivers down my body.

He tenses slightly when he feels my shiver and slowly unwraps his arms from my waist. Still standing behind me, he runs his hands down both of my arms, sending another quivering wave through me. There is something in his touch that triggers a response in me. Slowly, his hands reach mine, and he moves around to the front of me. Taking my hand in his, he tugs me forward slightly.

"Follow me," he whispers as he guides me through the dark, down a paved walkway to double French doors. Turning the handle, he pushes one of the doors, and I feel a rush of cool air escape from the room and brush across my face. Stepping inside, he pulls me closer and guides me through the room. The room is dark, but I can make out large objects: a bed, a dresser, nightstands, and an oversized chair.

I can hear him open another door as he runs his hand up and down the wall. He flips a switch and light appears, filling the small room that I see is a bathroom.

"There you go. I'll wait right here for you."

I step inside the bathroom, turning to close the door behind me, but I can't because he's still standing in the doorway, staring at me. When I tilt my head at him, he finally backs up slightly.

"Do you need water?"

"I'm okay; just a little wobbly." I giggle, shutting the door and flipping the lock on the handle.

"Be careful," I hear him say through the door.

Shaking my head, I can't help but smile. "Over protective much?" I say back through the door.

"You're killing me, woman," he mutters back at me. I can't help but giggle.

After I'm done relieving myself, I adjust my almost too short denim skirt and straighten my black lace-trimmed tank top. Washing my hands, I check myself out in the mirror. I grab a tissue from the box on the counter and wipe under my eyes where it looks like my eyeliner is bleeding. The damn humidity does not help my make-up situation.

My cheeks are pink and flushed, probably from drinking, or it could be from the way my body reacts when Landon touches me. Swallowing hard, I turn to the door and open it slowly. Landon is sitting on the side of his bed, waiting for me, and a small lamp on his bedside table is on.

"Feel better?" he asks, handing me a cold bottle of water. Unscrewing the cap, I nod my head yes at him and take a small sip of water. Landon stands up and moves closer to me, watching me drink the water. We maintain eye contact as I continue to drink. A small smile crosses his face, and before I even realize what is happening, large arms wrap around me and push me up against the wall.

The bottle of water falls from my hands and splashes both of us on its way to the floor. Landon kicks the bottle of water out of the way, and presses himself closer to me. Since he's taller than I am, he lowers his head slightly and, without warning, presses his warm lips to mine. Not moving, he leaves his lips pressed against mine, waiting for my reaction.

My heart feels like it's going to beat out of my chest, but my body reacts differently. My body relaxes slightly under his grip, and a low moan escapes the back of my throat. My lips separate slightly, inviting him in, and he accepts the invitation, devouring my mouth.

I taste the slightest hints of cinnamon and tequila; his lips are soft and intoxicating. Gently nipping my bottom lip, he runs his tongue over my top lip, and my breath hitches. My legs are wobbly, and if he wasn't holding me against the wall, I know my legs would fail me.

His arm is snaked around my body, resting along my lower back. Pulling me forward slightly, he presses me against the front of him. My head falls back against the wall, and he immediately moves in to assault my neck. As he gently kisses and sucks, my body tingles and trembles from his touch.

He begins walking backwards and pulls me with him at the same time, while never taking his mouth off of my neck.

Twisting us around, I can feel the edge of the tall bed just behind my thighs as he pushes us down onto the soft mattress.

For a split second, thoughts of Gabe fill my mind as I feel Landon's firm body on top of mine. I've never slept with anyone other than Gabe, and my body has never reacted this way to anyone other than him. It was always supposed to be Gabe. Me and Gabe. No one else. Landon uses his hips to push me further up into the middle of the bed, and his mouth has moved from my neck to my chest. He pulls my leg up and wraps it around his waist, and naturally, my other leg follows.

Pulling my arms above my head, he uses his hand to hold them in place, lacing his fingers through the fingers on both of my hands. He shifts his hips and presses his erection into me. My denim skirt is above my waist, and the only things that separate us are my thin silk panties and his khaki cargo shorts.

My body is tingling, and I feel close to losing control. My hips are rocking slightly, and he gently squeezes my nipples through my tank top, causing me to gasp. My hips rock faster, and he continues to press his erection into me. My hands are still above my head as he presses kisses across my chest and back up to my lips.

"Landon," I whisper.

"Shh…don't talk. Just feel."

"Oh God, please, Landon…"

"Shh…"

The only sounds in the room are the deep breaths and the light noises our bodies are making. Kissing me again, he presses his erection into me harder, and I realize how close to the edge of losing it I am. My breathing quickens, and I wrap my legs around him tighter, holding him firmly in place.

"Don't come," he whispers across my lips.

My legs aren't doing a very good job of holding him in place because he thrusts again, and I'm on the cusp of losing it and giving in to the throbbing between my legs. A moan escapes me.

"Not yet. I will tell you when you can, understand?" he demands. My panties are soaked and my legs are shaking. "Open your eyes and look at me," he instructs. It isn't until he tells me to open my eyes that I realize I've kept them so tightly closed.

"Open your eyes now," he mutters again against my lips, pressing firm kisses on me.

When I open them, our eyes meet, and we stay focused on each other. I'm trying to ignore the pulsing between my legs, the goose bumps across my skin, and the rapid beating of my heart. Without blinking, he presses himself up against me one more time, causing my body to shudder. My legs clench around him.

"Not yet. Do you understand me?"

"Please," I beg.

"No. I will tell you when."

"Oh, God," I moan again as I begin to feel the tingles start spreading through my lower half.

My eyes roll back, but I shake my head yes in understanding. His hand pinches both of my nipples again, but slowly, he moves his hand downward. Lifting his hips away from my center, he offers me a temporary reprieve until his fingers push away my panties to one side. With a gasp, his fingers find that center of nerves that is about to explode.

"Please," I beg some more. My legs are shaking, and I can't stop moving my hips. If it didn't feel so good, I would consider this torture.

Gently rubbing me, he reminds me again, "Do not come yet. I will tell you when." The pad of his thumb is working my clit, rubbing it side to side with gentle presses, and I honestly can't breathe anymore.

"So wet and so swollen," he mutters, continuing to strum me with his thumb. Sliding back in one fluid motion, he settles himself on his knees between my legs. "Leave your hands above your head." I obey. There is something in the way he orders me that I don't question, I don't refuse.

He pulls my panties down and off of my legs. I begin to panic. I can't do this yet, not with him. My legs are shaking, but he finds that spot again and pinches and presses, bringing me back to the edge, and it feels so good.

Running his fingers down through my swollen lips, he continues rubbing me. "So wet." A low growl escapes him. "I need to taste you."

"Landon…" Before I can say no, his tongue is wreaking havoc on me. I gasp for breath, arching my back off the bed. I feel his tongue brush my clit, and I can't hold it any longer. My legs are shaking and everything between my legs is pulsing.

"Please. I have to now," I beg.

With one last swipe of his tongue, I begin my fall. Just as ecstasy takes over my body, I feel him slip two fingers in me, and this is where I'm not ready to go. My chest caves like it has a ton of bricks on it. I can't breathe and my throat tightens.

"Stop. Please," I cry out, snapping my legs together as tightly as I can. Tears leak from my eyes and roll down the sides of my face and into my hair. "Please," I cry, pulling my hands over my face.

He freezes, but does exactly as I ask him. He crawls up to me in a panic and pulls me into his arms.

"What's wrong? Did I hurt you? God, please tell me I didn't hurt you." I can hear the panic and concern in his voice. He's squeezing me into his chest, hugging me and rocking me.

Shaking my head no, a giant sob breaks free; I pull out of his arms, rolling to my side. Pulling my skirt down, I still feel so exposed. Landon pulls me into him again as I fight him, trying to break free from his grasp, but he won't let me go.

"Shh... it's okay," he says over and over again, holding my head to his chest while I shake and cry. "Jess, talk to me. What happened? What did I do?"

I can't answer him, because it's not him; it's me. I cry for what seems like hours. Landon never loosens his grip on me, but every few minutes, he squeezes my arm, or kisses the back of my head to let me know he's still there. As embarrassed as I am, I feel safe with him, and I'm not ready to leave the safety of his arms. It's the same feeling I felt with Gabe—safe—and that's comforting to me, yet selfish, I know.

My breathing finally settles as my crying subsided minutes ago. Landon shifts slightly on the bed, still holding me, not loosening his grip on me. In one swift move, he pulls us up to a sitting position. He rests his back against the large wooden headboard on his bed and pulls me tightly against him, my back to his chest.

Loosening his grip a little, he runs his hands up and down my arms in a move to comfort me. I feel him press his lips against the back of my head, leaving them there before pulling his lips away and resting his forehead against the back of my head.

"Talk to me, baby girl, please," he begs. His voice is full of concern. "Please tell me what happened."

I don't know if it's the alcohol, or the fact that I'm hiding behind a façade that I am okay because I'm not. Something inside me actually wants to tell him, to be honest with someone other than Dr. Peterson. My heart races, but this time, I force myself to calm down. Taking two deep breaths, I clear my throat and, with a swallow, I murmur, "I was raped."

Chapter Thirty-Nine

-LANDON-

I honestly don't know if I heard her correctly. I push her forward slightly and, turning her by her shoulders to face me, her head drops forward and her long brown hair hangs loosely, covering her beautiful face. I realize I'm gripping her upper arms rather tightly, but I'm so afraid she'll run away from me.

"Look at me," I say quietly, yet firm. I mean it. She shakes her head from side to side in little movements.

"Jessica, look at me." I pronounce each word softly. Her chest is heaving in and out, and I see tears dripping from her face onto her bare legs, which are crossed in front of us. Slowly, she lifts her head, tears running down her cheeks like little streams, and our eyes finally meet. The large green irises appear even greener, as the whites of her eyes are stained pink from her crying.

Releasing one of her arms, I use my free hand to wipe the tears from each of her cheeks, and then place my hand back on her arm to hold her up gently. "I need you to repeat what you just said to me." I swallow hard. My mouth has gone dry as I wait for her to repeat what she said. I know what she said, but I fucking pray to God that I heard her wrong. Her head drops again slightly, but this time, I catch her chin and hold her head in place.

"Baby, talk to me." As I lift her chin a little higher, her eyes finally meet mine. With a deep breath, she mutters those three words that cause my stomach to clench again.

"I was raped," she whispers again. This time, her head doesn't fall forward, but she shifts her eyes away from me; she doesn't want to look at me. Large tears continue to fall from her eyes and down her cheeks. I've never seen such large tears. I can feel her body trembling underneath my grip as I watch her lip and chin quiver. My stomach is in knots, and if I wasn't so concerned about her state of mind, I'd fucking punch something. To see this perfect girl so scared, so broken, kills me.

"When?" I ask, not sure I really want to know the answer or that it really matters, but it's the first thing that comes out of my mouth.

"Three months ago," she replies quietly, in between short gasping breaths, and I inhale sharply at how recent that was.

My body is overcome with anger, and hate roils its way through my veins. I pull my hand away from her chin and release her arms. Wrapping both of mine around her, I pull her into my lap, cradling her. Without thinking, without asking, I kiss her forehead repeatedly. Small, soft kisses. Holding her, I think about the animal that could do this to another person, but especially to Jess. As a police officer, my mind is flooded with many questions I want to ask her; Did they catch him? Did she know him? But as the man that loves her, I just want to comfort her.

I replay every encounter I've had with her, thinking about the last couple of months of getting to know her. Her behaviors and moods make more sense. Every bad mood, every snarky response, every downcast eye, every time she's pulled away; her trust issues have all been the walls she's constructed to protect herself. I know these walls, but for very different reasons.

She pulls herself out of my lap, and I let her go. I want her to feel safe and not constrained. She positions herself cross-legged in front of me and grabs a small pillow, placing it on her lap, over her short skirt. Her hands are twisting around each other, shaking on top of the pillow. I reach out and stop both of her hands with one of mine. Looking up at me, I see it. The sadness that has always been there, but now I recognize the pain behind it.

"I need you to listen to me for a minute and not say anything, please," I beg her. I need for her to let me talk before she says anything. But most importantly, I need her to trust me.

"Okay," she says, her voice still trembling.

"If I had any idea, whatsoever, that this had happened to you, I would never have touched you like that. I need you to know that I would never take advantage of you, or pressure you to do anything that you weren't comfortable with."

She nods her head at me and maintains eye contact. "You also know that what happened to you wasn't your fault, right?" She nods her head again, and her eyes fill with tears.

"Will you tell me what happened?" I ask her, hoping that she trusts me enough to tell me. Dropping her eyes again, she looks at our hands intertwined on the pillow that is sitting on her lap. For what feels like minutes, we sit. Her eyes are downcast and focused on our hands, which remain linked in a tight knot. With a gentle squeeze and a deep breath, she quietly starts talking. I hold my breath and hang on every word she's speaking.

With her bottom lip quivering and her chin in a small pucker, I see the strength and bravery in the words she's whispering to me. I take in every minor detail from the name of the park she's running in to the song she's listening to on her phone.

For the next hour, she tells me every last detail of what happened to her. There are times I don't know if I can bear the details, but I don't stop her. This is her story and she needs to tell it. At times, I'm overcome with sadness and other times, I'm overcome with anger…for her. But it's when she speaks of Gabe that I'm overcome with jealousy.

Silence fills the space around us. I don't know if she's done talking or gathering her thoughts, so I give her time. She releases her death grip on my hand and lies down on the bed, her head propped on my pillow. She just stares at me, blinking slowly. She has spoken nonstop for the last hour and didn't cry. I'm overwhelmed for her. Sliding off the bed, I walk to my dresser. I pull out a white tank top undershirt and pair of boxer shorts that will undoubtedly be too big for her, but I take them to her anyway.

"Change into these. I'm going to go get you some water and Tylenol." I hand her the tank top and boxers.

Opening my bedroom door, I find her sitting on the side of the bed, her long legs dangling out from the wide opening of my boxer shorts. My tank top fits her snugly, showing every curve of her upper body. I hand her the two Tylenol. She pops them and swallows with a sip of water. She stands up and starts walking toward the door.

"Jess, take my bed, please. I'll sleep on the couch." With a slight smile, she doesn't argue, but walks over to the far side of the bed. Pulling the covers down, she stands next to the bed, looking at it. I turn to leave the room and hear her slide into my bed and under the covers.

"Wait. I don't want to sleep alone tonight."

For just a moment, I'm overcome with happiness. Not because she wants me to sleep with her, but because she feels safe with me. She trusts me. I feel a tug at my heart, which is such a foreign feeling for me, as I walk back toward the bed. Sliding into bed, I leave my cargo shorts on and reach to shut off the small table lamp. Careful as I lie down, I am sure to keep my distance from her to give her as much space as she wants or needs.

Raising my arms above my head, I relax into my place. Within seconds, she wiggles over and wraps herself around me, her arm across my chest and her long legs twisted in between mine. She's pressed up against my side, and her face is pressed to the side of my chest.

I lower my arms from above my head and twist slightly to wrap myself around her. It's comfortable and peaceful.

"Landon?"

"Yeah, baby girl?"

"Thank you," she whispers, her lips pressed to my chest.

"For what? I didn't do anything."

"For not running away from me. For listening to me and caring about me," she replies.

"It sounds like you have a lot of people that care about you," I whisper. Listening to her breathing settle into short, shallow breaths, I know she's asleep. Feeling her heart beat against my chest, I close my eyes and feel a sense of contentment. For the first time in my life, I decide that I'm going to do the right thing, even though it may be the hardest thing I ever do. I'm letting her go.

I could love waking up to her warm body wrapped all around me every morning. Her long legs are still tucked in between mine, and her arm is tightly wrapped around my chest. There is absolutely no way I'm going to be able to slip out of bed without waking her. Running my index finger down her arm, I quietly whisper, trying to wake her without startling.

"Baby girl, time to wake up." I continue to run my finger up and down her arm as she starts to rouse. Rolling her arm and chest off of me, she slides her legs out from mine so that she is now lying flat on her back. Rubbing her eyes, she mumbles something inaudible and rolls over onto her stomach, burying her face in the pillow.

I want so badly to touch her, to finish what we started last night, but then I remember the promise I made to myself. *Let her go.* I rub her back gently and lean in close to her ear.

"Time to get up, baby girl," I whisper again, brushing her hair off of her shoulders and back, sweeping it over to one side, so I can see her face.

"Why?" she grumbles.

"We've got somewhere to go," I say, pushing myself off the bed.

Rolling over, she opens one eye and scrunches her face at me.

"Who's 'we'? Because I have nowhere to be this morning." She smiles the cutest smile at me. Sitting down on the edge of the bed, I'm cautious of how close I am to her. I grab her hands and pull her up into a sitting position.

"I have an appointment and I want you to come with me."

"An appointment? It's a Saturday. The dentist is closed and the doctor's offices are closed." She's so damn cute when she gets all sarcastic. "What kind of appointment?" she asks curiously.

"It's a surprise. Just please get up. I need to get you home and changed so you can go with me, okay?" She grumbles and throws herself back down on the bed.

"Fine," she mumbles as I hop off the bed and walk toward the bathroom.

"I mean it; we'll be late. Up! Get dressed and be ready to go when I'm done. I'll take you home so you can shower and change."

Shutting the bathroom door behind me, I hear her grumble again. The shower is on and steaming up the bathroom. Brushing my teeth quickly, I step out of my shorts and into the hot shower. I didn't sleep well last night. I couldn't stop thinking about what Jess told me, and I just wanted to hold her, and remember how she felt in my arms. Rinsing the shampoo out of my hair, I feel a rush of cool air drift across my body, and I hear the click of the shower door before I see her standing in front of me. All of her naked, tanned perfection.

"What are you doing?" My voice is tense. Sighing, she takes two small steps forward, and our bodies are mere inches from each other.

"You're in a hurry. I thought this would save us some time." Taking a step back, I reach above me to adjust the showerhead so that the water is coming down right between us. Turning around so her back is to me, she tips her head back, letting the hot water run through her long brown hair. I can't help but look at her long back, all the way down to her ass. Every inch of her screams "sexy."

"I don't think this is a good idea," I say, trying to be gentle in my delivery. Turning back around, she closes her eyes and steps forward into the stream of water, letting it run down her face. I watch the trail of water as it runs down her face, over her chest, and off her tight nipples. My mind wants her out of this shower, but my body wants to take her up against the wall. It's a battle of willpower for me. *Fuck*.

Reaching around me for the bottle of shampoo, she leans in, pressing her breasts against my chest. I can feel her nipples brush against me. I try to act unaffected, taking a step back from her, but my body defies me. I'm instantly hard. *Fuck*. Again.

She takes notice of my condition and smirks, lathering the shampoo in her hair. Turning around again, she tips her head back into the water, rinsing the shampoo from her hair. Reaching for the sponge, I flip the cap on the body wash and squirt a decent amount. Flexing my hand, I work the body wash into the sponge and press it to her back.

She freezes at my touch. Looking back over her shoulder at me, she takes a step backwards into me, and I start circling her back with the sponge. Pulling her hair over her shoulder, I work the sponge over her shoulders, down her arms, and to her lower back. I want so badly to drop the sponge and use my hands lathered in body wash to cover every centimeter of her tanned flesh.

As I stand up, our mouths are inches apart, and even with the hot water, I can feel her hot breath against my lips. She presses her hands against my chest and, this time, I tense under her touch. I want so badly to wrap my arms around her and take her right here, but I stand still. Closing my eyes, my head drops back into the stream of hot water.

"About last night, I'm sorry. I would never have gone as far if I had…"

She cuts me off, pressing her index finger against my lips to shush me. "I should have told you before I let it get as far as it did." Her voice trails off and she looks past me, her eyes heavy.

"I just wanted to feel your lips on my lips and your hands on my body before you knew what happened to me. Before you decided I was too damaged to touch." I flinch at her comment. "I'm so fucked up. One minute, I want you to touch me, and the next, I can't handle being touched." Her hands move down my chest, to my stomach, and back up. With a small step forward, she's pressed up against me. Both of us are standing under the water, eyes locked on each other. I want to make a move so badly, but the promises I made to myself last night are flashing through my mind. *Let her go. Let her go. Let her go.*

"I've been working through this with my therapist." She pauses, staring at my chest. Her hands move down as she wraps her arms around my waist and presses the side of her face to my chest. Without hesitation, my arms instantly wrap around her in return. Standing for minutes in this embrace, I don't want to ruin the moment, but I know we are running late. I pull back from her, reaching for the handle to shut the shower off.

She steps out of the shower and grabs two bath towels. Tossing one at me, she smiles a sweet genuine smile while she wraps herself in the other towel. I love seeing her like this: happy, confident, and beautiful.

"Like what you see?" she asks with a little giggle. I realize I've been staring at her.

"Always. You're beautiful." Her cheeks blush at my compliment. "You're stunning, Jess." She looks back at me and bursts out laughing.

"What are you laughing at?"

"Are you going to stand there and drip dry with that towel slung over your shoulder and toss compliments at me all day, or are you going to dry off?" She laughs.

"Shit." I grab the towel off my shoulder and wrap it around my waist. Walking past her, I give her ass a hard smack through the towel she's wrapped in. I grab my clothes and head to the bedroom to change. She's still in fits of giggles as I close the door behind me.

Once again, she is looking at me like I have two heads.

"Why can't we just take your car?"

"Because we're young and wild and free, and we only live once. Hop your sweet ass onto the bike, or we're going to be late."

"Whatever, Wiz." She rolls her eyes and mumbles at my reference to being wild and young and free, but she hops onto the back of my bike and gets settled in. She pulls an elastic band off her wrist and pulls her hair into a big messy ponytail, and puts her small Ray-Ban aviator glasses on. There is nothing sexier than she is at this moment.

"Ready," she says as she stuffs a tube of Chapstick into the front pocket of her cut-off jean shorts that she borrowed from Lindsay.

"Let's do this," I say, getting on the bike and starting it up. Selfishly, I know I should just drive my car, but I love the way she feels pressed up against me, her thighs bracing me. I know that this will be the last time I will have her on the back of my bike, so I'm going to enjoy every minute of it.

She wraps her arms around me and presses her cheek to my back, and her fingers press against my stomach as she holds onto me and we wind through the streets. Pulling into the parking lot of a small brick building, I park my bike and cut the engine.

"Where are we?" she asks, looking around while sliding off the seat.

"Told you. It's a surprise," I say, grabbing her hand. She laces her fingers with mine, and I pull her toward me. Walking up to the small building, she sidles up next to me, unsure of what we're doing. The building has no signage except for a neon sign in the front window that flashes "open."

Opening the front door, I motion for her to enter first. She puts her sunglasses on top of her head, and eyes me tentatively.

"Joey!" I announce and look around for my friend.

"What is this place?" she whispers. The front reception area has a leather couch and loveseat, but is non-telling of where we're really at.

"You'll see." I smile at her. I know that the nondisclosure is driving her crazy.

"Landon!" Joey announces, rounding the corner from the hallway that leads back to the four stations in the back. Joey walks up to me and shakes my hand. "And who do we have here?" he asks, looking at Jess, which causes her to press herself closer to my side.

"Nice to meet you, I'm Joey," he says, offering his hand for her to shake. Politely, she reaches out and shakes his hand, but does not remove the death grip she has on mine.

"Jessica," she replies. "Nice to meet you as well."

"Well, let's do this, shall we?" Joey smiles, his voice full of energy and enthusiasm. Leading the way, Joey turns and begins walking down the hallway, and we follow suit. Turning into the large bright room, she gasps when she sees where we are. Her eyes are large, and she squeezes my hand, turning to look at me. Her lips curl into a smile.

"You're getting another tattoo?" she whispers. Leaning down, I rub my nose into her hair and kiss the top of her head.

"Yes, and I wanted you here with me while I did it." Her smile is huge and her eyes light up with excitement.

"Have any ink?" Joey asks her.

"I've always wanted one, but I'm too afraid," she admits quietly.

"Nothing to be afraid of, I tell ya. Once you get one, you can't stop. Just look at our guy here." Joey smirks. "I'll be right back. In the meantime, lie down on the table and take off your shirt," he directs me.

"Pull up a chair, sweetheart." He barks orders as he leaves the room. I pull back my t-shirt over my head, and my white gold crucifix I'm wearing dangles from my neck. Jess walks over and places her hand over the top of the cross, pressing it against my chest. I wonder what she's doing, but I don't ask.

"What are you getting?" she asks quietly.

"A saying that I tell myself every morning," I whisper back.

Her eyes find mine. "What is the saying?"

"*Vive ut vivas.*"

"What does it mean?" She moves closer, not moving her hand from my chest or from the crucifix.

"Live so that you may live." There is silence while she takes in the meaning of the saying. I take her hand off of my chest and bring it to my lips, kissing each one of her fingers. I take my time because I know, after today, I won't see her or touch her again.

"Live so that you may live," she whispers.

I tug on her hand, pulling her down to me. I place small kisses on the center of her forehead between each word, "*Vive ut vivas*," as if I'm pushing those words into her subconscious.

"Live so that you may live," she whispers again. She pulls back from me when Joey comes bounding back into the room, carrying a sheet of transfer paper. I lie still on the table. Joey hands me a small pillow that I tuck under my head with my free hand, still holding Jess' hand with my other.

"Ready, big guy?" he asks. Sitting down in a chair that is next to the table, she's right by my side. I give her hand a small squeeze, willing her to calm down. She's been running her thumb in a fast movement across the top of my hand. My squeeze slows her thumb considerably. Joey preps my chest, shaving the area and cleaning it. She gasps when she looks at Joey press the transfer sheet to my chest.

"Jesus Christ, that's huge," she bellows. Joey laughs at her reaction, but doesn't flinch as he places the paper across my chest. Pressing it on, he removes the paper and hands me a mirror.

"It's perfect." The large font follows the curve of the top of my chest, from just under each collar bone. Joey grabs the tattoo gun and begins working. Since it's black and in a simple English-style font, it won't take long. Jess watches the needles glide across my skin.

"Does it hurt?" she whispers, squeezing my hand.

"No. I'm used to it. This is my eighth tattoo." I point to the others that mark my arms and chest.

"So it doesn't hurt?"

"Not really. Some pinching here and there, and every once in a while, he'll hit a sensitive spot, but for the most part, it doesn't hurt; it's just uncomfortable at times." Joey continues his work across my chest, not talking while he's working; he's focused intently on the job at hand. He's a legend in this town when it comes to tattoos. He has done every single one of mine. Jess sits, impatiently bobbing her legs up and down, chewing on her bottom lip.

"Hey, Joey," she asks.

"What's up, sweetheart?" He stops, looking up at her.

"Got time for one more when you're done?"

"Really?" I ask her.

"Live so that you may live," she responds with a smile, and I can't help but want to jump off this table and pull her into a hug.

"I think I can squeeze you in, sweetheart," Joey responds, looking at me, then chuckling as he puts the finishing touches on my chest.

CHAPTER FORTY

~Jess~

Looking at my inner wrist, which is wrapped with a thin piece of gauze, I catch him looking out the corner of his eye at me.

"You said it wouldn't hurt," I growl at him.

He bursts out laughing. "I don't have a tattoo on my inner wrist. I didn't know it was one of the most painful places to put a tattoo." He can hardly speak, he's laughing so hard. "I can't believe you cried." His roars of laughter just keep coming. Shaking my head, I narrow my eyes at him, trying not to laugh along with him. I can't believe I cried either, but it hurt, bad. Fortunately, the single word I put on my inner wrist in a delicate script took Joey all of ten minutes from start to finish.

"So are you going to tell me what it means?" he asks, shaking off his fits of laughter, trying to be serious with me.

"Maybe," I say, still pissed at him for making fun of me. When he raises his eyebrow at me, I roll my eyes at him. "Fine, it says *Infragilis*."

"Yeah, I got that much. But what does it mean?" he asks.

"Google it," I respond, my mood lightening a bit, but giving him a hard time.

"Even though I don't know what it means, I like what you chose," he says, trying to lighten my mood some more. "It looks nice."

"I do too. Joey made a great recommendation with the white ink." I smile at him. We left the tattoo shop and drove to a little burger shop here on the beach. Ordering dinner, we eat at a small table on the patio, overlooking the beautiful green water.

"Let's walk," he says, his tone somber. Kicking at the sand as we walk the beach, he reaches for my hand, and I reluctantly take it, lacing my fingers through his. We walk for a bit, not saying anything, but just enjoying the comfort of each other's company. Tugging at my arm, he sits down in the sand and gently guides me down next to him. It's late afternoon and there is a light breeze. It's warm and comfortable, and the sand is warm underneath us. The sun is slowly descending out above the water, and there is no one else on this stretch of beach.

We sit side by side, watching the small waves lap at the shoreline. "You need to call him," he says, not looking at me, but staring straight ahead out at the water. I turn my entire body to face him and lay my legs over his.

"Call who?" I ask.

"Gabe," he sighs. I feel his hand inadvertently clench. Turning his head, he looks at me. For the first time today, there is no happiness in those beautiful blue eyes. His face is devoid of any emotion, and I see the muscles in his neck clench when he swallows. I don't say anything as I study his gorgeous tan face.

"What are you afraid of?" he asks me quietly, running his finger over the bandage on the inside of my wrist. Looking back to me, he waits for his answer.

My throat tightens as I form the words. "Everything. I'm afraid of everything. I'm afraid to feel again. Being numb is easy." Now I'm the one looking out over the water. His grip on my hand tightens.

"Look at me." I turn back to meet those perfect blue eyes. Where they are normally full of life, they are full of sadness and hurt. His day-old stubble sits perfectly along his chiseled jaw line and around his chin and mouth. "Never be afraid to feel. It's the only way to really live. If you don't feel, there is no way you can love, heal, or forgive. You'll never move forward or get past this. You have to forgive, Jess."

"What if I'm not ready to forgive?"

"How do you know you're not?"

"Because I'm angry."

"You have every right to be angry, baby girl, but you have to let the hate and anger go. If you can't forgive, it will eat you alive. Trust me." Those words hit me like a ton of bricks. He continues to run his fingers over the gauze taped onto my wrist as we sit in silence.

"I can't call him. He hates me. I hope he hates me as much as I hate myself right now for pushing him away, for not talking to him—for running away. I don't deserve him or his love. I never did." I struggle with the words as tears spill from my eyes.

"I don't know Gabe, but I know there is no way he hates you. There is no hating you; it's impossible." His voice breaks. A small smile crosses my lips with those sweet words, but his face is still, sad.

"Why did you get in the shower with me today?" he asks.

My heart sinks as he asks me this. I shrug before answering, "I needed you."

"You don't need me, Jess. You need Gabe. I've been a convenient substitute. Are you going to call him?" he asks again. This time, his tone is more demanding.

"What about you?" I ask, my heart racing. I've never been one to be very direct, but I laid all my secrets on the table last night with him. He knows everything. Why not ask him about us?

"What about me?" he bites, his voice bitter. He turns to look directly at me. His eyes are narrowed slightly, and I can't tell if he's mad at me, or if the sun is in his eyes.

"What about us?" I whisper, almost hoping he doesn't hear me.

"There is no *us,* dammit."

I gasp quietly at his words. "Then what have you been doing for the last two months, chasing me around, kissing me, following me home, touching me last night. What was all of that if there is no *us*? Explain that, please," I cry. I'm hurt and upset about thinking of how I almost slept with him last night, showered with him this morning, and how I told him every secret I have. For him to belittle what I thought we had or the trust I had in him and then tell me there isn't an *us* is like a slap in the face.

"Jess." His tone has calmed, and he takes hold of both of my hands. "There can't be an *us* when your heart belongs to someone else." His voice cracks slightly. "The way your face lit up last night when you told me about Gabe, even when it was the bad stuff, the hard stuff, I knew you loved ... I mean ... love him." Tears trickle down my cheeks, falling onto my lap.

"Every time you mention Gabe, a soft smile crosses your lips, your eyes glimmer, and your face lights up. I don't do that to you." His words are laced with sadness. He reaches out and places his hand over my heart. "It's not me that's in there; it's him." My heart breaks with his honesty. Is it possible to love two men, but differently? Because in this moment, I know I do.

"I will never be that guy for you. I want someone who needs me to breathe, to survive, and to love. For you, that's Gabe. It took me two months to see that." Landon drops my hands and they fall into my lap. He doesn't move, doesn't look at me, or say anything else.

"Just call him," he says solemnly.

"I'm not ready," I whisper.

"You'll never be fucking ready if you keep waiting." Sliding my legs off of his, I pull them up to my chest, once again, feeling torn open, vulnerable, and rejected.

"I think I'm ready to go home now," I quietly announce. My statement catches him off guard, but he must see the hurt and sadness on my face, just as I see it spread across his.

"Please don't for one second think I didn't...don't want you," he says, grabbing my hand again as I'm brushing sand off my legs. "For the first time in my life, I actually care about, love someone...you," he pauses, gathering his thoughts. His blue eyes pierce mine as his hand squeezes mine.

"Tell me honestly. Last night when I was touching you...was it me you were thinking about, or was it him?" My heart stops. Remembering last night, my thoughts were of Gabe while Landon's mouth and hands were all over me. As much as I wanted to be touched, it wasn't Landon I wanted touching me, it was Gabe. Closing my eyes, I feel guilt wash through me.

"Tell me," he barks.

"Landon, please," I whisper.

"It was him, wasn't it? It'll always be him. If ever there was a day it was you and I, I want it all from you. I want your body, your heart, your soul. I don't have that. He has all of that. When I touch you and you close your eyes, I want you thinking of me, only me." His breathing is fast, his tone hushed, but full of hurt. "I may be making the biggest mistake of my life right now. But for the first time in my life, I'm trying to think of someone other than myself."

We sit in silence for minutes, neither of us saying anything, just holding hands. I can't deny that I have feelings for Landon, but he's right; it's Gabe that I love—that I will always love. Breaking our contact, Landon gives my hand a light squeeze, then drops it slowly onto my lap. Standing up, he brushes the sand off of his butt before reaching down to pull me up. Before he has a chance to drop my hand, I pull him to me, wrapping myself around him in a tight hug. Pressing my face to his chest, I feel his heart beating rapidly.

As I hold him, I realize his arms stay planted safely at his sides. He doesn't return the hug. He doesn't lower his head to kiss the top of my head as he usually does; he stands firm, hardened. Hurt rolls through me as I hug his tense body and get nothing in return. Releasing him, I quickly walk back up the beach toward the parking lot where his motorcycle is parked. Standing next to his bike, I realize he hasn't followed me. Turning around to see where he is, I find him standing where I left him, down the beach, watching the now-setting sun; his shoulders slumped with his hands in his pockets.

Reaching for my phone to shut off the irritating alarm, I can hardly believe it's Monday morning. The remainder of my weekend was quiet with the exception of the one hundred-plus text messages, phone calls, and voicemails that Lindsay left me, and I have ignored. Sighing, I kick the covers off of me and decide just to get on with this day and get to work.

Pulling into my parking spot at work, I grab my oversized handbag and trudge through the parking lot to the front doors. Weaving my way through the hallways and cubicles, I toss my belongings on my desk and boot up my computer. My head is pounding, and I'm not sure if it's from the emotionally exhausting weekend, the lack of caffeine, or a combination of both. Lindsay stands quietly, almost studying me, at the opening of my cubicle.

"Coffee?" she asks quietly. Turning to look at her, I nod and offer a small smile. "My treat. Let's go," she says.

Following Lindsay out the same doors I just came through, I fall into her car with a loud sigh. Pulling the sunglasses off of her head and putting them on, Lindsay backs out of the parking spot. "You look like shit," she tells me. "So does he," she offers without looking at me. Sighing again, I figure might as well get this conversation over with.

"Are you going to tell me what the hell happened, or am I going to have to sit and watch the both of you be miserable and have no understanding of why?" Lindsay snaps at me.

"Nothing happened and everything happened, Linds," I tell her, my voice breaking. "It's so complicated." Slowing to a stop, she turns to face me.

"He loves you, you know? And he doesn't love," she quietly informs me. Her hands are gripping the steering wheel and her knuckles are turning white. "There's a lot about Landon and me that you don't know, a *lot* of shit." She pauses for a second, looking away from me and out of her driver's side window. "I didn't think he had the ability to love anyone, but he loves you."

Guilt washes over me again, thinking back to Friday night and Saturday. The intimate, but also innocent, moments we shared. However, I'm more stunned at the information that she just spit out. What shit happened to them? Trying to swallow around the lump in my throat, I reach out and touch Lindsay's hand, which is holding onto the steering wheel.

"There is so much I want to tell you; I really do. Just know that where we left things…it's for the best, for both of us." Why is that so hard for me to say? I do care for him, but I know in my heart that I love Gabe.

When she nods slightly, a tear falls from Lindsay's eye and rolls down her cheek. She wipes it away quickly and offers me a tight smile. "I just want him to be happy," she says, pulling away from the stop sign and focusing her attention on the road in front of us. "He deserves it," she says quietly.

"I want him to be happy too," I whisper, and I really mean it.

CHAPTER FORTY-ONE

-Gabe-

As I pull up to my house, I see it looks like a war zone. There are so many cars and trucks parked up and down the street and in the driveway. I don't even know where to park my own damn truck. Luke is in the front yard, talking to a couple of men and appears to have things under control. Parking down the street at Mom and Dad's, I jog the short distance to my new house.

For six weeks, my house has been under renovation and the finishing touches are almost done. Luke and I have been working opposite shifts so that someone is always at the house, supervising the chaos. Even though most of these guys are friends of Dad's, I want someone around to answer questions and provide direction if needed.

Luke's head is tilted up, watching the men install a new roof while scaffolding covers the entire front of my house, providing a lift for the painters.

"Hey, bro." Luke turns toward me when he hears me jog up.

"How's it going?"

"Coming along. They're ahead of schedule. Man, look at how fucking good that new porch looks." Dad talked me into tearing the entire old porch out and spending a little more money to build a newer, larger one since the old one was impossible to salvage due to dry rot.

"It does look good, doesn't it? I want to go inside and see the kitchen," I say, patting Luke on the back.

Inside, the house smells of fresh paint and wood sealer. We kept the original wood floors and had them resurfaced and sealed. They look amazing all cleaned up and stained. Every wall was taken down to the studs, and new electrical and plumbing was run throughout the entire house. In a sense, this is basically a brand new home.

We ended up making larger structural changes, and I have to say, it was so worth it. In the kitchen, I went with all new cabinets in a dark rich cherry wood with light brown granite counters. A new large kitchen island was installed with a smaller second sink off to one side, and overhead pendant lighting that drops over the center of the island.

I hate cooking and don't plan to spend much time in this room, but I'd say that this is impressive. Top of the line stainless steel appliances complete the kitchen. Dad said it was important to have an upgraded kitchen for resale, as this is the room that will typically sell a house.

There are men moving all around the house, coming and going through every door. New tile was installed in the kitchen and the bathrooms, and now, all new fixtures are going into both bathrooms. I'm really happy with the results and how quickly the remodel has happened.

"So," Luke says. "You'll be around for the next couple of days to wrap up all the loose ends around here, right?"

"Yep." I nod as I take in all the small details that have really transformed this old house.

"After today, all that's left is new trim throughout the house and finishing up the exterior. I'm glad you went with all new windows," he says, turning around to notice the expansive living room. "Really opened up this room."

I nod my head in agreement. I went well over my initial budget, but every penny was worth it as I look around at how this bungalow was transformed.

"So have you decided what you're, ah, going to do with it yet?" Luke asks. We haven't discussed this part of it. Do I sell it? I designed this place with Jess in mind. All of this was what she mentioned she would love or showed me pictures of. Or do I stay for a while? Settle into the first home I've ever bought?

"Not sure yet," I reply honestly, because I really don't know what I'm going to do. Dad thinks I should list it right away, positive that it will sell and make me a large profit in the improving housing market. But this house holds a bit of sentimental value for me, and I'm not sure if I'm ready to cut it loose yet.

Luke nods in understanding, but doesn't press me further. Juan, the general contractor and foreman, walks up to Luke, asking some questions that I'll let him handle since my cell phone is vibrating in my pocket. Stepping out onto the front patio to take the call, I see that it's from an unknown caller.

"Hello?"

"Is this Gabe Garcia?" the voice on the other end of the phone asks.

"Yes, how can I help you?" I question the caller.

"My name is Landon Christianson. I need to speak with you about Jess." My heart stops at the sound of her name.

"Is she okay?" I panic.

"She's fine. Kind of. Do you have a minute to talk?"

I'm not even sure I heard every word Landon said. He spoke fast, and I mostly remained quiet, listening to him while trying to wrap my brain around everything he was telling me. Jess is in Wilmington, North Carolina. She's afraid to call me. She doesn't know he's calling. He's a friend, and she needs me.

Shoving my phone back in my pocket, I try to absorb everything that was just thrown at me. I feel my phone vibrate in my pocket with the text message I was just promised, providing an address of where I can find her. My thoughts and heart are all over the place. What should I do? What do I want to do? The front door opens and Luke meets me on the patio.

"Everything okay? You look a little pale," he says, concerned as he walks over to me. Shaking my head, I'm still trying to gather my thoughts.

"Who was that?" he asks.

"Landon Christianson."

"Who the fuck is that?"

"I'm not really sure. He called me about Jess," I say. Luke's eyebrows shoot up so high on his forehead, they almost meet his hairline.

"Jess, Jess?" he asks. "Our Jess? What about her? Is she okay?"

"I don't know. All I know is she's in North Carolina, and he says she needs me."

"North Carolina? What the fuck is she doing there?"

"I don't know. He wants me to go there."

"Fuck," Luke responds quietly, and I can't think of a better word at this time myself. "So are you going to go?"

Turning around to look at the house, I contemplate for a few seconds, but I already know the answer. "Yeah. She needs me."

"Don't worry about shit around here. We've got this under control. Go bring our girl home," he says as my stomach flips.

"What if she doesn't want to come home?"

"Well, you'll never know the answer if you don't go. Go pack your shit right now."

Sitting at the gate with my boarding pass in hand, I feel the exhaustion of the last twenty-four hours sink in. Work was a bitch; we had calls all night long, and I didn't sleep for more than an hour at a time. Within seconds of taking Landon's call, I knew there was only one option; I had to go to North Carolina. Spending the next few hours making arrangements for Dad or Luke to be around to oversee the final day's worth of work at my house and getting my shit packed, I'm dead tired, yet adrenaline courses through me at the thought of seeing her in a few hours.

Maybe I'm a glutton for punishment, but I know I have to see her and ask her one last time if she wants me out of her life. I know without a doubt that if she says "yes," I'll be gone. For good. But I have to ask her. I let her go too easy last time, but I had to let her go. I had to give her the space to figure out her life.

A slight jerk of the plane landing jolts me awake. The engines roar as we slow down. Opening the window shade, I'm met with the late afternoon sun in Charlotte, North Carolina. Deplaning, I follow the signs that lead me to the rental car counters. After a short shuttle ride and a few signatures, I'm walking out to stall B12 to find the car that is going to take me to Jess. Plugging in the address Landon sent me into Google Maps, I plug my phone in to charge and pull out of the airport. I have just less than two hundred miles and three and a half hours until I get to her.

The drive is beautiful and surprisingly fast. In just under four hours, I'm pulling into Wilmington and turning into the parking lot of a condominium complex that is situated right on the beach. I can't help but smile a little knowing that no matter where she ran off to, she'd find a beach. She loves the sand and the water.

Taking a spot in visitor parking, I kill the engine just as the sun sets over the water. A dusky darkness has fallen over the parking lot and large exterior parking lights have turned on. I take a moment to take in my surroundings and get my bearings as I've been traveling for over nine hours. Nine hours I've thought about everything I plan on saying to her. Yet here I am, and I still don't have the words. Nervousness sets over me, as in first time I kissed her nervous, first time I told her I loved her nervous.

Opening my car door, I step out and smell the salty ocean air. It's refreshing, and I can see why Jess would like it here. Immediately, I notice her SUV parked in a space marked #101. That matches the condo number that Landon sent me, along with her address. Walking up the sidewalk, I notice the door with #101 on the wall right next to it. Stopping for a minute, I turn to look back at my car and then at Jess' car and wonder if I'm making the right decision in coming here.

Reaching for the doorbell, I pause. My finger hovers over the small round button. I fight with myself internally over whether or not I should push that small button. Nothing but a door and some windows separate me from the woman I love with every ounce of my being. With a deep breath, I push the lighted white button, and my heart races. I can hear shuffling as she makes her way to the door. *Click, click, swoosh.* I can make out the sounds of the deadbolt, the handle lock, and the chain. My eyes move to the doorknob as I watch it slowly turn.

The door opens, and I lift my eyes upward, meeting the most beautiful green eyes I've ever seen. A small gasp escapes her lips, and she takes a step backward wrapping both arms around her waist. Her long hair is pulled up into a loose, messy, twisted ponytail. She's wearing a dark gray tank top and black yoga pants. I notice that she's still thin; you can see it in her arms and face. We both stand, taking in the sight of each other as my heart races. Swallowing hard, I decide it's now or never.

"Hi," I say nervously, my palms sweating. Her eyes are glistening and she drops her arms to her sides. Moving quickly towards me, she stops just inches away before throwing her arms around my neck. She pulls herself into me and lifts herself up, wrapping her legs around my waist. It may be the tightest hug I've ever felt from her. Wrapping my arms around her, I squeeze her back, taking in the smell of her hair. My cheek rubs against the side of hers, and I can feel her heart beating as wildly as mine against my chest.

Afraid to move for fear this moment will end, I forget everything I've rehearsed, everything I thought about for the last three and half months, and say the only thing that is in the front of my mind. "God, I've missed you."

CHAPTER FORTY-TWO

~Jess~

Am I dreaming? Is this real? I know it is when I hear the word "hi" roll off his tongue. Jumping into his arms, I hold onto him for dear life. He doesn't immediately hug me back. I deserve that. But when I feel his arms finally wrap around me and squeeze me back, the tears that are pricking at the backs of my eyes form.

Hearing him say he missed me melts my heart. Tears are rolling down my cheeks, and my body starts shaking. I didn't believe I'd feel him like this again.

"Don't cry," he whispers, turning his face into my hair. I feel his lips press against the side of my head for a second, but he pulls his face away. Untangling my legs from his waist, I drop them to the floor and loosen my arms from around his neck.

"What are you doing here?" I mumble, wiping tears from my face with the back of my hand. When he looks at me like he doesn't know what to say, I grab his hand and pull him inside the condo and out of the doorway. He takes a few hesitant steps into the kitchen area, and I notice him looking around the condo.

"Can we talk?" Gabe asks. "Is now an okay time?"

Extending my arm toward the living room, I nod. "Yeah. Have a seat." He finds a spot on the loveseat that sits perpendicular to the couch and I see him fidgeting with his hands. I sit at the end of the couch nearest him and take a deep breath.

"Landon called me," he says immediately, and my heart stops again.

"What? Why?" I question him.

Shaking his head at me, he continues. "He didn't say much. Just that you needed me, but you wouldn't call."

Closing my eyes, I remember every word Landon said to me on the beach last week. The words are ingrained in my memory.

"There can't be an 'us' when your heart belongs to someone else."

"I will never be that guy for you. I want someone who needs me to breathe, to survive, and to love. For you, that's Gabe."

"You need to call him."

I hear Landon's deep voice whispering these words to me again. I close my eyes and listen to those words repeat in my head.

"I will leave right now if you want me to," he says, looking at his hands.

"No," I whisper. The tears are back in my eyes, threatening to spill over once again. "I need to talk to you, and I owe you an apology."

He shifts slightly on the couch. "Before you start, there is something I need to say." I make direct eye contact with him and he clears his throat. "When you came to say goodbye that night, I know you thought something was going on with Heather. There's not. Luke and Heather are dating. She had just walked up and given me a hug, and that's when I saw you.

Jess, for three and half months, all I have done is think about you. For the rest of my life, I will regret not fighting harder for you. I should have fought harder for us."

Tears are literally spilling in buckets down my face. Listening to the words he is speaking is breaking my heart. He isn't to blame for any of this, yet here he sits trying to own wrongs that he didn't commit.

"I should never have let you go that easily. But I was so scared for you. I still am," he admits, pausing. "I know you needed time, and I tried to give that to you. But please, don't for one second think that the time and space I gave you was any indication that I didn't love you. Until the day I die, I will love you with my last breath."

Sliding off the couch, I lay my head in his lap and cry. He places his hand gently on the back of my neck and lightly rubs. Through the tears and sobs, all I can muster out is, "I'm sorry, I'm so sorry," over and over.

For hours, we sit and talk. I don't know how many 'I'm sorry's' I said, but I'm certain it will never be enough. We talk about my therapy, my internship, and even Landon. I am surprised to hear how Landon contacted him, but with every beat of my heart and every breath from my lungs, I'm so thankful he did. I haven't talked to Landon since he dropped me off after our talk on the beach. Something in my gut told me that night would be the last time I talked to him.

For the first time in months, I wake up excited. Gabe is asleep in the guest room, and I feel a sense of hope. I don't know where this will lead us, but it felt good to talk to him and apologize. It felt good to explain my feelings and thoughts, and why Dr. Peterson called me a "runner." I've never faced my issues head on, and for the first time, with Gabe here, I did.

I slowly open the door to the guest room and peek my head inside. He is sprawled across the top of the bed, wearing nothing but his boxer briefs. His jeans are on the floor in a pile with his t-shirt. He didn't even pull the comforter back on the bed. I know the three-hour time difference is hard, and we talked until the early morning hours. Closing the door, I lean back against it and smile.

Shuffling through the fridge, I realize that I have nothing except coffee creamer. Jotting down a small list, I grab my keys and wallet and head to the grocery store. Filling my basket with fruit, eggs, bacon, bread, and muffins, I grab a few extra items to snack on throughout the day. Unloading all of my items onto the belt, I reach for the last item. Setting it down on the belt, something, actually, someone catches my attention out of the corner of my eye. Landon is standing three lanes down, holding a few plastic bags full of groceries. We make eye contact for a brief second before he shifts his eyes and turns to walk away.

"Landon," I holler at him. I know he hears me calling his name. "Landon," I yell again. I see him slow for a second, dropping his head back slightly, but then he continues to walk away. I'm left standing in the grocery store as I watch him walk away from me for a second time.

Making the short drive home, the sadness of watching Landon ignore me for the final time dissipates with the happiness and excitement, knowing that Gabe is waiting for me. I can't help but feel a sense of peacefulness and contentment with him being here. I line a cookie sheet with parchment paper and bacon, putting it in the oven to cook. I whisk eggs and some milk in a bowl, while I warm up a pan to scramble the mixture in. I also prepare French toast and a large fruit salad. Lastly, I start the coffee.

After setting the table, I get back into the kitchen to finish the eggs and French toast. Reaching into the cupboard, I grab two large coffee mugs. Turning to set them on the breakfast bar, I see Gabe sitting on one of the barstools. A small smile is spread across his face.

"What?" I ask, smiling back at him.

"You look good, really good."

"Thanks. So do you," I respond quietly. It's like I'm meeting him for the first time with the butterflies in my stomach.

"Let me help you," he says, jumping up from the stool. He grabs the coffee mugs and fruit bowl while I plate up the French toast, bacon, and scrambled eggs.

"This looks amazing, but you didn't have to go through the trouble," he says before taking a sip of coffee.

"It wasn't any trouble. Plus, I wanted to. I like cooking for you." I smile at him. "How did you sleep?" He still looks tired. I notice the dark circles under his eyes and see the way he is sucking down his coffee, like it's the drug that will keep him alive.

He's quiet, contemplating how to answer my questions. "Actually, for the first time in months, I slept well," he says quietly. I feel guilty, knowing that I was the cause of so much stress and many sleepless nights for him.

I reach out and place my hand on top of his, just a small gesture, an unspoken apology. "So how long are you here for?" I ask, hoping he'll say "forever."

"I leave tomorrow. I have to be back at work on Monday. You know, that boss of mine is a real slave driver." He laughs. Laughing back, I can't help but think of my dad. Even though he's not a man of many words, I really do miss him.

Picking up our dishes from the table, I carry them to the sink. Gabe follows behind with the few I couldn't carry. It feels good to be standing next to him, falling into old routines like we used to, except I have no idea where this, or rather us, is going. Bending over, I stack the plates side by side into the dishwasher. Standing up to retrieve the remaining dishes in the sink, Gabe pulls me to him, pressing his soft lips against mine.

"I'm sorry. I just can't look at your mouth any longer without tasting it," he mumbles against my lips. Relaxing into his embrace, I let him kiss me, relishing the feel of his lips on mine. He devours my mouth like it might be the last time he ever kisses me. For all I know, it might be.

I kiss him back while wrapping my arms around his neck. Lifting me gently to the breakfast bar, he sets me on the cold granite countertop. I gasp when the back of my warm thighs press against the ice-cold granite.

"And I love how you look wearing my t-shirt," he says, brushing his hand across his name, which is silk-screened over my left breast. I smile against his kiss.

Pulling out of his kiss, I run my hands down both sides of his face, holding him. "I wore it almost every night since I've been here," I tell him, wanting him to know that just because I ran, he was never far from my thoughts. Pressing his forehead against mine, he leans in one last time to press a firm kiss to my lips.

"I've missed you more than you'll ever know or understand," he whispers.

"I've missed you, too."

"Hey, I'd love to show you where I'm working, if you're interested," I say.

"I'd like that," he says with a smile.

It's Saturday afternoon and WXZI should be fairly quiet. It'll be a great time to show him the station without being in the way. Using my keycard, we enter through the front door to the always-empty reception area. Gabe gives a little whistle as he takes in the leather furniture and swanky desk that no one uses.

Rolling my eyes at him, I grab his hand and pull him down the hall to the area where all of the offices and cubicles are. Weaving our way through four-foot cubicle walls, I lead him into my cubicle.

"Very fancy," he says with a smirk. "You've hit the glass ceiling, haven't you?" he kids with me.

"Don't be mean," I fire back. "This internship was all but given to me on a silver platter in exchange for counseling," I mumble out.

"What?" he asks, confused.

Flinging my purse onto my desk, I fall into my desk chair and slouch down. "When Janet called me to tell me I had to make a decision on my internship right away, I went to her office. I was still pretty bruised up, and with a few questions and a mini-mental breakdown in her office, I told her what happened. Kevin, the News Director is her brother. She told me the internship was mine if I wanted it, but she made going to counseling a condition of my internship," I explain.

"Can she do that?" he asks.

I actually laugh. "No, I don't think so, but I was so desperate to escape, I took her up on the offer." I realize how those words must hurt him. "But Dr. Peterson has been wonderful; she's really helped me work through a lot of my issues, but I know I still have a long road ahead of me."

Gabe nods his head in understanding. "So that's why you left so quickly, to escape?" he asks timidly. I know he fears overstepping his boundaries.

"Kind of. The other reason was you. I know I hurt you when I broke up with you." I feel a lump form in my throat, but I need to tell him this. "Every day when I would look out my window, get in my car, or lie in my bed, all I saw was you."

Interrupting, he snaps at me, "And what was wrong with that?" His eyes are squinting and he looks angry.

"Nothing is wrong with that, and everything was wrong with that," I offer. "I felt at that time you deserved better. Mentally, physically, and emotionally I was broken," I mumble. "You deserved someone who wasn't—me."

Moving closer to me, he bends down so we're eye to eye. Sitting forward in my chair, I lean into him, our faces mere inches apart. "Do you still feel that way? That I deserve someone better?" he asks quietly, his eyes softening.

"Sometimes," I say honestly and divert my eyes to a picture hanging on the wall of my cube.

Grabbing my chin lightly, he turns my head back toward him. "All I have ever wanted was you and is still you. You are what I deserve," he whispers. Pressing his lips to mine, he offers me the softest, sweetest kiss. "Understand me?" he asks, still not releasing his grip on my chin.

"Understand," I quietly return.

"Good."

With that, he stands up, pulling me up out of my chair. "Now show me around this place so we can go to the beach." He laughs and takes a hold of my hand. For the next half hour, I show him the ins and outs of a small TV station. He genuinely seems interested and smiles when I get excited about teleprompters and newsfeeds.

The afternoon is spent lying on a blanket in the soft sand at the beach just outside my condo. Conversation is easy, just like it used to be. But there is an unsettling feeling that hovers around us. I know he feels it too as he's been a bit more quiet and restless for the last few hours.

Lying on our backs, his fingers are laced through mine, just like we used to do. Pulling my hand to his mouth, he runs his lips over all of my knuckles and places gentle kisses to the top of my hand.

"Jess," he says. "Come home." It's a quiet plea. "I need you with me in California."

"So much has changed," I say. "I've pushed everyone I care about out of my life: you, Ava, Mom, and Dad. I'm almost embarrassed to go home." Sitting up, he looks down at me as I fling my arm over my eyes to hide the tears rolling down my temples and into my hair.

"Everyone misses you and wants you to come home, not just me," he says.

"I know," I whisper. "I'm just not sure I'm ready yet."

"Will you ever be ready? Or will I be waiting forever?" he asks quietly.

"I don't know," I tell him through my tears and in a shaky voice. The look on his face is desperation, and sadness. The damage I've caused is heartbreaking, and I hate myself for it. The rest of the evening is filled with moments of awkward silence. We're tiptoeing around the delicate subject of "us."

"What time do you have to leave tomorrow?" I ask him as we sit on the living room floor, picking at our Thai take-out.

"Eight o'clock. I have to drive back to Charlotte and return the rental car before my two o'clock flight," he says, pushing his food back and forth across his plate.

"Gabe?" I say quietly. Reaching out, I place my hand on his arm, stilling him. Looking at my hand, he drops his fork and places his other hand over mine, but he won't look at me.

"I'm really happy you're here," I say.

"Me too." He squeezes my hand.

I don't sleep for all but ten minutes over the course of the night. I toss and turn and watch the minutes tick away on the alarm clock that sits on the bedside nightstand. Finally, around seven in the morning, I pull myself out of bed and take a quick shower. Putting his fire department t-shirt back on, I pull on some clean yoga pants and head downstairs to make coffee. By the time my feet hit the second stair on my way down, I see him. There he sits on the loveseat with his already packed bag lying on the floor. He's staring at the wall, deep in thought.

"Hey," I say.

"Hey." He turns toward me and responds with a half smile.

He looks as bad as I feel. The dark circles under his eyes are even darker. He looks exhausted. Sitting down on the loveseat next to him, I run my hand over his unshaven face, stopping to run my thumb over his lower lip. His hand stops mine and pulls it away from his mouth.

"When did you get this?" he asks, running his finger across my barely healed tattoo on my inner left wrist. "I noticed it yesterday, but forgot to ask," he says.

"Last week."

"What does it mean?" he asks, tracing each letter of the script that is barely visible against my skin.

"Unbreakable," I whisper.

"Unbreakable," he whispers back, running his fingers back and forth, over and over again across my wrist.

"I finally decided that I can't let circumstances or events that I have no control over break me," I offer. "No better reminder than to have it front and center every day where I have to see it and can't forget it," I explain. A small smile crosses his face, and he pulls my inner wrist to his lips. He closes his eyes and gently presses small kisses along my wrist and over the tattoo.

"I have to go." His voice breaks. Clearing his throat, he stands up, still holding my hand. He pulls me into a hug and I wrap myself around him.

"I love you," I whisper in his ear. "Thank you for finding me."

"I love you too. God, you have no idea how much I love you."

Pulling away from me, he saunters over to his bag, picks it up, and turns back to me. "I will wait for you. When you are ready to come home, I'll be there. I will always wait for you." And that's when I knew there is no one in this world for me other than Gabe Garcia.

CHAPTER FORTY-THREE

-LANDON-

"Turn down Beach Avenue," I direct Matt as I do every shift we work. Driving past her condo has become a ritual for me when we're on duty.

"Have you talked to her?" Matt asks, his voice masked with sympathy.

"Nope," I reply abruptly. "Only two more days of you driving my sorry ass past her place," I reply quietly. "She's moving back to California." The patrol car is silent except for the radio broadcasting calls. Matt has turned the volume so far down, that it's almost inaudible.

"Sorry, brother," Matt says.

"It's okay. It's what's best for her." Saying those words, even thinking them, is fucking killing me. I keep my attention focused out my window, trying to not get emotional. "She was different," I say, turning my head to look at Matt.

"I know," he says, nodding his head in agreement. "I've never seen you like this over any woman. She has to be something. I really am sorry."

"Thanks," I reply, knowing he's right. I fuck women. I use them and dispose of them. I don't care about their feelings, and I certainly don't fall in love with them. Until Jess.

"You need to say goodbye to her, man. Don't let her leave without talking to her," he says. I listen to him and take his words to heart, but I don't know if I can stomach seeing her. I don't let people in, and she is in a place I didn't know existed.

"Yeah, we'll see."

"Do it, man," he tells me.

"Let's go eat. I'm starving," I say, changing the subject and taking my mind off of the one thing that has consumed my every thought for the last three months.

"Hey, big brother," Lindsay announces as she rounds the corner into the kitchen. I'm sitting at the small table, drinking coffee and reading the latest *Sports Illustrated*.

"Hey, little sister," I respond. "You look nice," I say, looking at her in a little black dress with knee high black leather boots on. Pouring herself a mug of coffee, she joins me at the kitchen table.

"Thanks. We're all taking Jess to lunch for her last day," she says quietly, looking down at her mug and blowing the steam off of the coffee. "You should meet us," she says timidly, awaiting my normal tense reaction.

"Nah. Have a great time, though. You really do look nice," I say, laying the magazine on the table and taking my mug of coffee with me to the living room.

"Just call her, Landon. Text her. Say goodbye to her. Neither of you will talk to me about each other. I've never seen you like this," Lindsay pleads with me, her voice becoming more faint the further away I walk. My throat dries up, and I swallow hard. I've honestly never felt like this. All of these emotions are new to me as well.

"We'll see," I toss back over my shoulder.

I've only ever dealt with losing one person I cared about: my mom. I vowed to never let a woman into my heart to the point where I'd get hurt, but I did. My gut tells me to just let her go, but my heart tells me to say goodbye. The decision is simple really; I only ever listen to my gut, but fuck if my heart isn't trying to win this battle.

CHAPTER FORTY-FOUR

~Jess~

Shoving the last suitcase into the back of my SUV, I slam the door and pray I can still see through the rearview mirror out my back window. Kevin is shipping a few boxes back to me in California that won't fit in my car. Walking up the sidewalk, into the condo to get my purse and lock up, I can't help but remember what it felt like to walk this same sidewalk three months ago. What a different person I was then. A shell of what I am now.

I have grown immensely, moving across the country for an internship, meeting some of the greatest friends I know I'll ever have, and for the therapy that has helped me forge a path to healing. I know I have a long way to go, but I feel hopeful for my future. I know that my leaving California, on the terms I did, was selfish, and I hurt many people. I'm ready to make amends, but I won't regret my time here in Wilmington.

Taking one last look around this beautiful condo, I can't help but wonder what everyone will think when I show up in California. No one knows I'm coming, not even Dad. Gabe and I text and talk daily, working to repair the damage I did by shutting him out, but I needed to make the decision to move home on my own accord. This is about me, not Gabe.

Locking the door to the condo, I place the key under the doormat as Kevin has instructed me. Holding the key to my SUV in my hand, I take one last look at the amazing beach that lies straight ahead. I will miss the sounds and smells of the ocean. It's become a needed form of therapy for me, to sit on the soft sands of its beaches, and just think.

My heart stops when I see him, leaning against the side of my car. Wearing dark jeans and a tight white t-shirt, his sandy brown hair is messy, and a five o'clock shadow outlines every ridge of this jaw. I can't help but smile when I hear that sweet Southern accent drawl out, "Hey, baby girl."

My pace quickens until I'm standing right in front of him. "What are you doing here?" My pulse is racing.

"Wasn't going to let you leave without saying goodbye." He smiles at me with his perfect mouth. Reaching out, he pulls me into a firm hug. I will never forget his smell; light, masculine, and comforting. We stand, hugging each other for at least a minute. I can feel his heartbeat against my chest. Finally pulling back, I look into his beautiful blue eyes.

"Thank you for calling Gabe," I say, my voice finally breaking and tears spilling out from my eyes. "You were right, you know."

"I'm always right, baby girl," he says with a chuckle, wiping the tears from under my eyes with the pads of his thumbs. "I should be thanking you," he says with his eyes focused intently on mine. "I didn't know I had the capacity to feel love for anyone, and somehow, you broke down those walls that were barricading my heart. So, thank you."

"FFLs?" I ask him.

"FFLs? What the hell is that?" he asks me, laughing.

"Friends for life," I say.

"Always. FFLs."

"Oh, and hey," I raise my left arm and flash him my inner wrist. "It means 'unbreakable.'"

Grabbing my wrist, he presses his lips to the white script tattoo just like Gabe did. Slowly releasing my hand, he moves to open my car door, waiting for me to step in. I toss my purse over to the passenger side seat and he moves closer so that he can close the door after I get inside. Before I sit down, he wraps his large hand around my upper arm, pulling me toward him. Standing there, just inches from him again, he leans in and presses a soft kiss to my forehead.

"Bye," I whisper as I pull away from him and get into my car. With a nod, he closes my door. Backing out of my parking spot, I roll down my window.

"Take care of Linds for me."

"Always have, always will, baby girl. Be safe." He forces a smile. Memories of Landon will be etched in my heart forever. I will cherish his honesty, trust, and friendship for the rest of my life. With a raised hand, he mouths "bye" to me, and I leave him standing next to his motorcycle, beginning my three-day drive back to California.

Time stands still as I make that last turn onto Lawson Street, the street where I grew up between two different homes. Dad's truck is gone, which means he's at the fire station—shocker. At this hour, I will go unnoticed. It's after midnight, so I grab just my purse and small bag with clothes and toiletries. Checking the hanging planter for the house key, I find it exactly where it was left. Some things never change.

Letting myself into the house, I take in the surroundings that I left just over three months ago. Everything seems different here. I feel older, like I've been gone much longer. Finding my way down the short hallway in the dark, I open my door to find my bedroom untouched from when I left. Throwing my purse on the white wooden desk, I quickly shower and change into my pajamas. I want to get a few hours of sleep before I drive to the fire station to see my dad.

Waking at six, I actually feel refreshed. Even with a few hours of sleep, I'm excited to go announce my arrival back in California. I pull a short cream dress from my closet that has eyelet cutouts around the neck and sleeve line. Putting the finishing touches on my make-up, I'm out of the house before seven.

My heart is racing, and adrenaline is running through my body, not because I'm nervous to see Dad or Gabe, but because of the stop I need to make first. Driving back from California, I decided this was something I needed to do for me and my healing. I must face my fears and forgive, let go.

When I pull into the small gravel parking lot at Washington Park, the sun is up, casting its bright rays on the green park. Walking the path I used to run, I clutch my phone and car keys in my hand while passing women and men running, just as I did that day. Winding through the park on the paved trail, I find the spot where my life changed so suddenly. No one is around this morning—the irony.

Sitting down on the grass at the edge of the creek where it meets the water and cattails, I finally let go. I lie down in the grass and the tears slide from the corner of my eyes at the same time that I let go of the hatred, the fear, and the anger. I let go of the anxiety that has suffocated me for more than six months. I finally forgive my attacker, not because he deserves it, but because continuing to harbor the anger, the hurt, and the fear isn't allowing me to heal—and I'm ready to heal. I know that this is one small step in my healing, and I still have a long road ahead of me. Taking in a deep breath for what feels like the first time since I was lying here nearly six months ago, I feel like I can breathe. I let hope take over that place in my heart where I harbored anger, hatred, and resentment.

Sitting up, I wipe away my tears away with the back of my hand and toss a small rock into the creek that my feet are almost touching. I'm ready to get my life back and ask forgiveness of those I hurt in my attempts to heal. I'm not running anymore. Dr. Peterson would be so proud. I take a picture of myself sitting on the bank of this creek, and I plan to text it to her. Collecting myself, I stand and feel lighter. It is truly amazing the weight that anger and resentment has on a person. I walk quickly to my car. I'm excited and hopeful, and surprisingly, at peace.

Pulling into the fire station, I drive around to the back and punch in the gate code that I'm glad I still have memorized. I pull through the metal gate as it slides open, and find an empty spot in the back and pull in. One of the large stall doors is open, and I see the ladder truck inside with boots and pants lying on the floor next to it.

Walking toward the open door, I see him standing there, talking on his cell phone. He looks like he's aged in the three months since I've seen him. His hair is a little grayer, and a few more wrinkles have crept in around his eyes. When he looks up and spots me, a smile crosses his face. He begins walking towards me as he stuffs his phone in his pocket.

"Hi, Dad," I say as we approach each other.

"Jessie, what are you doing here?" he asks, lifting me off the ground and into a giant bear hug.

"I'm home," I respond, squeezing him back.

"You look good, kiddo," he says, and I notice his misty eyes.

"Thanks. It's good to be home." Pulling back from him, I study his face, remembering the resentment and anger I left at the creek. I know he did the best he could, raising a daughter alone while grieving the loss of my mom.

"There's someone inside who I think would be really happy to see you."

"Yeah, I figured," I say, excited to see him.

Jackson, another one of Dad's crewmembers is standing in the open stall near the fire truck and happens to holler, "Hey, Garcia. There's someone here you might want to see."

My heart races at the anticipation of seeing him. I sense him before I see him; I always have. From around the dark corner, he steps out of the bay and into the sun shining down on the driveway. Looking at me, he shifts his eyes to my dad and then back to me. He stops momentarily. With a quick walk, his pace picks up, and I start running towards him at the same time. Jumping into his arms as I meet him, I wrap my arms around his neck and my legs around his waist, not even caring that my short dress has probably exposed my ass.

"Jess," he whispers, spinning me around. "What are you doing here?" he asks in shock. Setting me down, I lean in and press a kiss to his lips.

"I'm home," I say, watching a smile spread across his face. He pulls me into another hug and spins me around again.

"You're not going back to North Carolina?" he asks hesitantly, searching my eyes for answers my mouth hasn't been able to provide every other time he's asked me. Shaking my head no, I let the words he's wanted to hear fall from my lips.

"I'm home for good—if you still want me here."

CHAPTER FORTY-FIVE

-Gabe-

The expression "It looks like you've seen a ghost" couldn't have been truer the moment I stepped out onto the back driveway. Jess was standing there with her dad, a huge smile spread across her face. I wasn't expecting her to be anywhere other than North Carolina. I second-guessed what my eyes were seeing at that moment. She was beautiful, wearing a dress, her long legs peeking out from underneath it, and her long dark hair blowing slightly in the morning breeze. But what stopped my heart was the sense of tranquility on her face and the genuine smile I was used to seeing there.

Walking towards her, my mind was filled with thoughts of why she was here. I couldn't help but wonder if she was here to collect the remaining items she left behind the first time she left for North Carolina—to settle into her new life, and sever her ties here in California. But it was her smile that calmed me slightly as I walked faster towards her. I felt, for a fraction of a moment, that my Jess was back.

It was when she jumped into my arms and wrapped her legs around me, the erratic beat of her heart against my chest, that my nerves turned into waves of adrenaline. But it was hearing her tell me that she was home that really allowed me to breathe for the first time in six months.

"All I've wanted since you left was for you to come back. Don't ever doubt that I don't want you here."

I press my lips to hers, taking in the taste of my world. The catcalls, hoots, and clapping are what finally bring us from our moment. Chief is laughing, and Jess buries her face in my neck, trying to hide her embarrassment, but I hear her giggling. All of the guys on our shift are now outside, making a scene and ruining our moment together.

"Come on. You better go say 'hi' to everyone, or I'll never hear the end of it," I say, pulling her hand and tugging her towards the firehouse. Her cheeks are flushed, but she smiles at me and laces her fingers through mine as she follows me. Once inside, she spends time talking to all the guys. Most of them she's known for years, but I introduce her to a few of the newer guys.

Leaning against the wall, I stand back and watch her as she interacts with everyone. I see glimmers of the old Jess as she smiles, laughs, and talks about her time at the TV station interning, the friends she made, and the beach. In a way, I know that this experience was good for her. I just wish it had been on different terms.

Finally sneaking away from the guys, she walks up to me and presses a light kiss to my lips. "I missed you," she whispers.

"I missed you too," I say and kiss her back.

"Please tell me you didn't just start a forty-eight hour shift," she says, laying her head against my chest and wrapping her arms around my waist. Still leaning against the wall, she wiggles her arms between my back and the wall.

"As a matter of fact, I was off at seven. If I had left on time this morning, I would have missed all this." I run my hands up and down her back.

"Did you have a lot of calls last night? Are you tired?" she asks. Even if I had been up for thirty-six hours straight, there was no way I was going to go home and sleep now that she was back.

"It was actually pretty quiet last night. How about I go shower and change and then we can go grab some breakfast?" She's nodding her head yes against my chest.

"Sounds perfect," she says as she pulls away from me. She glides over to the large group of leather sectionals we have in the day room and sits down next to Tony. He's her Dad's age, and she has known him since she was four. They fall into easy conversation, and as much as I just want to stand and watch her, I want to get her out of here more.

"Almost finished?" I ask as she sips on her third mug of coffee.

"What's the rush?" she asks. "I love my coffee." She winks at me.

"Then I'll ask for a 'to-go' cup." Clearly I'm anxious, and actually, slightly nervous for what I'm about to do. What will she say? What will she think? *Fuck.*

"Forget it. I'm ready," she says, pushing her chair back from the table and grabbing her large handbag.

"Where are we going?" she asks as she pulls her sunglasses off the top of her head and places them over her beautiful green eyes. Lacing my fingers through hers, we walk through the diner and out to my truck.

"It's a surprise." She laughs and shakes her head at me.

Driving through Santa Ruiz, I turn down Lawson Street and pass our homes. I pull up in front of the house I bought and remodeled that still has the 'For Sale' sign in the front yard.

"Why did you park here?" she asks me, looking confused. I open the door and slide out of my seat, meeting her around the front of my truck.

"Remember this house?" I ask her, studying her face as she takes in the remodeled house.

"I can't believe Old Man Johnson finally fixed this place up and is selling it," she says as she walks through the yard and closer to the front porch.

"Remember when we would run and how I always stopped in front of this house?" She continues her walk through the front yard, closer to the porch steps. "How I used to tell you that a wrap-around porch would be perfect on this house?" she says, stepping up the front steps onto the porch. Gasping, she turns to me as I still stand, leaning against my truck.

"Gabe, look." Her hand is pressed against her chest over her heart. "He added a porch swing." Her voice is excited. The sight of her taking in everything she had once told me she wanted sends chills over me. She sits down in the swing and gently pushes herself back and forth.

"This house is absolutely beautiful," she says. Finally walking across the lawn and up the steps, I meet her on the front porch. She's still rocking back and forth in the swing, her head tipped backward just slightly, and her eyes are closed.

"Want to see the rest of the house?" I ask, dangling a single key.

"How did you get that?" she asks, jumping off the swing.

"Oh, I know a guy who knows a guy," I say, laughing at her.

"Come on." Opening the glass door, I insert the key into the large wooden door and push it open. Holding the door, I let her in first and watch her eyes take in the large room. Closing the door behind us, I follow her as she walks slowly through the living room.

I see her mentally taking notes of the new windows, the original floors, and the crown molding. I study her as she sees every little detail that I worked on for months. I stay in the living room as I watch her light steps taking her into the kitchen. When minutes pass and she hasn't returned, I walk to the kitchen. There she stands with her back against the kitchen island, her arms on either side of her, holding her still. She's looking out the large windows into the backyard—tears falling down her face. Turning to meet me when I walk into the kitchen, I keep my distance.

"This isn't Old Man Johnson's house, is it?" she asks, swiping at her tears.

Shaking my head, I simply answer her honestly. "No."

"It has everything I ever mentioned to you." Her lip and chin are quivering as she stops speaking.

"I know," I whisper.

"Why did you do this?" she asks.

"Every second that I was away from you, every overtime shift I picked up, was so that I could provide you with everything you ever wanted: a house, a ring, a family. If I had known what was going to happen that night, I would never have taken that shift."

"Stop," she interrupts me. "What happened to me was not your fault. It wasn't because you were working that night. I don't blame you."

"I know that, but if I had slowed down, if I hadn't picked up that shift, you wouldn't have been running alone."

"But you picked up that shift because you were thinking of me," she whispers, wiping more tears from her face.

"I can't remember a time when I haven't loved you. You have been a part of my life for over fourteen years. When you were younger, it was a different kind of love, but now, it's the kind of love that won't let me breathe if you're not with me. It's the kind of love that makes me not want to live if I can't be with you," I say, meeting her at the kitchen island.

She's crying harder now, and I need a moment to swallow the lump that has formed in my throat. Holding both of her hands in mine, I know I need to finish this.

"Jess, this house is for you. Everything I do is for you. I want to give you everything. I know we have a lot to work through, but I never want to spend another day apart from you. I'm not asking you to marry me yet, but one day, I will give you everything—everything you have ever dreamed of, if you'll let me."

Through her sobs and hiccups, she plants herself directly in front of me. "Gabriel Garcia, there is no other man in this world that I will ever love as much as I love you. You loved me when I didn't even love myself. I don't deserve your love. But there is nothing in this world that I would love more than being with you for the rest of my life."

Pulling her into me, I hold her. I remember the last time I cried—I cried when she left. Today, my tears are for new beginnings—for days with her I thought I'd never have.

"I'm home. Forever," she whispers against my chest—
and I know she is.

EPILOGUE

~Jess~

I can hardly believe it was three years ago that I packed up my life and moved to North Carolina. Driving away from everything I knew was the scariest, yet most liberating experience of my life. I was broken in every way possible and needed to find out who I was amongst the shattered pieces.

Reflecting on where I've been, I'm thankful for my experiences in North Carolina. I wish I hadn't hurt Gabe in the process, but I learned important lessons about myself while I was there. The most important lessons I took away: it's okay to hurt and to be broken, but it's also imperative to forgive and heal. You have to *feel* to be able to love. But most importantly, every girl needs a tattooed bad boy to teach her to really *live*. That boy needs to kiss her like she's never been kissed, to put her on the back of his motorcycle so she can feel the wind on her face and in her hair, take her for her first tattoo—and to let her go when he knows he's not the man she really needs. Landon will always be that man, an important part of my life; my friend forever.

Dr. Peterson and I still talk weekly. We "Skype date." She helps me process feelings that occasionally surface, but I can say for the first time, I am truly happy. Finding a therapist to help me, talk to me, guide me, and ultimately teach me to love myself, was single-handedly the most important part of my recovery process.

A year and a half ago I rediscovered my love of running. I run with Gabe or a friend—always, never alone. It's been my largest hurdle in my recovery. As for my attacker, he has never been found. The case is still open and active, and with the DNA collected and processed, it is still in the hands of the detectives.

Learning to forgive is the hardest barrier in any relationship, including the one you have with yourself. I had to learn to forgive my dad for not knowing how to grieve my mother's death and throwing himself into his career as a way to cope. I had to forgive my rapist for taking trust and security from me. But the hardest person to forgive was myself.

I hurt Gabe in ways that are hard to comprehend. We've made amazing strides in our relationship, and now marriage. Gabe proposed to me on the beach in Santa Barbara a year to the date after I returned from North Carolina. We've been married for two years now. Gabe is the one person I trust with my life, but most importantly, my heart. Gabe is my everything. Well, one of my everythings.

Olivia London Garcia was born eight weeks ago. With a full head of dark brown hair and intense, deep brown eyes, she is the love of Gabe's and my life. There is a sense of peace that Olivia brings to us that words cannot describe. You never know unconditional love until you hold your baby in your arms, look into their eyes, and hold their little hand.

I spend hours on the front porch swing with Olivia, holding and swinging her while she sleeps and when she's awake. I look at the beautiful house Gabe worked on for months and feel a sense of *home* for the first time in my life. I've never had a home that was mine, where I felt that I truly belonged, but this is it. My heart is finally home.

Every day, I thank the heavens above for Gabe and Olivia. No matter what the future holds, what is thrown our way, the love that binds us is unbreakable. That little white tattoo that reads *"Infragilis"* across my inner wrist reminds me of that daily.

For anyone that has experienced rape or sexual assault of any kind you can find information and help at 1-800-656-HOPE or RAINN.org*

A SNEAK PEEK AT THE COMPANION NOVEL "UNDONE" (LANDON'S STORY)

-PROLOGUE-

Sifting through the clothes that are strewn about my darkened bedroom, I find my boxer briefs and slide them on, then start collecting her bra, panties, shorts, and shirt. This is never the fun part of my evening, yet I feel no guilt in asking her to leave. She fell asleep shortly after I fucked her senseless, and for the last hour, I've been awake contemplating how long I should let her sleep before I kick her out.

Sideling up to the edge of the bed, I nudge her shoulder gently.

"Hey, Maria," I call, nudging her until she shifts slightly. "Time to go." I drop the pile of her clothes on top of her as she wakes and walk to the bathroom connected to my master suite so she can have some privacy to get dressed.

I lean down and splash my face with the cool water, repeating it again. I grab the hand towel from the hanging towel rack and dry my face, looking at the man staring back at me in the mirror. He looks worn. Hearing her moving around my room, I toss the towel onto the counter and open the bathroom door. The light from the bathroom illuminates the dark bedroom and I can see her sitting on the end of my bed, leaning down to fasten the straps on her sandals.

I rest my body against the doorframe while she finishes up and collects her purse; I can't help but feel nothing for her. This isn't unusual for me; I don't connect emotionally with women. I let a women "in" once—to a place in my heart I really didn't know existed, but I let her go, knowing she needed something I could never be. I don't do romance, I don't do relationships, and I definitely don't do love.

"Thanks for coming by—it was fun," I offer as I usher her out of my house and out of my life for good. I never sleep with the same woman twice; it complicates things. I open the front door for her, holding it open so she can leave.

She plants herself in front of me and moves to kiss me, but I turn my head, successfully dodging her lips—I rarely kiss women, either; it's just not something I do unless I care about them, and there's only been one woman I've cared enough about to kiss.

"Bye, Maria." I nudge her towards the open door.

"Maria?" She laughs bitterly. "It's Mariana, asshole." As she says it, a hand connects with the side of my face.

Fuck. I deserved it; I usually do.

"Mariana...Maria, same thing," I say, closing the door behind her. For a brief moment, a flash of guilt washes through me. Then it all but vanishes and I feel nothing. Again.

ACKNOWLEDGEMENTS

There is not enough space on this page to thank everyone who deserves to be recognized, but I will try!

My family: I love you all more than is humanly possible. Thank you for allowing me to chase this crazy dream of mine. Your patience and giving me "quiet time" to write did not go unnoticed. I couldn't do this without your love and support.

A.L. Jackson: Thank you for inspiring me, and offering me endless advice and encouragement. In this cut throat world, your kindness and support mean everything. Love you, friend.

My sprinting buddies: A.L. Jackson, Molly McAdams, and Kristen Proby. Thank you for allowing me to wiggle into your little sprinting group. I've learned so much from all of you, and the laughs are endless. I love "us."

To my betas: Your feedback, guidance, and encouragement meant the world to me. Thank you for your brutal honesty.

Bloggers: I can't name you all, but thank you, thank you for believing in me, promoting me, and helping me! I adore you ALL.

Aleksandra Kirievskaya: Thank you for giving me the beautiful cover photo. That photo inspired the most emotional scene for me to write. Thank you! Thank you!

CONNECT WITH REBECCA SHEA

Facebook:
www.facebook.com/rebeccasheaauthor

Twitter:
@beccasheaauthor

Goodreads:
www.goodreads.com/goodreadscombeccashea

Email:
rebeccasheaauthor@gmail.com

31511984R00206